MW01354207

Acts of Closure

NT Anderson

Tepris Press

USA

Acts of Closure

Book 1 of the Acts Series

NT Anderson

ISBN: 978-1-7361950-3-1

Editing by John Painz and Jon Ford
Cover art by Marlena Mozgawa
Formatting by Jon Ford

www.ntanderson.com

For...

Chris – My rock, my woobie, my safe haven in every storm...no matter how rough the road. All that I am today is possible because of you. Careful...your wings are showing!

J – A priceless friend through all seasons, you have given me immeasurable support. This book never would have seen daylight without your wisdom and humor to guide me through.

Jon – An unexpected gift of this journey. The bright light who matches my every creative ebb and flow with invaluable input and cherished friendship.

PROLOGUE

I took a deep breath and, index finger slightly shaking, hit send.

`Sexy picture!`

Staring at my inbox wasn't going to expedite a reply...if I was even going to get one. I felt myself falling into the trap of agonizing over my brazen choice of words and decided to click around, checking on what some friends were up to in an effort to distract myself.

Laurie was posting about her adventure in day drinking. Jason was sharing some new artwork he would be showcasing that weekend.

I navigated to the page that always drew me in for the tunes, playing what were sure to be 'top ten' sounds even before the radio stations caught on. The playlist started. Investigating Caleb's shuffle on a regular basis was a surefire way for me to find music I liked by artists I wouldn't normally listen to.

I was tapping my foot to a Lady Gaga tune when the notification caught the corner of my eye.

My finger started shaking again, and I accidentally clicked Caleb's photos causing me to curse under my breath.

I had a message. Was it one of the 200 people I was friends with on Myspace? Or was it him?

A quick move of the mouse gave me the answer. And simultaneously made my heart race.

Um, thanks. I never really liked this picture much, but had to put something up, right?

So, I have to ask - do I know you?

I should have expected that right out of the gate he'd ask a question I didn't want to answer.

You must be very modest. I think it's a great photo!

No, you don't. Sorry to be so bold. I was just looking around here and stumbled across your profile and wanted to tell you that I got a little shiver when I saw you.

It was only my second message to him, and I was already throwing yet another line into the water. Maybe I *was* being too bold, but I felt like I had run out of patience.

Minutes ticked by. I clicked around some more while mentally kicking myself for leaving it so open-ended. I should have asked a question!

A new notification.

Well, again, thanks. Not quite sure what to say about the shiver. Are you sure I don't know you? I don't mean to sound suspicious, but I'm not used to being contacted by strangers.

He may not have known what to *say* about the shiver, but at least he acknowledged it, and kept writing to me without chalking it up to a bizarre internet character in search of kink.

The friend request was a small wrench for which I was prepared. It was a commonplace move among most people to send one within the early stages of communication. *Delete* was a quick and suitable recourse if you decided your new friend wasn't all you thought they'd be.

I can understand your suspicions and I don't blame you for being careful with online connections. Maybe we could just talk a bit and not get into anything too personal.

Speaking of which, if it's okay with you, I'd rather not do the friend request thing. That may not seem very forthcoming since my page is locked up and private, but I think it would be nice to get to know each other without internet personas coming into the mix.

While waiting for his response, I prepared to carry out my plan of purging all identifying information off my profile just in case he insisted on being 'friends.' I had finally arrived here. We were talking after all these years, and I wasn't going to drop it. If deleting photos and anything else that gave me away was the price to pay to keep the momentum going, so be it.

Okay. I guess I can go along with it (for now) if you want to be mysterious. Or at least anonymous. Since you have the advantage here, I'll have to put the ball back in your court...what would you like to talk about?

CHAPTER ONE

Turning my rented sports car into his neighborhood, I immediately recognized that it was an undeniably high-end area. Located in Westchester County, New York, not far from the city proper, it consisted of large, older homes, massive, manicured lawns, and impeccable landscaping. Even the sidewalks here were well-maintained. The streets were spotless. Some of New York's highest paid tax dollars hard at work.

Expensive cars filled every driveway, including several I recognized as Ferraris, Rolls Royce, and the like. I couldn't imagine there were that many people in one place who earned a living worthy of this lifestyle, but I only cared about one person in this community. His notoriety aside, he was my sole purpose for even setting foot in this area.

As I slowly passed each residence, I noted that a few of the more opulent homes had gated driveways. I nervously tapped my fingers on the steering wheel as a new potential hitch in the plan crossed my mind. The whole concept was contingent on simply walking up to his front door. The possibility of a gate, or worse still, some form of security blocking my access, was a barricade for which I had not considered.

It was hard for me to see him as the successful person he had become. Not that I had doubted he would accomplish it. To me, he was oddly frozen in time. The same person I had known back when his apartment, he told me, was littered with rejection letters from agents, publishers, and film studios. His current lifestyle was a good example of what perseverance could do for a person.

He seldom gave interviews or talked to the press, but from what little I had seen, I believed he was the same man I had gotten to know so well through our correspondence. And that meant he was still harboring his deep passion...and pain. Maybe that was the key to his success – he was channeling it into his writing. Instead of being the man he wanted to be with a woman, he directed that energy toward his quirky, clever story lines.

Now he had a voice the world heard with every screenplay-turned-blockbuster he sold. Had that changed him? From everything I had heard and read, it didn't seem so.

Twelve years earlier, I logged onto MySpace and sent a private message to a man I had never met...although he wasn't exactly a stranger. I was the acquaintance of someone close to him, and I had heard about him in casual passing conversation.

I knew his full name was Jack Perry, but my friend always referred to him as J, as he apparently preferred the simple initial. By all accounts, he was handsome and witty, and a little off-dead center from a societal norm perspective. Described as 'quirky,' J was a writer, and a bit of a hermit, but also a strong, soulful type. And, as reputation had it, a pool shark. At my tender age of twenty, I was his junior by just a few years.

The first mention of him provided ample enough detail for me to be intrigued to find out more. Whenever I saw our mutual acquaintance, I found subtle ways to strategically encourage them to speak of him, if only a few words here and there. I wanted to consume all the information I could without point-blank asking.

This dance went on for almost ten years until J was in his early 30s, and I had recently crossed the line into my third decade. He had been married and divorced. My life had been as it always was – a series of unusual circumstances, bad choices, and good times. Then, technology finally caught up with my long-time fascination, gifting me a newfound golden opportunity to connect with J – and maybe more – when MySpace hit the scene.

The World Wide Web revolutionized how people interrelated to each other, but up until that point it had been baby steps. MySpace was a game changer. Now the whole planet seemed to be socializing in one small corner of the internet.

On a whim, I sat down at my kitchen table on a Saturday night in Louisiana, and through this new miracle of technology, found J in New York City. To my immense joy, there were pictures. My acquaintance was right – he was handsome. More than that, in fact. Dreamy, sexy, and in one picture, I could see a whole world behind his eyes.

A world I *really* wanted to know.

He had sandy colored hair and a long, fit build. I already knew he was tall – six foot three, I had been told. Perfect lips – not too thin and not too full. Sitting at my table, looking at his profile picture, I saw a seriousness in him that had the potential to run deep, but I also recognized a playfulness, as if, when he relaxed and let go, he was a lot of fun.

And so, it began.

With a simple one-line message to tell him I thought he was sexy, we were off and running on what would become a year of emailing letters, getting to know each other, and sharing everything we could think of. There was no shame, no fear – just honesty.

We bounced feelings, thoughts, and ideas off each other about everything from relationships to careers. We delved into each other's fantasies, finding we held common ground, and more than once, his words brought me to orgasm.

Through it all, he worked on his writing career in private, but during our correspondence together he chose to share with me a short story that would never be developed for shelves or screen. Up to the point that it found its way to my inbox, it had been an expression of his deepest desires meant for his eyes only. It was a side of himself he had explored at one time but vowed never to do again. So, he held it close to the cuff as he poured that fiercely passionate energy into his mainstream writing.

As the story goes, there was a girlfriend from the days of his mid-twenties to whom he had begun, gradually and slowly, to open himself up to. Eventually, he found the courage to be exactly who he wanted to be with her in the bedroom...and she encouraged it.

From what I garnered in his writing, to say he was a considerate lover was an understatement. He was a giver in the territory of sensual matters, but he also wanted to call the shots. I imagined that if you let him do so, disappointment was an emotion you would never feel. Sadly, by the time I was finally connected with J, it was a vulnerability he was unwilling to risk.

So, this former girlfriend took all he had to offer and then, without warning and with a savage viciousness, turned on him, engaging in a verbal warfare that wounded him to his core. All because she became interested in a new and more socially popular lover. As if giving up on him for another wasn't enough, she launched a personal attack against him using everything they had shared as ammunition, including their sex life.

For the introverted, sensitive J, it was emotionally devastating. He never recovered. He had entrusted her with all of himself and she returned the favor with contempt. As he cautiously, piece by piece, revealed this to me in our emails, he told me he didn't care about the fact that she found someone else. Had she simply moved on quietly, he could have accepted it, and healed.

It was her hateful expressions that caused the damage.

As a writer who intimately understood the power of words and the meaning behind them, it caused irreparable damage when she used those tools against him for the sole purpose of justifying her retreat to a new admirer. A successful stockbroker, this latest lover placed her into the role as the woman behind the man, and she fell into it with ease. J had given her the fire he now held within and she had traded it for high society, leaving him feeling shameful of himself and his desires.

Words that had been turned into a venomous weapon created a rift between him and every woman he had been with since. Not that there had been many. Trusting had been difficult enough for him to begin with. After this, it became almost impossible, and he had engaged in only a couple of attempts at rudimentary relationships. Remaining the caring person he was, of course, but holding the rest of himself at bay from anyone who thought they could be close to him.

All he wanted was to be the thoughtful, considerate man he was within the day-to-day customs of a relationship...and then take control in the bedroom. Nothing obnoxious, nothing kinky. Just to be in charge of this one private, intimate aspect of his life. But the experience left him unwilling to display that kind of vulnerability again. He had endeavored to lock up his true nature, throwing away the proverbial key.

I was an exotic dancer at the time, a career choice I never thought I'd make. However, when my boyfriend kicked me out of his house without notice, I discovered I had few options. I found myself going on thirty years old with every last dollar devoted to keeping a roof over my head. Being down to pennies with no time to waste on sending resumes and going to interviews, I responded to an ad for a bartender at a local strip club. I had some bar experience and immediate cash was what I needed to regain control of my life. Tip money would do the trick.

Having a very outgoing, up-for-anything type of personality, I thought I could handle working in a place like that...as long as the bartenders didn't have to take off their clothes. I wouldn't do that.

Meeting with the owner of the club, who treated me more respectfully than I anticipated, I learned the position had been filled just the day before...but, he said, I was welcome to come back and dance. I laughed and told him how old I was – isn't this a life for kids who are trying to put themselves through school?

Without drooling on me or being rude, his response was flattering. "I don't care how old you are. You're beautiful and you would do very well here."

Well, I should probably start by telling you that I'm a dancer. Exotic, that is. It can be frowned upon by some people, so I'll be honest and put that out there for you now.

The fire of independence burned within me. In hot pursuit of personal sovereignty, I seized the words of Dylan and had no intention of going gently into that good night. Out of time and short on options, I began my entry into the world of selling the idea of sex. I willingly accepted this career change, resolving to approach it as a learning experience.

On this new path, I embraced my co-workers, avoiding the petty nonsense that often circulated in the dressing room as I constructed foundations of friendship. It was an education, and I carefully considered their advice and instruction. Absorbing the minutiae of the lifestyle, I found a comfort zone within my choices. Throughout the process, I learned more than I could have imagined possible about the male psyche and what makes them tick.

I had unsavory customers. But I also had thoughtful and kind ones. I pushed the former aside as soon as I was done performing for them, but I appreciated the ones who were there for a deeper reason – they needed an outlet. I made time for them, made an effort to get to know them, talking about what had gone wrong that day at work, or why a wife hadn't shown love in years. Some of them even spoke about God and the meaning of life.

I sipped expensive wine spritzers as they ruminated, and I listened. To many of them, having a sounding board was more important than any sexy performance I could offer.

The physical nature of the dancing itself came easily to me. I always had a natural proclivity for body movement, and I performed well on stage, even staying after hours to work on getting to know the pole and all the acrobatics associated with it.

In a profession of sin, I was an innocent, avoiding the high-dollar offers of sex-for-money, working against all that surrounded me to keep my core values in place. I was, the other dancers said, the girl next door.

I was educated, and the men who paid to spend time with me one-on-one recognized this immediately through our conversations. I was different, they said. Above all else, I stayed away from the drugs. My location, in conjunction with the job itself, placed me in an arena rife with women working for their next fix, so my steadfast commitment to the clean life fascinated my customers.

My success became well known, and the tellers at my bank soon understood it would take three of them to double and triple check my weekly deposit...in cash.

The world I was accustomed to had changed, and my outgoing personality evolved to one of being bold. The choices I had to make on a daily basis now were not for the faint of heart. There was no room for feeling shame, no time for hiding the truth of the life I was living. Acceptance was the only way forward, fully grasping the twists and turns of the inky playground where I spent my nights, well past the witching hour, and into the wee hours of the morning.

My new career was an education in psychology. And, locked and loaded with this confidence and knowledge, that's when I made my move to find J online.

He was in a bad place. The girlfriend who had torn him down was long gone. There was a failed marriage in the wake, and nothing else was going right in his life.

Little by little, J told me everything. Perhaps it was because I was an internet stranger with a story of my own that I was willing to share with him. My anonymity made me trustworthy. Meanwhile, unbeknownst to him, my fascination had endured for ten years to that point. However, letting him in on my secret was never a consideration.

Now that we were finally connected, I eagerly read every word he wrote, immersing myself in his pain and frustration and helplessness. I was all too familiar with the struggle to regain individual characteristic foundation after handing the building blocks to someone else for safekeeping. I hurt for him.

I told him all about myself, without giving away any clues as to who I was that could be recognized by the acquaintance, should he ever mention me. I was determined to keep this between us and only us.

From my online profile, he came to know me by my stage name. This worked well because it was an everyday name, although not my own. He accepted it and respected my insistence for anonymity, including my refusal to share photos.

Everything I said was embraced without hesitation or judgment. His caring personality was everything I had imagined...and more. Our friendship expanded, and eventually, he found himself to be comfortable enough to share with me his erotic writing.

Interesting. No problem with it here. Can't really understand why anyone would be bothered by it. We all have to do what we have to do, right? Do you like it?

I'm a writer. Starving, that is. Most people don't take it seriously. I guess it doesn't mean anything until some level of success is attached.

I sat at my computer, reading about his cravings, feeling pained that he had been rebuffed, and ever since, was accepting a basic sex life. Beyond basic. Virtually non-existent. He couldn't, he told me, share anything more than that with someone. No one else would ever know there was a primal instinct within him that wanted to take what he craved. This secret, this fantasy, had been entrusted to me...and I would be the last person, he swore, who would know.

As life and distance intervened and it came time for our correspondence to fade out, it wasn't discussed with any definitive ending. Instead, we entered into an unspoken mutual agreement that moving on was for the best. There was no fear that either one of us would reveal the secrets we had shared. Enough had been said on both sides to respect the privacy of the other. We could safely conclude our time together, our written relationship, and move on. Separately. Tucking away our musings into a protected vault. Guarded, and not to see the light of day with anyone else.

His attention had turned to Rebecca who, while not the best fit for him, was real and there and in front of him. She accepted his drive toward his chosen career, and although she didn't know about what lay beneath the surface, she was supportive.

J wasn't alone in his discovery of a new horizon. My interest also shifted to a new focal point. His name was Robert. He was solid and stable, but there was more than that. He shared my interests, passions, and intensity for life. We fit together like a puzzle, and it was a good match.

And, so, when neither J nor I made a move to meet and progress our mutual interest in each other, it became time to let go and explore these different horizons. We made no silly declarations, like "If it doesn't work out, let me know."

Now, here in his neighborhood, within minutes of finally meeting him, I was contemplating what may have possibly changed for him, other than his career recognition. Reflecting back on the man I knew from our emails, no amount of success would have pulled him out of the very private, highly protected cave in which he dwelt. Was that still the case? I imagined him feeling immense satisfaction in his achievements, but what had become of him on a personal level?

If the soulful man who wanted, desired, and needed was still in there, and if he was still hiding it from everyone, then I was determined to move forward with this exploratory mission. He had, after all, shared it with me all those years ago. Now I needed to know if it was possible to bring an end to our story. This was my choice – to put *myself* first. However misguided the decision might have been, I was taking control of the wants and desires that infiltrated my mind.

Having never seen a picture of me, he wouldn't recognize me upon arrival, but once it was revealed, I was willing to open a chapter for him, should he choose to take the leap. An experience that would bring to light all he had exposed to me, once upon a time.

Rebecca was still a fixture in his life, although I heard it had become more of a mechanical arrangement of convenience. Robert and I got married and started a family. But I never forgot J, and while I seldom see the acquaintance these days, it was a matter of a simple phone call to find out where J was and a little about what had been going on with him.

This became necessary when, six months ago, and on the heels of an unexpected detour on the road of life, J crept into my dreams in a deeply personal manner. Ever since, the urge to know how this story ends had been uncontrollably overwhelming me. I tried to do away with my thoughts of him, but to no avail.

All efforts to distract myself led me right back to the place where I knew I shouldn't be. My long-lasting crush in conjunction with our written time together made sure of that. Finally, feeling too compelled to resist my need for answers, I made the difficult decision to do something about it. And I am about to find out.

Over two decades of fantasizing about one person was going to come to a pinnacle. Tonight.

CHAPTER TWO

I glanced at the piece of paper with his address for the fiftieth time as my GPS announced I was turning onto his street. It was early fall in the northeast and the day had been warm, but the evening was expected to be cool. This was my favorite time of the year, and even though I wasn't able to experience it often, my kind of weather.

There was a twelve-lane, bumper-to-bumper traffic highway going on inside my head, and I wasn't paying attention to what I was doing, so I had to stop short when the navigational voice declared, "You have arrived at your destination." Hitting the brakes, I cringed a little at her choice of pre-programmed words.

I turned my head to take a good look at the destination in question and said a silent thank you to no one in particular when I saw a driveway that was easily accessible.

No gate. Perfect.

There was no one else driving on the street in either direction, so I paused a moment before pulling into the driveway. I was hoping he wouldn't hear me, prompting him to come to the door to see who was dropping in unannounced before I felt ready. Or as ready as I was going to get. As much as I disliked the analogy that was running through my head, I had to admit I felt like a cat preparing to pounce on a mouse.

How the evening played out would be up to J, and I anxiously anticipated where he would lead us. For now, though, I needed to maintain my plan, which included a clandestine approach. I felt the element of surprise was critical to piquing his curiosity, and interest, at just the right time. It wasn't my intention to be devilishly calculating, but the strategy called for precise execution. After all of the thought I had invested in getting to his door I wasn't about to settle for anything less.

Among those who knew me, I was regarded as spontaneous, often acting on spur of the moment decisions. On the flipside, I was also passionately loyal and reliable. The act of going to J's house spoke to my uninhibited reputation, but this was out of character with my position as a wife. Keeping my eyes and actions focused, I had never wandered.

J was an obvious exception to this. Having recently been driven toward a reevaluation of my priorities, the need for closure with him was too overpowering.

He'd always been there, in the back of my mind, enticing me from a distance. At this stage of my life, pushing him aside was no longer an option. J had resumed an old, familiar orientation, invading my thoughts, my dreams.

I knew we could never be together in any traditional sense, but I had to get answers. Maybe he wouldn't even be interested, and that would be okay. It would still be an ending to my decades-long preoccupation. In order to move forward, I needed to first take a step back.

It unnerved me to no end that doing this was the solution, but I had tried to work it around in other ways and none of my ideas gave me the blend of responses for finality that I required.

It had occurred to me that maybe I should have just emailed him. But that would not have offered the resolution I needed. What would he have said in reply?

"Hey! How have you been? I'm good. Hope all is well with you. Thanks for thinking of me. And take care."

Such a reply would have done absolutely nothing to hush my need for a conclusion. Without a definitive ending, my fascination would continue to burn through me, leaving me always wondering, always speculating.

The memories of what we shared were in place. The time for emailing had come and gone. Now, action was required, and this was the only answer that made sense to me. Meeting him, finding out if the perceived chemistry existed... and doing something about it. That was the conclusion to our story.

Funny thing about memories. Once you've made them, they stay tucked away in a place where they can always be found...and unearthed. Some of them can be pesky little buggers, resurfacing at times when you need them to stay locked away. Some of them not only emerge, but nag away at the heart, mind, and soul. This was where I had arrived with my memories of J. As much as I tried to push them away, they chipped away at me until my values were impaired and my restraint was broken.

I was not the first person in history to whom this had happened, and I certainly would not be the last. But I felt alone in this. Here and now, it was happening to me. In a short time, I was going to take my shattered resistance and continue forward with my plan. I needed this for myself, and I hoped J would welcome the opportunity to be himself, if only one more time. If I was wrong, I would at least know.

Dancing was something that I just kind of fell into out of necessity, so not exactly a choice, but yes, I do like it. 'Interesting' is an understatement most nights. Ha!

That's really cool that you're a writer! Although I'm sorry to hear about the starvation. And the lack of credit you get for it (the writing - not the starving). Everyone has to start somewhere. What do you write?

I looked over at the house and saw that it was a sprawling stone ranch. There weren't any cars in the driveway, so I couldn't be entirely sure he was home. There *was* a three-car garage, however, so maybe whatever he drove was safely parked in there, out of plain sight. Alternatively, recalling our past conversations about his transportation preferences, it was possible he still didn't like to drive and simply did not own a car.

Perhaps, as I remembered everything I had been told, J still catered to his reclusive tendencies. Not to the point of an official diagnosis, and perfectly capable of socializing when necessary, he simply preferred a solitary lifestyle. He used to, anyway. Now, the matter of his success may have put a different spin on it.

Without the answers to these questions, I had to stay in the moment and continue to operate solely on a wing and a prayer.

The house had many windows of varying sizes in the front, all with blinds that were closed, but behind them I could see faint lights in a couple of the rooms. Stone surrounded the front door that was shaded in a deep red. The entranceway was dark. The evening sky was just getting to be dusk.

On the long front porch, I noted two separate sitting areas, each with a pair of cushioned chairs arranged around a low table. Small, rustic metal pails in various colors adorned the tables and speckled the stone floor around the chairs.

Cute, I thought. *Candles.*

Several large potted plants completed the front porch scene.

I pulled into the driveway and quickly remembered my concern that he would hear the car and get to the door before me. This forced me to make one final brief makeup check in the rearview mirror, even though I had already confirmed everything was just right only a mile back. Satisfied with my appearance, I jumped out of the car without allowing myself too much time to dwell on what I was about to do. It was a good thing.

Leaning back in, I retrieved the bottle of wine and my purse that were sitting on the passenger seat. I had no idea if sauvignon blanc was a good choice for him, but a big glass of it was definitely what I needed right then.

I tucked the small handbag carrying only my essentials under one arm. My phone sat, turned off, in a leather overnight case in the backseat of the car. There would be no disruptions on my end. My bag would stay right where it was until needed. *If* needed. To present myself at the door with that in hand would have been downright alarming.

My legs felt like spaghetti, and I was wondering what possessed me to wear four-inch heels in a situation like this. On top of that, I had on a mini-skirt that I was sure was going to give away my nervous and weak knees.

The attire for the evening was a carefully chosen dress of fire-engine red. I hated to wear the crimson shade, convinced that it made my fair skin look washed out, but compliments always indicated I looked great in it. So, even though I didn't consult a soul about this plan, I took the collective advice from over the years and wore everyone else's favorite color.

At first glance, it would grab his attention, but I wanted more than that, so I chose the style for the purpose of commanding his full focus. It was something I would have worn at one point in my life, but those days were long gone. Not that I couldn't pull it off; it simply didn't fit my lifestyle these days.

The heels accentuated the curve of my calves, and the dress gave a great view of my bare legs up to mid-thigh. The lower portion of the skirt was fitted, but the stretchy material had just the right percentage of give to allow me a little wiggle room. Moving up from there, it was a smooth, flattering fit right to my navel, where the deep, plunging neckline separated to reveal my stomach before flaring to cover my breasts while still showing the invitingly naked skin of my chest.

As for the back, there wasn't one. And I had never been more grateful for breasts that were full, but small enough that I could still get away with not wearing a bra. Like the dress itself, I wouldn't normally have entertained the idea, but for this scenario, it would be just fine...as long as reality cooperated with my fantasy and no one else was there to see me.

When I found it at a boutique that was known for selling high-quality imitations of what some celebrity had recently worn to an awards show, I was very hesitant. First, I wasn't trying to fit into his current lifestyle, and A-list attire would seem that way. Second, I feared what might happen when I moved around in this thing. Would I end up with a Super Bowl wardrobe malfunction that looked like I was asking for trouble by wearing it in the first place?

The Hollywood impersonation concern left my mind the minute I saw myself in the fitting room mirror. Color aside, I had to cautiously admit I looked good. Conceit was not a word on my list of personality traits, but I had enough internal confidence to know when I felt comfortable with my appearance. The dress did have the potential to swing toward trashy, but I knew with my hair down, the right accessories, and the assertive way I planned to enter this situation, I could turn it to all class.

My second concern was eliminated by the sales associate who was helping me when I stepped out of the dressing room, pointed at the narrow swatches of fabric covering my breasts, and asked, "How does this work?"

Her mouth dropped open. "Wow! You look great! You have to get this dress and wear it somewhere spectacular."

That's the plan, sister, I thought.

"Thanks. But, seriously, what about this?" I asked again, still pointing to my chest.

"Oh, that's quite the clever and simple fix," she said. "Hang on a minute."

She jogged over to a set of drawers tucked away near the fitting rooms, coming back with two small adhesive strips.

"Check this out," she said, reaching her hands toward me. "Do you mind?"

"Nope. Go for it," I answered.

Turning a small piece of the fabric away from my left breast, she attached a thin strip of matching tape to the dress. She then stepped back, looking carefully to be sure she was about to place it exactly where it should be on my chest, and once she pressed the fabric to my skin, voila! It stayed in place. The same process was mirrored on the other side. I was then instructed to move around to confirm what the sales lady already knew. I shimmied, and even shook a little, but everything stayed where it should.

"How hard is it to get off?" I asked, envisioning sticky residue that would take an act of congress to remove.

"It comes off really easily. Seriously. Try it when you go back in the fitting room – just a small tug on the fabric and it will peel off. The strips usually stay on the dress, too, which is nice. The trickiest part is making sure everything is lined up and even," she said. "So, it's really best to have someone help you get dressed in this."

Yeah, that wasn't going to happen, but I was confident I could pull it off on my own with enough patience and a full-length mirror. And I did...and there I stood on J's walkway, dressed to kill in my fiery outfit and black heels, with long blonde hair flowing over my shoulders, and just a touch of makeup.

Red toenails and clear polish on my fingernails did the trick for that part. Mid-sized silver hoop earrings and a loose silver link bracelet rounded out the ensemble. I opted for no necklace, believing the amount of exposed skin should be the focal point.

I wore no rings.

Yeah, I can imagine that 'interesting' puts it mildly. You must have a million tales to tell. Have you always been a dancer?

I have lots of short stories, a couple of novels that have been through my own editing, and some screenplays. I think writing for films is where my real passion lies, but so far, I'm not getting anywhere.

Halfway up the path to J's front door, I stopped to compose myself for perhaps the zillionth time since I had left my hotel. I knew all the psych tricks – take a deep breath, count, find five things in my surroundings.

Yeah, yeah, okay.

Enormous maple tree in the front yard to the right of the walkway, brightly colored leaves dropping from it courtesy of the fall season. Rose bush closer to the house on the same side, with just a few yellow flowers remaining. Like the red maple leaves, they would soon be gone until spring. A rectangular, brick-bordered garden on the left with a variety of little shrubs, exotic-looking grasses, and flowers. Antique front porch light – unlit.

Damn, I needed one more. Cat in the window. A cute, orange tabby watching me as if he – or she – could read my mind.

What is it with cats and their ability to sense when humans are up to no good?

I had read somewhere that he lived alone, but just in case, I quickly rehearsed my line in the event the girlfriend answered the door – "I'm sorry...is this the Millers'?" She'd probably wonder what the hell the Millers were up to, having company dressed like that, but I would apologize and leave, and no one would be the wiser. Unless he answered, and she was in the house somewhere. For that scenario, I had no plan. All I could do was take my chances.

I was ready, and I needed to make my move.

I rang the doorbell, listening to its deep tones sound out inside the house.

Footsteps.

My back was turned toward the entrance as I thought, *Let him get that view first...*

CHAPTER THREE

Still facing the street, I was desperately trying to control my nerves, when I heard the over-sized door open. A moment later, the sound of his baritone voice made my heart flutter with anticipation.

"Hi, can I help you?"

All attempts to prepare for this had done precious little to address the reality of it.

Composing myself, I turned slowly, flashing him a slightly crooked smile. "Hi, J."

He was more stunning in person than in any photo I had seen of him.

He was older now than our Myspace days, of course, but he hardly looked it. A well-trimmed goatee framed his mouth with the hint of deliberate stubble following his jawline. The slightest peppering of silver whiskers peeked through. If anything, that enhanced his sex appeal.

His hair was a little longer than the super short style

he used to prefer. I could see some waves and had the impression that if it grew much longer, it would probably get very curly. I was willing to bet he would hate it that way, but I thought it might be cute to see.

His body looked as phenomenal as if he had still been in his early thirties, as opposed to the forty-four he was, according to my calculations. And those eyes. I could tell from every picture that they were penetrating, but to experience it in person was enchanting. His gaze was locked on me, the intensity of sparkling hazel daring me not to look away. I didn't want to. I was captivated.

He was wearing jeans and a black t-shirt with charcoal grey socks that appeared to be thick and soft. The shirt fit beautifully, and I quickly soaked in the sight of firm arms that indicated he was still working out a lot. He wore a silver watch on his left wrist; an actual watch and not one of those smart watch things, and I loved that.

In person, he was a magnetic presence, and I found this to be no surprise. He wore his clothes very well. Even in this most casual of looks, he was alluring. I needed to internally compose myself in order to regain my mental traction, and I did so hoping he didn't notice.

Neither of us spoke for several seconds. He settled himself against the doorframe, arms across his chest, crossing one foot over the other.

He was taking me in, assessing the display that was there, without invitation or announcement, on his front porch.

For my part, I was struggling to catch up with the reality of the scenario. It was a surreal feeling to see J in person. When the door opened, this man gave life to my persistent fantasy, leaving me spellbound by the mannerisms and animation with which I was unfamiliar.

His presence seemed larger than life to me.

If there were any straggling thoughts of uncertainty over my decision, they were now gone. I was committed to my course, fully in the moment, and it would take no effort on my part for me to stay there as long as he would allow.

My legs still felt weak and shaky. More so now that he had become a tangible reality like never before. No longer just a fanciful dream and a digital persona. Now J was something, someone, I could *physically* touch.

I knew it would take a miracle for me to move without stumbling. The anticipation for J to know who was standing in front of him was killing me.

"I'm sorry – do I know you?"

He appeared to be using a lot of restraint to stop himself from openly looking me over. I wondered if he was still in there. If the real J, the old J perhaps, was still inside him, I had a pretty good idea what he was thinking. Maybe he was pushing it deep down, trying to snuff the wick, but my plan for the night was riding on the belief that it *was* still a shrouded piece of him. And that the initial attraction I was feeling was mutual.

Sidestepping his question, I lifted the bottle I was holding to show it to him and said, "I brought wine. Can I come in?"

I knew that was going to come across as awfully forward on my part, but there was only one way to do this.

J looked utterly confused...yet intrigued. So far, so good.

He stood to full height again, keeping his arms crossed, looking around beyond me, as if trying to find someone else, and stammered, "I'm...I'm...what's going on here?"

On unsteady legs, I slowly stepped up to him to test

the waters. He stood his ground but didn't seem alarmed as I approached him. I was practically pressed against him as we both fit in the doorway.

Looking down at me, I could see the slightest hint of amusement in his eyes, so going for broke, I gently pushed myself against him, brushing past into the house.

No, I haven't always danced. I have a background in marketing, but the company I was working for downsized and I was going through…some stuff…and needed something fast. By the time I was back on my feet, I was kind of enjoying it, so I decided to stick with the dancing for a while. It's actually rather…empowering.

What are you doing while you're waiting for your big break?

My heart raced as I moved deeper inside his home. I pictured him behind me, watching me walk casually through his large foyer and onward down the hall, all while he was trying to comprehend exactly what was going on.

At the end of the passage, the house revealed a semi-open concept layout, and I saw a horseshoe-shaped kitchen to my right. Putting on an air of confidence I didn't truly feel, I leisurely headed there, disappearing from his view. I heard the front door close, and then the fast-paced footsteps that told me he was quickly following.

This was a gourmet kitchen unlike anything I had ever experienced in person. With an eight-burner professional stainless range, double ovens, and a refrigerator large enough to whisk me away to Narnia, J was set up for entertaining the masses.

There was a butcher block cutting board, a wooden stand branded with what looked to be a German logo housing every size of knife imaginable, and a ceramic container offering a variety of cooking spoons, spatulas, and ladles.

On the opposite side of an expansive counter stood four large stools. I wondered if he actually utilized all of this, or if he simply settled onto his favorite seat to eat takeout.

Before he arrived at my side, I made short order of taking a deep breath while closing my eyes to gain a foothold on my composure. I had to keep going, pushing through the whirlwind of emotions I was feeling – excitement, heightened sense of awareness, impatience, and apprehension. And that wasn't even taking into consideration my physical desire for him which, now that I finally had a personal visual, had increased tenfold.

Making that inceptive contact with him all those years ago had been nerve wracking, but it was child's play compared to this. My head was spinning as I quickly darted back to hearing about him for the first time, long before writing to him had ever been a consideration. Such a winding road from those early days to finally meeting him.

Tonight, I would finally reveal that we shared an acquaintance, but I was determined to stand firm on maintaining my continued anonymity as well as that of our mutual friend. I trusted J as much today as I did when we had been in the midst of our emailing relationship, but I still didn't want any outside interference.

I also felt there was no reason to divulge my real name. It was an identifier and nothing more, having no bearing on the woman he knew, nor how I felt about him. Keeping the mystery alive in this separate world that I was in with J seemed like a good idea. Maybe it would help me to split reality from what I was about to do.

I was taking in the expansive granite counters and a sea of dark wood cabinets when J turned the corner and said, "I really need to get some answers here. Who *are* you?"

There was a hint of annoyance in his voice, but his expression was still more curious than anything else.

The kitchen wasn't overly bright and, from where I stood, soft lighting was visible in the other rooms that were in my line of sight. Dimmer switches, perhaps. Regardless, I couldn't have asked for better ambiance.

Unknowingly, J had provided the setting, and the atmosphere was just right. Now I had to move this forward, carefully pacing these early moments to preserve his intrigue without causing too much frustration. I knew I was capable of the necessary performance, but first I needed to calm my nerves. That would require a glass of wine. Soon.

Placing the bottle and my purse on the counter, I faced J head on. "Corkscrew?"

He shook his head as if trying to clear a fog.

I turned my back to him, leaning over the counter, shifting my face from his view. Balancing on one four-inch stiletto, I wrapped my other foot around the back of my lower leg, running it up and down, slowly, as if absentmindedly. While I was waiting, I decided giving him another opportunity to view the back of the dress might be an enticing idea.

In this position, I couldn't see him directly, but I could practically feel him watching me while not even trying to hide the intensity of his observation.

I shifted position subtly, pulling my hair over my shoulder, allowing me to see him in my peripheral vision. As I twirled a lock playfully around my finger, I noticed J shake his head as he moved toward one of the drawers.

I couldn't even begin to guess at the thoughts running through his mind, but he was clearly going to let me get away with this...at least until he got more information.

After some shuffling of kitchen gadgets, he came up behind me, a little to the side, as I continued to lean over the counter. I made sure he was getting an eyeful, and that the dress was sending him all the right signals.

And, if I'm wearing it right, just a little glimpse of the curve where my back meets my ass.

I didn't hear any movement for a few seconds, and I hoped he had stopped to take it all in. I counted to three, tossed my hair back over my shoulder, and let him consider that for a brief moment before I turned. With any luck, a number of sensual thoughts were streaming unchecked through his head. Like a flash before my eyes, my mind fast-forwarded through several carnal scenarios. But we had a long way to go before that happened.

If it happens, I reminded myself.

Confidence was one thing, but I wasn't naive enough to make assumptions about what would take place this night. I knew what I wanted and what I was willing to do to get it; however, overindulging in the belief that it was a given would be foolish, potentially leading me down a rabbit hole of disappointment. I needed to hold tight to realistic possibilities. At the very least, I would have closure, one way or another.

Turning slowly, I rested my palms on the counter behind me as I cocked my head to one side.

"Any luck with that corkscrew? I'm really ready for a glass of wine."

Among other things. But wine first. These nerves aren't

going to settle themselves.

Even though I planned and orchestrated this outline, I was still having a hard time believing that I was standing there with him, face-to-face...for the first time. This moment had been years in the making. My focus stayed on him as I absorbed all I could of his every movement. Even if his answer was no, I wanted to be able to revisit him in my mind's eye.

'Empowering' isn't really a word I expected to hear associated with that world. How so?

Marketing is cool. My mother has a small company and I help with her marketing.

You say it like that 'big break' is right around the corner - ha! Oh, for now I just take on some odd jobs here and there. I should probably figure out something more solid, though, since I'm not getting any younger and the writing hasn't panned out. I'm 33, by the way...

J remained silent as he showed me the corkscrew in his hand. Taking it, I turned back to the counter where I had set down the bottle and began to open it with swift, experienced motions. He noticed.

"You're pretty good at that," he remarked, half mumbling.

This was a bizarre puzzle. One that he couldn't put together without the pieces.

"Thank you. I've had a lot of experience. Glasses?"

"Hmm? Oh, yeah." He was playing along a bit now, but I needed to keep this moving before he snapped out of it and started demanding answers about who I was and why I was there. I didn't want this to be unmasked with a frustrated tone.

As he opened a cupboard, reaching in for two glasses, I asked, "How are you doing? It's been a long time."

Sounding relieved and apologetic at the same time, he said, "So, I *do* know you? I think I'd remember meeting you, and I'm sorry, but I don't recall."

A little more relaxed now, he reached past me for the bottle, pouring two glasses of wine. The scent of his cologne lit up my senses. My legs trembled. I gripped the counter a little tighter.

The quicker J solved the riddle of who I was, the closer I moved to finding my own answers. To solving the enigma that I had nervously travelled so far to crack.

"Well," I started slowly, "you do *kind of* know me. We confided in each other once, years ago. You shared something with me...something that no one else was privy to. At least, at the time."

So much time had passed between that moment of intimate confidence and where we both found ourselves today. I had to accept the fact that *maybe* he had found someone with whom he shared his secrets in the intervening years. Someone who had changed him, possibly even given him the passionate love life he had once confessed he craved. He was a handsome man, the kind who would have opportunities thrown at his feet on a constant basis.

The gamble for the evening was based on the knowledge that, at one time, he definitely didn't want anyone to know the details of his preferences for private pleasures. I'd wagered that the pain of betrayal had stayed with him through all these years, that he still wasn't letting the truth be known to the women in his life. That somehow, a decade later, he was still suppressing the side of himself that I wanted to release.

My thoughts wandered back to our emailing days, and

how I had gently drawn out of J what was on his mind. It had taken a lot of sharing on my part, about my life and the world in which I worked, to encourage him to even begin talking about what ignited him physically.

I snapped back to the present, seeing that now he was the one cocking his head. He looked perplexed.

"You mean...a secret?" he asked with a bit of a furrowed brow as he tried to recall what he could have shared with someone he didn't recognize. But he had never seen me before, so this was going to take just one more gentle nudge.

"Yes, a secret. But more than that, really." I paused. "A...desire."

No more visual groping. His attention was now focused, searching my eyes for confirmation as realization slowly dawned. Yet, I could also see his bewilderment. It seemed so impossible. Surely it couldn't be...not after all these years.

His confusion and hesitation were my confirmation. I knew, with certainty, that nothing had changed for him in this regard. He still kept it hidden, accepting missionary mediocrity, most certainly allowing his partner to dictate the plays of the game. That was, after all, safer than letting someone see his raw side again.

He had been with the same girlfriend for a long time. If he hadn't shown it to her by now, no one was likely to be let in. No one except, hopefully, as he had said a long time ago...me.

I was searching him, too. Penetrating him. Striving to read him as I tried to gauge just how far down he had buried that secret fragment of himself. We were standing in this time and place more than ten years after he had shared it with me, and it had been even longer since he wrote his erotic pieces. Did he have to put those yearnings into a proverbial box, tucking it away in the attic of his mind, where our deepest desires are held in storage? Dust collects, webs are built, and life goes on. We allow distractions to creep in, taking from us the animalistic tendencies we have, even if they aren't behaviors on which we are acting.

He cleared his throat. “Okay, so, I really don't know what you're referring to. You're going to have to give me something else to go on here.”

He shuffled his feet as the epiphany advanced. It was all there, bubbling just beneath the surface. One more inch and he’d break through.

I smiled. Not coyly this time, but a truly warm, friendly smile. The kind of signal that told him to relax, that it was going to be okay. And it worked – it was barely visible, but some of the tension left him.

Well, for one, dancing really solidified my independence. I will never lean too heavily on someone else again. And when it comes to the future, my definition of ‘partnership’ has changed. For the better, I think. Or at least in my favor.

That’s really great that you’re helping your mother!

I’m 30...

Taking my glass, I walked out of the kitchen, looking around at what I could see of the house from where I was standing.

To my left, a long, wide hallway angled and disappeared out of sight. In the opposite direction, there was a large archway to a dark cavern. Squinting slightly, I thought I detected the outline of a dining room table. Doors along the wall to the side of it led to parts unknown.

The house was impressive, yet modest for someone who was so accomplished. That didn't matter to me. I found it endearing to learn he hadn't been caught up in the fame and money.

Absorbing the tasteful and welcoming décor, my mind wandered to thoughts of the bedroom, wherever it was, and what I was hoping would be taking place in there later. Or anywhere else in the house he desired for that matter. I felt the heat between my legs, tried to stifle a shudder, and reminded myself that I needed to remain in control of this situation, at least for the time being.

"I'm referring to something you shared with me a lifetime ago, J," I said, and spun quickly to again look him in the eyes, but only briefly.

The living room was a few steps ahead of me at the back of the house. Without invitation, I walked toward it as he continued to process. I heard him quietly sip his wine, which reminded me that I hadn't touched mine. I started with a small taste, then took a larger, though ladylike, drink. Having bought it on my way, it was still cold and tasted delicious. Thank goodness because I was about to come unglued on the inside.

I stood, taking in the layout of the living room. It was a large room, slightly more rectangular than it was square, with lots of overstuffed furniture. There was a vast stone fireplace on one end, an enormous flat screen television in a corner, and some end tables with various décor on them. A number of the pieces looked decidedly imported. Possibly remembrances of his travels to the four corners of the earth.

Opposite the end with the fireplace was a big couch. Placed perpendicular to it, I noted a matching armchair. Another over-sized piece. There was a large, square coffee table positioned within reach of both, but the overall size of the room left more than enough space to navigate around it.

The tones were earthy and masculine, with little splashes of muted color here and there. It was all very warm and inviting.

Oh, cool. So, where do we go from here? I'm Jack, by the way. A few people who are close to me call me J, but most use Jack.

Also, you've probably already seen it on my page, but I'm in New York City. And you are…?

J walked over to stand in front of me, not trying to block me from going further into the room, but still assessing me and the odd situation in which he found himself. What had probably started out to be a typical Sunday night for him had been altered.

My instincts told me that if I stepped in closer, possibly making a small, suggestive gesture giving him the green light to escalate this to a physical dimension, he just might respond. The calculations taking place behind his eyes told me he suspected my identity, and with that knowledge, perhaps he was feeling the draw of our past connection. But J needed to be in control of the game-changing call, if and when we arrived at what he deemed the appropriate moment.

It was essential for us to be patient, to feel the ebb and flow of our conversational tide, watching for when the right wave would break. I hoped to coax J into riding the surge until finally it crested. Then, and only then, he would take what he wanted. Rushing it would do a terrible disservice to this time I had stolen for us.

"Can I at least get a name? Maybe that will help me," he said with a hint of frustration.

I was moving slowly, gracefully, looking at knick-knacks, twirling my hair on my finger again in an absent-minded fashion. I was in his house...drinking a glass of wine...and I knew I couldn't hold out the mystery woman routine much longer. One more quick round before I was going to give up the ghost.

"Is there a particular name coming to mind?" I asked, turning to look at him.

J hesitated before answering me. "Maybe...but you go first," he said firmly, setting down his glass and crossing his arms in front of his chest.

"Look, I understand this is highly unusual and I *have* caught you off guard here. But please tell me the name you're thinking of. If you're not right, I'll tell you who I am, and it will be no harm, no foul. Okay?"

More hesitation, but I could see him considering it. We both held our ground, staring at each other for what seemed like an eternity. There was a clock ticking, and I was suddenly aware of the absence of music. Once we got this part settled, I needed to ask him to turn on some tunes.

A loud sports car drove by, outside in the real world, and when that sound faded into the distance, we were back to only that damnable clock...and our own breathing.

He opened his mouth, started to say something, then closed it firmly.

I will have those lips on me before this is over, I boldly thought, my desire for him mounting as I observed his expression.

The seconds ticked by. It was clear the staring contest needed a conclusion that included an answer.

I glanced down at the floor, on the verge of giving in, when he suddenly whispered, "Natalie."

CHAPTER FOUR

Raising my head ever so slightly, I flashed him a bashful, playful sideways kind of look. His educated guess had been correct, causing him to shake his head in stunned amazement. At least he didn't seem angry. A flush of relief surged through me. For the time being, it looked as though my plan was moving forward. At the very least, confirming his suspicions hadn't gotten me thrown out on my ass yet.

"Hi, J," I whispered. I was playing shy girl now.

"But... What... How... But..." There was a heavy sigh followed by a sharp intake of breath through his teeth. "I am *so* fucking confused right now. What are you doing here? How did you find me? Why are you here? I'm...I'm..."

"Hey, I get it," I simply said, taking a sip of my wine.

Of course, this didn't answer any of his questions. Other than why I was there, though, the rest of the queries were, in my mind, rather irrelevant. I was also confident that once he slowed down and focused, the reason for my presence would become abundantly clear. When he came to *that* conclusion, what happened next would be in his hands...literally, with any luck.

He sipped his wine and grimaced. “I need something stronger for this,” he muttered. “Do you mind if I switch to bourbon?”

“No, not at all.”

He started to turn toward the kitchen, stopped, looked me briefly in the eye, then turned again. After another step, he faced me once more, this time taking a long, slow look...from head to toe and back up again. As if I was the bourbon, and he was savoring it.

He's in there. I know he is.

After a second of hesitation he walked from the room, still shaking his head as he went, leaving me momentarily alone. Just me and the sound of my heartbeat, thudding heavily in my chest. The thump of cupboard doors and the clinking of glass broke the silence, and I called out, “Hey, would you mind putting on some music?”

“Yeah. I guess,” he mumbled as he walked back into the living room holding bourbon in a rocks glass...minus the rocks. “What do you want to hear?”

“Oingo Boingo?” I teased with a mischievous grin and a raised eyebrow.

It was a subtle nudge of familiarity, telling him that I remembered his favorite band. His eyes grew wide with the realization.

“No, I'm kidding,” I said with a giggle. “Anything but that. Something a bit...more...less enthusiastic. Please.”

He was staring again until he finally turned toward the stereo and started fiddling with the buttons. As I watched his hands, I could feel the heat rising in my belly, burning, teetering me close to the brink just from being in his presence.

This direct proximity to him, after all that time we had spent getting to know each other, had my senses on a razor's edge. I was captivated by the way he moved, and it created a tangible feeling of anticipation deep within me. Could he sense it? I anxiously hoped I wasn't outwardly projecting the nerves I felt.

A fleeting thought told me to be grateful that we didn't meet back then. We would have had fun together, but I don't know if we would have been ready for each other. In fact, I was fairly certain that, as much as I wanted him, with everything I had going on personally and professionally, the timing would have been all wrong. I think I instinctively knew it, and that was why I hadn't done anything about advancing our relationship beyond the emails.

Now, the timing was still all wrong, but from here on out, at no point in our lives, would it ever be just right. So, taking this brief moment in time I had appropriated for us was all we had left.

At least now we had gained more wisdom; processed life and what it had to offer a little more. Although, as I stood there, desperately trying to hide from him that I was physically trembling, I was questioning my sanity.

Disregarding a mental health check, cat-and-mouse continued...

He was still pressing buttons and working on the stereo, so I said, "Hey, how about some Jackson Browne?"

J may not have remembered, but I did, and a few seconds later, I heard it...the song he had on his MySpace page when all of this started – "Doctor, My Eyes."

Even with all the planning and preparing I had done for this night, I couldn't have executed that any better if

I had been swiping through the playlist myself. It brought me right back to one of our first exchanges, right after he officially introduced himself and sent me a friend request, which I declined.

J,
I like the idea of calling you J...do you mind? You can call me Natalie. Or Nat. Whatever you're comfortable with.
I'm in Louisiana. Acadiana region. Cajun territory.
How about music? I was just listening to a new Lady Gaga song when you answered my message and now I'm digging your Jackson Browne tune. What else are you into?
Natalie

When he turned to face me, I could see he had reached his limit. He was done complying until he had more information. I had my wine, and he had granted my request for music – enough.

He held out his hands as if to say, *"Explanation now, please."*

Natalie,
Sure, you can call me J. I think you'll be the first person I don't know really well who's done that.
I'm not into Lady Gaga. Sorry. Oingo Boingo is my favorite band. Lots of others, too. I have a wide range of tastes, for the most part. Is Lady Gaga your thing? (Not judging.)
J

Aware that I was probably appearing very tense, I reminded myself to relax my shoulders, and took a deep breath.

"Okay, I know this is mind boggling..."

"More like mind blowing," he interrupted.

"We can save the blowing for later." Known for shooting from the hip with off-color jokes when I was nervous, it slipped out before I could stop myself. He didn't seem amused and gave me a look meant to circumvent any further wisecracks on my part. As much as I hoped to reignite our flirtatious tone of the past, now was not the time. Now, he wanted answers.

"All right," I began. "We have a friend in common."

At this, he looked startled and very unsettled, so I quickly continued.

"This friend doesn't know anything about us. I promise you that. But I found out where you were and I was going to be in the area, so I decided to finally come meet you. I know it's been a long time and things just kind of faded out when I was seeing that guy and you had a girlfriend, too, and... Well, I don't know. Here I am.

"It probably doesn't make any sense and if you want me to go, I absolutely will and I'll never bother you again, but I thought if you wanted me to stay, we could get to know each other, you know, in person and just hang out because we were pretty close back in the day when we used to email and all that and..."

I stopped myself. I had babbled, and now that I couldn't undo it, my wishful thinking was that this would come across to him as cute. He didn't say anything.

My trembling had increased, and my nerves were shot, so without thinking, I asked, "Do you want me to? Go?"

Damn – why did I say that? I needed to hold myself together better than that if I was going to get through this. So far, the way I was presenting it was veering off in a much different direction from the way I had rehearsed it.

"What? Oh, no. No, you don't have to go. I'm just still trying to process all of this. You being here and all." *Thank goodness.* "Who is the friend?"

"It's not important, J, other than to say that they were how I was able to find you."

"Well, if someone I know is giving out personal information about me..." I saw the inevitable light bulb flicker in his head. "Is this why you contacted me years ago? Is all of this some kind of joke?" There was a hint of anger building in him now.

"I promise you, this is not a joke. They don't know that you and I have ever talked, written, whatever. And trust me, they're not giving out your personal information."

"Why would someone tell you where I am if they don't know we have a history?"

"Please trust me. I'm not some star-struck groupie who—"

"—who is just going to turn up on my doorstep out of the blue," he finished.

Suddenly, I could see how bad this endeavor was beginning to look to J. My objective was to be honest with him...to a degree. I had felt that telling him we shared a person was necessary, but as with my babbling, the way it had played out in my head sounded a whole lot less cryptic than the course it was taking. Evidently, knowing for myself that I had no nefarious purpose wasn't the same as J understanding it. Contrary to what I had envisioned, none of this was settling very well with him.

"Okay, cards on the table." *Some of them.* I took another deep breath. "In order to answer your question, yes. Years ago, I was talking with a friend and you cropped up in conversation. You sounded...attractive, and I wanted to get to know you..."

"So, you didn't just find me by sheer chance?"

"No. Admittedly, I didn't..."

J stood looking at me, taking in all of it, still confused. "And you're here today because...?"

"Because things felt unfinished between us," I told him. "Look, it's not all that outside of the box, is it? I heard about you, and I was interested, so I found you and we wrote. And when our correspondence...ended, it left a nagging little question in my life. One I feel a need to answer."

I could see J was trying to take in this information – that I had been fascinated enough to go in search of him. That his impact on my life had been profound enough for me to find him again, a decade later.

His eyes scanned over me as he took a few steps in my direction, but then stopped as if he didn't want to get too close to a flame. I casually shifted to the side, giving him space, pretending to look at some artwork on the wall. He walked to the couch and sat down.

I had my back to him, and trying to make a comeback from my chattering, ever so slightly shook my long, straight hair. This was an invitation...for later. If we could get past our present topic.

J,

Sorry to say Oingo Boingo isn't my thing. Truth be told, neither is Lady Gaga. No judgment on this end either, though. Although judging seems to be a favorite pastime of others I encounter.

Natalie

"Sit," he finally said, waving a hand at the multiple seating options in the room. I was happy to see he was moving on from the friend topic for the time being.

I was also grateful that he didn't ask how long my preoccupation with him had been going on before I found him online. In the situation we were now in, he thought we had a history dating back twelve years. I would have been rattled to have to tell him, on my end, it was over twenty years.

I turned to see J leaning his elbows on his knees, the bourbon on a coaster in front of him. He was looking in my direction, focused on the floor.

"I'm good with standing, thanks. I don't sit well." Nervously, I followed with, "I guess I spent so many years on my feet for work that it became my comfort zone."

"Right," he said slowly, his gaze finding mine and holding steady. I could see he was debating on whether or not to verbalize what he was thinking. After a few seconds, the forward approach won. "Stripper, right? Exotic dancer."

With this, his eyes were all over me again, finally resting on my chest. Being without a bra, I knew exactly what had caught his attention, and the intense scrutiny made them harden further.

This small gesture told me I was already getting a response from him that he wouldn't normally show anyone else. I knew from what he wrote to me that he was a watcher, an observer. He wanted to take what he wanted in the physical form, but he also desired the freedom to openly view his interests without fear of shame. It was just another intricate piece of what he kept hidden.

"That's right," I said.

"And you were in Louisiana," he remembered.

"Yes."

"And now?"

"Now? I'm...still there. Status quo." I took a sip of my

wine, recognizing this line of questioning as expected ground.

"You were getting serious with someone the last time we wrote," he said, more in the form of a question than a statement.

"I was. We got married. We're still married." I hesitated, shifting my weight from right to left foot. "Happily. And your girlfriend?" I asked, only to be polite.

"She's fine. If you're so happily married, why are you here?"

Fair enough.

Thoughtfully, even though I had prepared for this inquiry, I said, "Because no matter how hard we try...no matter how successful we are at burying them...fantasies don't die."

I was telling the truth while leaving out the main reason J had been catapulted back into my mind. Depending on how the night went, maybe I would mention it later, *if* I needed to, but I didn't want to bring it up just then. Mentioning my husband and his executive decisions would only serve to launch me into a bitch fest that I didn't want to get into until we better established where this was going.

To this, he raised one eyebrow, taking it in. He seemed to be settling into the evening and my surprise arrival. Feeling more comfortable in his own home again.

Now that he knew who I was, I had no doubt that the connection we had was flooding back into his memory. He was remembering that I *knew* him, and that opened the door for more unrestrained communication. Now, he was ready to be more bold.

"So, married women still have fantasies. Okay. I don't think most of them put on come-fuck-me dresses and show up on the doorsteps of men they had bizarre email flings with a decade ago, though."

I internally flinched, unsure if my reaction was because he had called our past "bizarre," or if I was a little stunned that he had called me out so quickly. Probably both.

He stood up and went to a window, looking out at the darkness that had now completely fallen over his backyard.

"I mean, isn't it more in keeping with the times to look up an old high school boyfriend and have an affair with him?"

"Who said anything about having an affair?" I asked.

Quickly, he turned and moved in front of me.

"Well, honestly, Natalie. What is this? Why are you here? Totally out of the blue, wearing...*that*. You're talking about something that happened years ago...and now...this. And you're married. And, well, what the fuck?" J let out a heavy sigh. "This is ridiculous. I don't even know if Natalie is your real name. I don't know a godforsaken thing about you other than the stripper story, which, now that I'm seeing you in person, I believe, quite frankly."

While I realized his comment was likely intended as a positive, and my history had presented me with my fair share of backdoor compliments, I made no effort to conceal how off-putting this sounded.

He looked frustrated. "No, not like that. I mean, you're definitely attractive enough."

I winced, exhibiting that being attractive was not indicative of being a dancer.

"Fuck," J said. "I'm sorry. Nothing is coming out right. Sorry. I just...I don't get it. Who the hell am I? And who the hell are you?"

In an effort to diffuse the situation while accepting

his frustrated apology, I cautiously approached him, putting my hand on his arm, touching him for the first time. *Ever.* The electricity was sharp. I felt it course through me, causing a slight ankle wobble that I tried to offset with a step to the side.

"Maybe we should just slow down, take a step back and we'll start at the top, okay? I think I already answered why I'm here. And you *do* know me, J. There were a lot of components to what we shared. You got me to open up about more than just the dancing revelation, and I know you're aware of that."

I paused, reluctantly removing my hand. He looked at the spot where I had touched him, making a face that told me he had felt the power of our physical connection, too.

Good.

"Fantasies," J flatly replied, focusing on my remark about why I was there while leaving alone my statement regarding what our knowledge of each other actually entailed.

"Regarding why now...well, why not? Do you remember back in the day we once talked about meeting in Florida? You were going to see your mom and I was going to be a couple hours away at the same time? We weren't able to make that happen because of my schedule. I thought maybe this was...opportunity knocking...again."

He looked into my eyes for a moment and faintly nodded.

"As for what I'm wearing, I have a bag in the car, and I can get changed...if you'd like."

I stopped there, the ball now firmly in his court. I had no intention of speaking again until he answered that because it *was* a question, even though it wasn't formed as such. I was hoping he would decline my offer, but I had thrown it out there, aiming to exhibit that I was willing to accept any concessions necessary to make him comfortable.

"You have a bag in the car," he repeated.

"I'm traveling, J."

"Right."

He moved in to close the gap between us. J had about nine inches in height on me, but with the heels I was wearing, it was more like five. I looked up into his face, making every effort to keep any expression from my eyes. I wasn't going to beg for this, but I was also pretty sure that it wouldn't even come close to being necessary.

He reached out, running one hand down my hair before brushing it away to my back, off my shoulder. I felt his fingers graze my skin. It was all I could do to stop myself from shuddering.

Stepping back, he looked me up and down again.

How many times was this now?

It didn't matter, and he was past caring if I saw him do it. He knew why I was dressed like this, and he knew that undressing me with his eyes was expected. Encouraged.

"I'm not crazy – don't change," he finally said.

J turned and walked back to the couch, but before sitting this time, he said, "Sit. Please. I don't want to stand right now, and I'd be more comfortable if you'd sit down, too."

I was feeling the urge to kick off my heels and curl up in the big armchair next to the couch, but I thought it might be a bit too soon for such a casual maneuver. Instead, I approached it and sat down, careful to keep my knees tightly together, slowly crossing my legs. I didn't want to be so crass as to pull a *Basic Instinct* move on him.

Not yet anyway.

"Who's the mutual friend?" he asked again.

"J, I already told you I'm not getting into it."

"Why not? How could this person be telling you about me and not know about us?"

"I promise, no one knows. You needn't be suspicious of any of your friends. They don't know anything about us. Not that we've ever written to each other, not that I'm here...nothing. I have to ask you to *please* trust me and leave that there."

"Trust you," he said in a slightly high-pitched tone, as if it was a ludicrous request. "No doubt you remember my affinity for privacy?"

"Yes, J, I do. I absolutely do, and that's why I am asking you to believe that my appearance here has nothing to do with anyone else. It is honestly not my intention to cause trouble for you."

Our related friend would never deliberately stir the pot for J, either. That said, I knew their personalities were night and day, and that Mark sometimes had a tendency to meddle in places J where didn't want advice. There were only the best of intentions behind the mild intrusions, but I had been told on numerous occasions that they felt very differently about life, love, and relationships.

Divulging to J who it was that we shared could prompt a phone call that might elicit...what? I didn't want to find out. Mark wasn't aware of my feelings, and J didn't need to know about the friendship, beyond grasping it was what had brought me there.

Two very different men holding two very different places in my life. Neither J nor I needed counsel in this matter, and always wanting to insert his two cents, that's exactly what we would both get from Mark. These worlds did not need to collide.

J gave it some thought, and I could tell that, for the moment, he was considering extending me the benefit of the doubt. While it would only be natural to feel compelled to know the source, it was feasible that his line of thinking was beginning to follow mine. I hoped his drive for solitude and privacy would supersede curiosity.

Between J's career – that put him squarely in the spotlight – and the personal relationships in which we were both committed, discretion was an important factor of what might take place as we moved forward with the evening.

His narrowed eyes scanned me, looking for signs of deception, perhaps. When he was done taking stock of that, he very slowly looked me over, drinking me in inch by inch, again. I fixed my eyes onto his, focused on keeping my trembling under control.

When he arrived back at my face and our eyes locked, something jogged his memory. “Shit,” he said, abruptly getting up to go to the kitchen. As an afterthought, on his way out of the living room, he followed with, “Excuse me for just a minute.”

I took this opportunity to stand again, as it was my preferred position for the moment. It allowed for movement, which dispersed some of the nervous tension within me.

Walking into his line of vision, I saw him leaning against the counter, holding his cell phone to his ear. There was no discernable countenance on his face.

The person on the other end answered, and J simply said, “Hey, man.”

Uh oh.

Even with the distance that was between us – he in the kitchen and I in the living room – I could hear a man's voice talking on the other end. I was relieved to hear he wasn't calling the girlfriend, but I had to strain my ears to determine that the tone and pitch weren't on par with Mark's sound.

Phew!

Whoever he needed to connect with had a lot to say, though, so J stood there, still expressionless, for almost a minute as he listened.

Finally, his patience wore thin. "Yeah, yeah, we'll take care of that, but listen, I have to cancel for tonight. Something came up."

He listened again, then said, "You could say that." He narrowed his eyes and kept them focused on me. "Yeah, man, I'll call you tomorrow to reschedule."

More listening on J's end. I thought I caught a glimpse of a small eye roll, which made me giggle quietly. J grasped it and gave me a little smile.

So sexy.

"Yup, all right. Thanks, man. Talk to you," J finished and put the phone on the counter.

He remained in the kitchen for several seconds, staring at me, before walking back to the living room. Coming to a stop in front of me, he brushed my bangs out of my eyes. "Okay, Natalie. You win. Let's get to know each other...face to face."

CHAPTER FIVE

After taking a deep breath, he asked, "What's with the Jackson Browne song?"

The stereo had long since moved on from "Doctor, My Eyes," but J had noticed my expression when it started, and his curiosity about it was evidently still in place.

"It was playing on your MySpace page when I found you. Ever since then, I always think of you whenever I hear it." Straight sincerity. Nothing more, nothing less.

He frowned. "Should I feel like I'm being stalked?"

"Stalked? No," I said, giving a small laugh. "I haven't made a single move to contact you or be near you in over ten years. Do you feel like I stalked you?"

"I'm not sure," he answered. "I've never been stalked, so I don't know exactly what it feels like." He paused; his brow still furrowed. Finally, with a tilt of the head, he spoke again. "What's the deal with this 'fantasy' talk? If I recall correctly, we shared some...thoughts. But it was just words. I'm a writer, and you seemed to have an affinity for writing yourself, so it was natural to share. It was fun at the time, but what's the point of bringing this up now?"

I walked across the room to put some distance between us.

"Honestly, J," was all I could muster for the moment.

Natalie,

I'm sorry to hear that you have people in your life who are judgmental, although I understand it. People can be difficult sometimes. Or at least I think so, anyway. I find it easier to avoid them most of the time. Except for pool league. For that I'll risk exposing myself to the human race.

Speaking of pastimes, how about hobbies?

J

I was not planning on hashing up his past and the emotional turmoil he had previously gone through, especially as it related to his bedroom activities. I knew about all of it. At this point, he was aware of my detailed memories. I hadn't gone there to spend time dredging it up and having a discussion about it. Physically addressing it and confronting it head-on, yes, but talking about it, no.

If he wanted to try to brush it aside as a non-issue now, that was fine. But he wasn't fooling me.

We stood staring at each other, and then I finally turned my back and leaned over, very deliberately, as I pretended to give my attention to a picture on an end table. In reality, I couldn't even keep my eyes focused on what I was looking at.

I could hear his breathing get heavier, even from

across the room. I stood up straight, keeping my back to him, and then there was the sound of his stocking feet walking across the carpet. My heart was racing again. I knew what I desired...but it was still too soon. There was much ground we needed to cover before the necessary comfort zone was achieved and the juxtaposed tension would be at its true tipping point.

He was behind me, his hand on my hair again, brushing my skin as an afterthought. His touch burned.

"You know, I spent a lot of time imagining what you looked like." A chuckle. "I couldn't tell you how many times I...read your emails, always picturing this woman I created in my head, from what you told me about your appearance."

"And? Do I live up to your expectations?" I asked.

I turned to face him and realized he was standing much closer than I thought. My breasts were only an inch or so away from him, and they were screaming for attention. I wanted to slip that t-shirt over his head and run my hands across his chest.

J let his arm drop down to his side and simply said, "Oh, yes."

For a fleeting moment, I thought I saw something melancholy in his eyes. And then he turned, walking away again.

"How old are you now?" he asked.

"Almost forty-two. How about you?"

He paused. "You don't look it. Just turned forty-four. And I look every bit of it."

I approached him, putting my hand up to his face to touch his goatee. The hair was soft, and this simple gesture felt intimate, further stoking the physical flames that I was attempting to keep internalized.

"You have the scruffy look going on now. I like it.

You're as sexy as you ever were...more so."

He already knew I found him to be very handsome, and I wasn't about to start mincing words.

He rolled his eyes, so I said, "Oh, stop. Men get better with age. Women just...get older. This...is all smoke and mirrors."

"Well, you're doing it right, if I may say so."

"Thank you."

He reached for me, hesitantly, yet stopped as quickly as he started. His hand slowly closed into a fist as he pulled away again.

Fingers running through his hair, he asked, "Do you need another glass of wine? I need some more..." and he wiggled his rocks glass.

I finished what little was left in my glass and nodded. He took it from me, heading for the kitchen. While he was out of sight, I slipped off my heels, placing them neatly next to the big armchair in which I had been sitting earlier. We were moving slowly but making pleasing progress. I didn't anticipate we would hit a lull anytime soon – the air practically crackled with the sexual energy between us – so it was time to get a little more comfortable.

J walked back in carrying the glasses, and I noticed both were much fuller than they had been the first round. He took a long drink out of his while handing me the wine. He looked irresistible. Our fingers touched, causing another spark.

At this point, a twinge of guilt poked at my conscience, but I swatted at it with reckless abandon. My decision had been made. I was going to give myself this *one* night. If J was on the same page, I was going to live this fantasy to the fullest. By the time I was walking out of his front door, destined for the familiarity of my life, I would *know*. And then I was going to go home and walk the line again. For the rest of my life.

I was okay with that. And I needed this in order to be able to concentrate on that line.

So, no, guilty conscience, I can't take your call right now. Leave a message, and I'll get back to you.

He looked down at me, noticing that our height difference had changed dramatically. Then he glanced farther down, saw my bare feet, and paused for a second before going back to the couch to sit.

J,

I never gave it much thought, but I can't say that I really have hobbies. Most of my time these days consists of working and sleeping with the occasional night out thrown into the mix. Sometimes I make notes about a future business plan I have on my mind.

Tell me about your writing. If you're willing to talk about it.

Nat

"So, what else? What have you been doing all these years? Did you start that business you were prepping for?" he asked, clearly attempting to make casual conversation.

Back when J and I were emailing, I was working on a business plan to start up an escort service. Living in an area that saw many executives traveling in from Houston, I thought it was odd that the nearest city didn't have such a thing. Surely these high-powered men would like a little arm candy to accompany them to dinners, keeping them entertained during their downtime from work while they were in town.

I had connections to beautiful women who would

have been happy to work for such a business. I also had links to the bodyguards I would hire to protect the girls from being forced to do anything they didn't want to do.

At the time I talked to J about it, I had already hired a lawyer and we had met several times to discuss the legalities of everything, from protecting myself from criminal activity, to the type of marketing that would be allowed. At that point in my life, I had spent enough time in a dark arena that my personal lines between right and wrong were becoming blurred. And I was leaning toward much riskier endeavors than I ever had before.

I walked toward the stereo, giving a brief thought to the principally questionable place where I once again found myself, before doing a small twirl to face him.

"No, that never came to fruition, unfortunately. Well, I say unfortunately, but in all likelihood, I would have gotten myself in trouble with it. I wasn't too concerned with observing the...finer points, so to speak...of it from a legal perspective. And, in hindsight, I probably would have made the headlines as the Cajun Madam or something like that," I laughed.

"I thought you had a lawyer."

Wow. I couldn't believe he remembered that much about it.

"I did, yes. But he was a little shady, and he knew what I was trying to do, so he was already preparing my criminal defense before the business was even up and running. I still think it would have been a big success, but I'm not sure I would have handled it right," I told J honestly. "That guy was also difficult to work with."

"How so?"

"Oh, you know. He was always getting a little too...hands on...for my liking. The idea of starting the business was so I could step away from actively working in the middle of that scene, but he kept treating me like a piece of merchandise." I let out a small, sad laugh and said to J, "I don't think I ever told you, but he even offered to waive his fee if I..." I trailed off. He knew what I was telling him.

J's expression gave way to one of sadness. He furrowed his brow and shook his head. "That really sucks, Nat. I'm sorry you had to go through that. I wish you *had* told me."

At the sound of my name – my name for tonight – being used so casually, and shortened to 'Nat,' like he always used to do when writing, I relaxed a little more.

"Why? Would you have come to my rescue?" I said, giving a wry chuckle.

Another look of sadness. "Maybe. I don't know. But we could have talked about it."

"I'm kidding, J. I didn't need rescuing then, and I don't need it now," I said evenly.

"I know. I just wish I had known. I thought we shared most things..."

"We did. I didn't mention that because it made me feel...dirty. So, I just handled it."

"And that put a stop to all of your ideas?"

"That and some of my own thoughts I had on the subject. First and foremost, I was questioning my plan to keep the girls safe with assigned bodyguards. If something ever happened to one of them, I never would have been able to live with myself.

"And then I was considering the morals of it. I mean, it was one thing when I was in the murky club world and watching my own back, but as the business started to take on a life of its own, it felt wrong to be talking about how to keep myself absolved of legal liability for their behavior."

J listened but said nothing.

I shrugged. "Maybe it's something that's hard to see unless you're actually in it since it *all* seems like morally ambiguous ground. But working for someone else and running a gig like that were two totally different animals in my head."

He nodded slowly. "I can understand that, I think."

While I was happy that J was remembering more of the things we had spoken of in the past than I thought he would, I really wanted to steer the subject away from it. This particular path of memory lane was not a place in which I wanted to walk at that moment.

Seeking a topic more conducive to the positive atmosphere I was trying to engender, I said, "I hear you've been doing great things with your writing. Screenplays, awards, accolades, all the good stuff. That's really great!"

"Hmm, yeah. Thanks." He smiled. "It's been a wild ride. Especially for someone like me."

I thought I knew where he was going, but I tilted my head and let him continue.

"I still struggle with the emotional stuff. You knew about that, right?"

Of course I knew all that. It was one of the reasons why I was there. His short comment skirted how serious the issue was for him, though.

"Yes, I remember," I said with another tilt of my head.

J was a highly sensitive creature, taking life to heart more than most people. He knew this, and because that in and of itself bothered him, he usually avoided too much contact with others. It wasn't that he *wouldn't* leave the house...it was more that it was easier for him to keep to himself.

"Eh. It is what it is. I'm happy here, and I have all the peace I need to do my writing. Order in food. Keep my own schedule. Can't complain."

"Well, when you put it like that, it sounds like something I would welcome on a lot of days. Peopling seems to be getting harder and harder, ya know?" I was hoping to keep my tone light in the face of what I knew was a very difficult subject for him.

"Oh, I know."

J very pointedly looked at me, leaving me unsure of where to go next with the conversation. How he'd been over the years mattered to me. I sincerely wanted to know. But the timing didn't seem right for this; it was too early for covering the deeper ground, and I was grasping for a more playful, seductive tone. If we went down this road in the beginning, I foresaw us falling into a friendship tête-à-tête while the rest passed to the wayside.

"Mind if I play a song?" I asked, motioning toward the stereo.

"Just type it in. Nothing cheesy allowed, though," he said with a smirk.

"Let's hope not."

A small touchscreen appeared at the tip of my finger. A few taps later, the dulcet tones of Shinedown started playing. I looked at J for approval and got a raised eyebrow and a shrug.

We had shared a lot of music with each other in the past. Both of us were moved by it and needed it to survive, more so than the average person. While we didn't agree on everything we sent back and forth, we enjoyed introducing each other to sounds we hadn't listened to before.

As "Second Chance" started, I turned up the speakers a little and my hips began to sway, just a touch, side to side. Brent Smith was getting ramped up into the first chorus as he sang about Hayley's Comet waving to him, while J sat still, observing, and said nothing.

I slowly put my glass to my lips and leaned my head back to drink. A long, careful swallow that exposed my neck as I tilted my head a little further. Putting my glass down on the end table nearest me, I gracefully raised my hands over my head. The music took me, as it always did.

My time on stage had taught me the key to dancing sensually was to move *slowly*, no matter what the music was doing. When I had first started out on that career path it took some getting used to, but I was now a master of it. I simply let the deep burning I felt for J dictate my small, focused movements.

Glancing furtively at him, I saw him recline into the comfort of the couch cushions and slowly cross his legs. He draped one arm across the back of it, as if placing it around someone, while his other hand raised the glass to his lips. He took a long, leisurely sip. It looked like he didn't take much of the bourbon, and his eyes never left me.

Excellent. I wanted his undivided attention.

With practiced precision, I balanced on the balls of my bare feet while utilizing every ounce of muscle control I had in my legs to gracefully lower myself to the floor. At the right moment of descent, I shifted my weight to my heels, executing a soft sitting motion onto the thick throw rug beneath me. My knees were pulled up to my chest, arms resting over them and out in front of me.

My primary goal – pulling off this particular move with the appearance of consummate ease – was accomplished. As was the second important factor – that I remain in a position so he had a side view only. Facing front would have given him a field of vision I didn't want him to have just yet. Facing away from him simply wouldn't have had the desired effect.

In an effort to mimic the look of the shoes I was no longer wearing, I raised my heels while pushing my toes into the rug.

As the music played, I casually stretched my arms straight above my head. While keeping toes pointed downward, I began to transition to a prone position, arching myself as the back of my head kissed the floor softly. I flattened out, hair fanning in a wave of blonde behind me. I arched again, unhurriedly, and just enough to mimic a position of ecstasy.

Shinedown was wrapping it up and in a nimble move, I rolled over, playfully kicked my feet, swung my hair behind me, and put my chin in my hands.

CHAPTER SIX

J was still leaning back, holding his rocks glass, and staring at me. When the next song started, a look came over his face like he was being snapped out of a trance, but he said nothing.

I stood and, as casually as I could, bounced over to the chair and sat down, tucking my feet underneath me.

I watched him for a minute. His intense gaze combined with his casual position caused a flurry of fluttering inside me. He looked so powerful, so strong, so *fucking* sexy...and all I could think about was climbing onto him, straddling him, unbuttoning his jeans, and finally...

Not yet!

If and when the time came, how it played out wouldn't be my call anyway.

He was absorbing what had just taken place in his living room. While I'm sure he could have had anyone he wanted perform for him with the wave of a wand, I would have been willing to bet it had never happened...until now.

When we were writing to each other, it had been my willingness to open up first that tugged on J to share some of what he harbored within. Now, I was hoping that my outgoing display would elicit a similar release. It was my aim that, as I openly gave myself, he would let me have small pieces in return...until we arrived at his moment of control. And then he would give me the rest.

"Hey, how about a house tour?" I asked, trying to sound casual. I desperately needed him to move. If he didn't, the pose he was in would have been my undoing in another two point five seconds.

Thankfully, it worked, and he sat forward. "Sure."

I exhaled, followed by a quick, shallow breath in, suddenly aware that this was my first taste of oxygen in...how long?

I had just aptly demonstrated my grace as a former professional dancer, hence there was an embarrassing irony in the fact that when I attempted to rise and follow him, my legs turned to jelly. As I moved into an upright position, I stumbled and fell into him.

Super graceful.

Fortunately, he caught me, and it was then that I discovered just how strong he really was.

As his arms reached out for me, I put my hands on his biceps, feeling his muscles. That's when I saw the future flash before my eyes. That body on top of me, those arms around me, his eyes gazing into mine – my whole existence consisting of uncontrollable planetary bursts of intense pleasure.

I can't stand, I thought. *You have to stand, Nat. Do it.*

"You okay?" he asked with a bit of a frown.

"Yeah. Oh, yeah. I'm good. Sorry about that...just a total klutz."

He gave a short laugh. "You're a dancer and you're also a klutz? Isn't that kind of an oxymoron?"

I smiled. "I once read that dancers are some of the clumsiest people. I don't know if that's true for all of them, but it definitely is for me...under the right circumstances."

He let go of me but kept his hands close just in case. To my astonishment, and relief, I managed to stand on my own. Satisfied that I wasn't going to collapse into a heap on his floor, he tentatively moved his arms away from my sides and began the house tour.

"So," he started, "you've seen the foyer and the kitchen." Here he stopped to give me a look that included one raised eyebrow, presumably pondering my forced entry into his home. "And this is, obviously, the living room."

He walked across the room to an entranceway and flipped on a switch that illuminated a chandelier over the dining room table. I came up behind him, just peeking in enough to see a table with eight chairs and a china cabinet. There were no dishes displayed in it, but the light danced off a huge set of matching stemware, all different shapes and sizes. Crystal, no doubt.

"I had the table imported from Italy," he said. And then kind of shrugged like it wasn't a big deal. As if to justify why he told me that, he continued with, "I was there a few years ago for a film and it was...well, there aren't words. Beautiful. I'm Italian – did you know that?"

J stopped and looked at me. I scanned the archives of my memory, finding a file that reminded me he had once emailed about his family tree. I nodded.

Satisfied with my brief acknowledgment, he continued. "So, I wanted to bring back something big and memorable. Something I could always have."

He gave a wave to the table and let his hand fall back to his leg with a small smacking sound.

The table looked heavy with sturdy chairs. Dark wood, masculine, almost thoughtful. I tried to picture him sitting at the head of it in one of the captain's chairs, presiding over a dinner party of witty friends. I wondered what his companions thought when he sat there looking at them. Does he have female friends? How can they stand to be around him? Do they beg him to make love to them? Do they squirm in his expensive imported seats as they look across the table at him?

On the walls, he had some artwork. A stark winter painting caught my eye, and I walked over to get a closer look.

"This is really interesting," I said.

It was a shadowy piece. One of those paintings that makes you feel like everything is devoid of life. As if creation never happened. Somber and cold, the planet rotates all by its lonesome, with snow falling, and no one to hear the soft sound of the flakes hitting the ground.

"Yeah, well, you know I can be kind of dark sometimes. This one really speaks to that side of me."

"I get it. I love pieces like this. I have a winter scene in my house. It's a hunting piece, actually, which is kind of weird because no one in my family hunts, and I obviously live in a place that doesn't see much of a winter. But it's snowing, and you have to look really hard to see the hunters and their prey and it just...I don't know...fascinates me. When I look at it, I feel like I can hear the snow falling in those woods."

He gave me a look that I couldn't really read before turning back to his painting. "Cool. Yeah, that's kind of how I feel about this one."

```
Nat,
 I hope I don't drive you crazy when I
hit these low points. I do appreciate you
listening, though.
J
```

Out of the corner of my eye, something moved, and I looked over to see a cat stretching. An orange tabby – the one I had seen sitting in the window when I first arrived.

J saw me looking at the cat. "That's Frederick. His friends call him Fred."

Fred was perched on a carpeted shelf that was attached to the inside of one of the windows.

"He's cute," I said, walking over to pet him.

Fred barely looked at me as he stood up long enough to turn around and then settled into a new position for another nap.

"He's really fucking lazy," J said. "But I guess I would be, too, if I was a cat. I mean, he has zero responsibility." He shrugged. "He'll stay in here all night."

I walked back to J. We stood for another few seconds looking at the room before he turned, putting his hand on the light switch, waiting for me to exit first. He wasn't rushing me, but we were done in there. And, while I was enjoying this glimpse into J's private life, I think he was acutely aware that I didn't *really* give a damn about his house. This was a suggestion I had made as a formality, to stretch the passing of time, because we still needed to wait.

He appeared to be processing what he was going to do about this married woman within his four walls. Assessing the purpose of my surprise arrival on his doorstep, and my current barefoot and seemingly relaxed presence.

J was a smart man. I was sure he knew why I was in

his home, but his decision regarding action, or inaction, had not been made yet. More time was needed before he concluded whether or not he was willing to cross a line, a boundary that had been put in place years earlier, and one that he had promised himself he would never breach. His inner wall was a solid, sturdy structure, and I knew from our history that scaling it was an Everest-like endeavor.

He also might have been gauging the collateral damage. While I was fairly certain he wasn't giving much thought to *his* relationship status, due to the purely habitual nature of it, mine may have been a concern for him.

You have your reasons for doing this, I reminded myself.

I looked at him and thought, there wasn't anything he could ask for that I would refuse. But the wheels were still visibly spinning, circling around what he was going to do when the inevitable moment struck. So, for the time being, it was back to the house tour.

Adjacent to the dining room, there was a short hallway leading to two doors that J dismissed as laundry room and garage. I let that slide. As much as we needed this tour to buy time, I didn't need to see every last nook and cranny of his house.

On the other side of the hall was a door that J opened revealing a large library. All of the walls were covered in shelves of books. Of course he would have an entire room dedicated to this, and it looked like there were books from just about every walk of life and genre. From where I stood, I could see history, classics, contemporary, horror, even comic books. He had it all.

In this space, there was a large, overstuffed armchair with an ottoman that was so big it looked like a backless love seat. Next to the chair was a small table with only a lamp and a coaster. No doubt he had plenty of bourbon-in-the-library nights.

I was an avid reader and would have loved to spend a month in this room, alternating my time between reading and an altogether more intimate pursuit. Visions of J sitting in that chair with me curled up on his lap, wearing nothing but one of his shirts, invaded my mind's eye. His hands roaming beneath the fabric, caressing my skin, my breasts, my thighs...

I shook my head to clear it, trying to return myself to reality.

"Wow," was all I could whisper.

"You like it?" J asked innocently, no inkling as to the thoughts running through my mind.

Like it?? I love it! I wanted to sign a lease and move into it.

"It's...incredible."

"Thanks. I like to come in here when nothing else is working."

I faced him, urging him to elaborate on what he meant – "when nothing else is working."

"Well, you know, I write more than I read these days. And then I have movies and gaming. I really like chilling with those. But when I find myself wandering around and can't get it figured out...you know...*it*...then I come in here and pull something off a shelf."

In the back of my head, I knew I was gawking, and I tried to snap myself out of it. I really didn't care about the money and whatever he had, but this room was something that impressed me.

Mercifully, J turned off the overhead light in the library, putting a stop to the silly look on my face.

There was another room, but he turned to skip over that one. My quizzical expression stopped him, and he said, "That's a home gym," pausing to see if it was okay to move on without showing it to me.

"Let's see," I said. Was he hiding something in there?

I hadn't intended the house tour to be any more than a delaying tactic, but my continued insight into J's day-to-day life had become so enjoyable that it even proved to distract me a bit. A quick look wouldn't hurt as we continued to build the anticipation I was feeling. He felt it too, I was positive. I could tell it was mutual by the palpable electricity in the air. With every step we took, every word we uttered, I became less concerned about where his decision would land, although I reminded myself to avoid assumptions. In the event he ultimately declined, I was determined to accept it with grace.

J,

Never! Tell me anything you want to share. I'm only a quick note away when you need me.

I've been wanting to share with you…you're on my mind a lot.

Nat

He turned to open the door without hesitation. It was another large room, this one filled with expensive workout equipment of every kind. There was a treadmill, an elliptical, a big weight set with different seats and pulleys around all sides of it, a rowing machine, and even an open area where I could see a television. Then I noticed the yoga mat and let out a little giggle. J looked at me to see where I was focused.

"What? It's good exercise," he said, feigning hurt feelings.

"Oh, I know. I just can't picture it." I giggled again.

"Hey, I may have my problems, but I'm nothing if not

well-rounded," he said as he gave me a gentle push on the shoulder.

"Yes, J. You're very well-rounded," I conceded in a mock tone, swatting him lightly with my hand.

His eyes locked on mine for a few seconds, and everything felt right and good and comfortable.

While I couldn't say for sure what was on *his* mind at that moment, my own imagination was working overtime again. I had a vivid image of J sitting on his weight bench, while I straddled him. My hands were braced on his shoulders, pulling him into me, as his hands gripped my hips, guiding my every move. The thought sent a shiver down my spine.

I shook it off as J closed the door to the exercise room and we made our way back to the living room. We crossed it, entering an unusually wide hallway, bringing us to what had to be the more personal side of his house.

J opened the first door on the left, flipping a light switch to reveal a welcoming bedroom with a king-sized sleigh bed that was perfectly made with a big fluffy comforter. The furniture was white, distressed wood with light shades of yellows and greens for all the accents. It instantly took me back to a collage of Easter mornings. The décor in this room was a lot airier and brighter than anything else I had seen in the house so far. Without needing to be told, I knew I wasn't looking at his bedroom.

On the far side of it, I took note of two doors. One, presumably, a walk-in closet and the other, most likely, an en suite.

"Guest room," he said. "Although no one ever stays here."

"That's a shame. It's a really pretty room. None of your friends ever stay over?"

"Eh. No one really comes here. You might remember that I keep to myself, embrace a reclusive lifestyle."

I tilted my head and looked at him. Yes, I did remember that about him, and it was the second time he had mentioned it tonight. I wondered if he felt that being a loner was an integral part of who he was as a person. It sounded so extreme, especially for someone who had finally caught his big film break and was one of the most sought-after screenwriters in the country.

"What?" he said. "I like it that way. Why do you think I'm living here, blending into suburbia on the east coast, and not out in California? I only go out there when I absolutely have to, and I sure as fuck wouldn't move there. Here, my neighbor on the left is some hotshot lawyer with his soccer mom wife and on the right, I have a retired couple. Everyone is too busy to be worried about what I'm doing, and they leave me be. I don't even think they know who I am...and I'm good with that."

Then he turned to look at me...and his face changed. He looked upset, angry even.

Uh oh.

Something had shifted, and I didn't know what it was.

"That's not why you're here, is it?" J had raised his voice, and it startled me.

I didn't know what he was talking about. Why did he think I was there?

"What?" I half whispered because I honestly couldn't see where we were going with this.

"Give me a break, Natalie. Are you here because of who I am now?" Again with the raised voice.

My mouth fell open. I couldn't answer him. I think I stuttered a few syllables, but anything that came out was nonsensical, I was sure of that.

He was running his hands through his hair as he

turned away from me. Of everything I had prepared for, of all the times I had played out this night in my head, this was the one thing I had overlooked. I was caught completely off guard, and I was not ready for this line of questioning.

Facing away from me, as if talking to someone else, J continued. "I have a hard time seeing myself like that. Like this famous...writer...who people want to get close to because they want something from me. This is why no one comes here. I don't want anyone here. If I don't let people in, I don't have to figure out stuff like this. I can't believe I let this happen!"

And with that, he exposed all of his old fears to me. But now I learned that his success had upped the ante, causing him to feel the need to further cloister himself, more so than ever before. I thought I had known what I was going to be up against, coming into his home, but all that I knew about him had actually been intensified over the years.

He turned back toward me. There was a fire in his eyes, and it wasn't the fire I wanted to see.

"I think you should leave now. I'm sorry. It was nice to meet you and all, but this cannot go any further, and you shouldn't be here."

He had lowered his voice, but he was dead serious. And I was still in shock.

"J...I...I mean..." I stammered.

He turned off the guestroom light, closed the door, and started down the hall toward the kitchen. Desperate to put an end to this line of thinking, I reached out, grabbing his arm.

Oh, my God, those arms again.

He pulled away but stopped and turned to face me. I could feel the wall he had put up between us. It was invisible, but it hung in our midst as if he had conjured up a concrete barrier out of thin air.

"J, listen. No, this has nothing to do with who you are now. I mean, what does that even fucking mean – 'who you are now'? You're you. You're the guy I wrote to for a year. Whatever this is," and I waved my hand around at his house, "has nothing to do with anything as far as I'm concerned. I'm happy for you. You made your dream come true – that's really great. But that is *not* why I'm here. I don't need anything from you...and I don't want anything from you."

Just as I got out the last few words, I could feel tears stinging my eyes. I balled my hands into tight fists and set my jaw. I'd be damned if I was going to cry in front of him. This train had totally derailed, and I didn't want him to see my disappointment. I felt deflated and angry at myself for not foreseeing this sooner.

I put my head down. I was quickly trying to come to terms with the destruction of the evening. Needing to accept it, I contemplated how I could compose myself enough to wish him well and go. I had come into this determined to maintain my dignity and if leaving was what I had to do to keep it intact, so be it.

Shit, shit, shit.

Even with my head down, I could see his stance soften. He reached out, putting a hand on my shoulder. We stood like that for a minute, maybe more, he with his hand on me, and me staring at the floor.

My thoughts were going way over the speed limit, trying to think of what I could possibly do to turn the situation around again, but I couldn't settle down enough to compose even one rational idea.

What I knew for sure was that, more than anything else, I needed to make him see that his achievements had nothing to do with my arrival. It would break my heart if I had to leave, say goodbye to him forever, knowing he believed I was one of *them*. But I was at a loss for the words to begin to explain this to him.

Finally, with his hand still on my shoulder and his posture relaxing a bit more, J spoke. "Hey, I'm sorry. It's just all such a pain in the ass for me these days, you know? It's like...fuck, man." Heavy sigh.

He took his hand away, and I felt a burning where his skin had been against mine.

"That one film took off and then everything changed. Here I was, one day living in this little apartment in the city, barely making ends meet, and then...I'm telling you – it happened overnight. Next thing I know, I've got all this money coming in and a high dollar agent and some people are looking out for me and others, I come to find out, are looking out for themselves. It's incredible who comes along to take advantage when something like this happens. I just wasn't prepared or equipped to handle it." J took a deep breath. "I imagine it's a lot like what lottery winners go through. Anyway, it was just...chaos."

I looked up at him to see he was running his hands through his hair again. It was clear how frustrated he was, maybe even slightly tortured. I mentally kicked myself again for not developing a plan to do a preemptive strike on this line of thinking. *Of course* he would be having these problems. Anyone in his situation would have to tackle issues like this. And, naturally, it would affect J in a way that would make it a serious struggle.

"J, I'm sorry. That sucks. You should be able to enjoy your success without having to worry about who's a gold digger and who isn't."

My words could not have been more sincere. And I was angry that anyone would treat him like that, causing him an even greater need for retreat.

"Yeah, well, that's not how it works," he said. "I'm sorry. I shouldn't have gone from zero to sixty on you like that. It's just...I don't always think about being careful, and then it hits me, and then..." His words trailed off, and he gave me a small sheepish smile.

"It must be very difficult for you to get close to anyone," I said quietly, further attempting to process how much his fame must have increased this dilemma for him.

"It was a hell of a chore to get me through the first year. My mom had to get involved. We talked about what I needed and what I wanted...as far as a lifestyle and a house and all that, you know? She found this house, and I moved in here and I just do everything by mail and computer. I go to meetings when I have to. Meet the producers and directors during pre-production. Meet the actors on set for a meet-and-greet. Then I come back here and go through the necessary rewrites. Outside of dealing with the film premiers, that's it."

"And then I showed up," I sighed.

I relaxed a little, now that he had opened up some more, but I wasn't sure yet if we were anywhere close to being out of the woods.

He chuckled a little before repeating, "And then you showed up."

Nat,

Sometimes I wonder if I'll ever be able to trust again. I mean, I trust you, but I don't know you, so that's different. With everybody else, I feel like a tourist in a world where I don't belong.

Same - you're on my mind, too.

J

That melancholy look was back in his eyes, and he was battling something within...I could see it. The avatars of good decisions and bad choices were practically visible, sitting one on each shoulder. It was time to gauge what raged deep inside him, assessing the many fears he had built up to a boiling point over the years. Then he moved, with only the slightest hesitation, and reached over to put his finger under my chin.

I wasn't about to stop him, but I also didn't know what this gesture meant.

Was this a "Hey, kiddo. Sorry for yelling. Thanks for coming, but we should call it a night now" move?

Or was it a "Let's put this behind us and continue on with the house tour" sign?

He stood looking into my eyes, as if he was searching for something within me that even I didn't know was there. Another heavy sigh. I paused, trying to decide if I should be the one to break this pose or if I should wait.

But while my reeling mind was struggling to reach a conclusion, my impatient body overrode my head and gave in to its base desires. I stepped into him and, in one fluid motion, pressed myself against his body, putting my arms around him. In my bare feet, the top of my head came to right below his shoulder. My arms easily slipped under his and around his back, and I thought, *This is comfortable.*

I sensed his resistance but held my position. To my relief, it only took a few seconds before I felt him reciprocating the embrace. His arms encircled me, but I could sense he was unsure of where to put his hands.

My back was completely exposed in the dress. His palms against all that skin probably seemed too physical, too intimate. I felt him link his fingers together, and when he did that, his biceps flexed against my shoulders.

Thus, the emergency crew showed up and the train was set back on the tracks. The conductor was blowing the whistle, and we would be back up to speed soon.

As we stood holding each other, with every second that ticked by, I became more confident that I wasn't leaving.

CHAPTER SEVEN

If he had held me like that thirty minutes ago, his touch combined with years of my fantasies would have pushed me precariously close to a climactic cliff.

I was working back up to that point.

While this had been an unexpected detour, now that I realized I should have seen it coming, I also came to terms with riding the hills and valleys as a part of this. It was the foundation of all the anticipation. While I knew the physical connection was a big goal of mine for the night, we were also friends first. He had just exposed a vulnerable side of himself to me...and I would hold that close, as I always had.

There was a special place for J in my heart. While I intended to follow through with this outlandish idea to gain some finality, I would never betray him or his trust. Everything he told me would stay locked away with my deep affection for him. There were different reasons behind our individual need for discretion, but it was essential all the same.

```
J,
I was thinking about you and I wrote a
little something. Show me yours if I show
you mine?
Nat
```

Pressed against him, I took a slow, deep breath, and as I released it, I moved in even closer. He didn't resist. I could feel the stirring behind the zipper of his jeans. This yanked me away from the friend-related feelings I'd just been having and steered me back to my other thoughts...the naughty ones.

It was impossible to stay focused on anything else when I knew what was behind that zipper. And the fact that he was physically responding to me made my head go dizzy with the whirling thoughts of where this was leading. The seeming inevitability of what was right around the corner in conjunction with his obvious arousal was ramping up my own excitement to new heights.

My fingers wandered with a mind of their own. They slid down his back. When I felt his steadily growing manhood pressing against my stomach, I couldn't resist inching them under the waistband of his jeans.

His muscles tensed. He pulled back slightly.

While his hesitation made my hands pause where they were, I didn't take them off of him. I looked up to discover his eyes were locked on mine. There was quite a distance between our faces, but evidently his desire was overriding his reticence as he started to lean forward, so slowly that it was almost hard to see he was actually moving.

I knew what was coming. And I was going to let it happen.

As he got closer, my eyes drifted closed. Waiting. Then I felt it. His breath, the gentle scratch of his goatee, and at last his lips, so very tenderly touching mine. It was a butterfly kiss. Incredibly light, soft, almost loving.

While I was enjoying this immensely, I also had the urge to put my hands behind his head, wrap them in his thick hair, pull him closer, open my mouth, and ravage him.

No! He's in charge! I sternly reminded myself.

It was a struggle, but I managed to maintain what was probably the last ounce of self-control I had.

His lips lingered against mine for a long time. When he finally pulled back, he ran his hands past my shoulders until they were both wrapped behind my neck. Leaning his forehead down to mine, we stood there, Peter Rabbit-style, as he gathered my hair into a ponytail and twirled it around his hand. His other hand moved to the side of my neck, caressing my cheek with his thumb.

My spine turned to jelly, and I whispered a moan from deep within my throat.

Of everything in the world I knew to be true in that moment, the sincerest verity of all was that I loved his hands. It was as if he was created to touch me. There was a strength in those long fingers that told me he would be able to anticipate exactly where I needed him to put them when the time came.

My hands were still on the upper part of his backside and I slid them around his waist to the front of his jeans. This prompted a small but sharp intake of breath from him as I eased my fingers into the pockets. Through the thin patch of fabric, his erection twitched again.

It was barely audible, but I heard J groan.

I lost track of time and a piece of my mind as we stood like that. Not that I cared. It was a beautiful moment. If only the clock could freeze, preserving us there forever.

Yet it also stoked the embers that were smoldering within, returning me to a heightened state of arousal. I was ready for him and all he had to offer. My legs felt weak, just like they had been when I first walked in the house. With the whole fame and fortune discussion firmly in the rearview mirror, we were moving forward. This was *going* to happen.

As if reading each other's mind, we both slowly and gently moved apart. He smiled at me, almost a sheepish, shy kind of smile. I winked at him in return and he laughed melodiously. It was a joyful noise; I loved it and wanted to hear more.

Not a word was spoken as he led me across the hall to another door that opened into a spacious, rectangular bathroom. The colors were rich, earthy tones with big tiles that led across the floor to a giant walk-in shower. Cabinets surrounded a long counter with two sinks, and there was a separate water closet for added privacy.

No comment was needed. It was a self-explanatory room, simply a small pitstop on the house tour that was leading to...what? The inevitable.

Nat,
Yes! Share!
J

The next door down the hall revealed a huge office. This was quite likely the biggest office I'd ever seen. There was a soft glow coming from a light on the desk. My eyes scanned deeper into the room, and I could see two separate sitting areas – one with an overstuffed sofa and the other with a huge recliner. The only time I'd ever seen that before was in stuffy corporate movie scenes, but this was much more casual.

"Wow," I said. "This is a damn big room."

"It used to be two separate bedrooms, but I don't need the one guestroom I have, let alone more, so I had a wall removed and turned this into my office. It's where I spend most of my time, so I figured why not, right? This is my life, you know? If I didn't have my writing, I'd have...nothing. I don't think most people get that. They say, 'Oh, step away from it. Take a break.' But I can't. This is my drug of choice, and I can't breathe without it. So, I wanted my space for it to be just right."

J's voice had taken on a tone unique to any other I'd heard from him that evening. It was evident that talking about the place where he crafted his ideas excited him. This was extremely personal, the center of his world, and I valued the glimpse he was giving me.

"Sure. It's great! So, this is where all the magic happens?"

He laughed again, sending another wave of heat blossoming between my legs.

"Yeah, okay, if you want to put it that way. Hey, have you seen any of my films? I mean, if not, that's okay, and you don't have to say you did."

He seemed nervous about whether or not I had seen the movies for which he had written the screenplays, and I thought it was cute and endearing.

"Actually, I have. I'm not sure I've seen all of them, but I know I've watched at least a few. They were really good. You're a fun, yet deeper, combination of Woody Allen and the Coen Brothers, in my opinion."

"Yeah? Okay, I'll take that," he said with a shy smile. "So, come over here and check this out."

We walked around the desk and turned to face a wall

where there were eight framed movie posters. I pointed at one of them and said, "Wait – you wrote that? I had no idea. I love that movie!"

"Ah, thanks. I went a little out of my comfort zone with that one. Glad you liked it." Again with the shy smile. "Actually, that was a book first. I tried to move away from the screenplay concept for a change. Funny thing is it did pretty well as a book, and I thought maybe it was a shift of direction for me, but then one of the studios bought it and I ended up having to turn it into a screenplay anyway. They backed me into a corner with that one because if I had turned it down, someone else would have done the screen adaption, and I sure as hell wasn't going to be okay with that."

J gave another one of those adorable shrugs.

I turned to a different wall and saw what looked like various framed awards and achievements. Underneath them was a table with the heavy hitters – Golden Globes, MTV Movie Awards, Cannes Film Festival, and the granddaddy of them all – his Oscar.

He saw me looking at them. "Kinda cool, huh?"

"*Very* cool." I turned to him and said with complete sincerity, "J, I am so happy for you. You've done a lot of great work, and you *really* deserve this success."

"Yeah, thanks. I appreciate that. It was a long road to get here, but I'm really happy I didn't give up. You know, at one point I threw up my hands and said fuck it – I'm going to end up being posthumously recognized!"

We both laughed.

"Well, I'm really happy you didn't have to remain a starving artist your whole life, only to have your work recognized after you die. It's pretty shitty when that happens and an artist can't be here to enjoy their success." I smiled. Then, being curious about this type of work, I asked, "How did you manage to get so many movies out in such a short amount of time?"

"Oh, I don't know. The stories just come to me really fast. Once my brain latches onto an idea, the majority of it rolls pretty smoothly downhill," he started to explain. "And after the first one got picked up, which by the way, is the one I was writing when we were emailing, it's been moving along pretty quickly ever since. I'm actually working on something right now, and it should be finished soon. Just having a little hiccup with the ending." He looked at me before continuing. "It'll come to me, though. It always does."

I nodded. I was sure the answer would present itself to him sooner rather than later. He was a creative powerhouse.

"What's with the two sitting areas?"

He turned to them and said, "Oh, so, that one is straight up movie time" – pointing to the couch. "And that one is for gaming. It helps to have it all right here when I need to take a break from writing. 'Cause, you know, I don't really want to get away from the room, per se, I just want to get away from the computer. It's nice to relax right here and then be able to jump up and make a note or something if the mood strikes."

He made a face as if he wasn't sure the explanation made sense to anyone but him.

"I get it," I said. "This room is like your one-stop shop."

"Right. I wander down the hall and grab something from the kitchen when I need to, but I'm usually in here, if I'm not in bed. Hell, I even nap here, so this is kind of a pseudo bedroom."

I looked at the big cerulean-colored sofa. There was a plaid throw blanket folded and draped over the back. I pictured his lengthy, firm body stretched out, maybe one ankle tucked behind his knee, watching a John Cusack movie.

As with the other rooms on the tour, once my imagination was off and running, the picture in my head started to skew toward something far more intimate. I could see him putting one of his muscular arms behind his head, watching me as I stood before him wearing nothing but one of his t-shirts. Carefully straddling him, I'd hear the TV remote fall to the floor as he reached to pull the shirt up and over my head, exposing my naked breasts to his gaze...to his touch...

Breathing heavily, I could feel my nipples reacting to the erotic fantasy playing out in my mind, hardening beneath the thin fabric of the dress that was feeling more restrictive by the second. I probably would have stood there and seen that fantasy through to the end, having a body-trembling orgasm on the very spot, if he hadn't snapped me out of it by asking, "Hey, you okay?"

"What? Yeah, yeah." I tried to smile. It was probably a crooked grin because all I could really focus on was the pounding in my chest and the increased twitching beneath my barely-there g-string.

Trying to train my focus anywhere else, I remarked that the gaming recliner was huge.

"Mhmm. Super comfy, too. I usually end up falling asleep in the middle of a game," he chuckled.

J,
Keep in mind that I'm no writer, but all right. Here goes nothing...
Nat

I walked over to his desk, still trying to shake off my daydream, and J followed, sitting down in his chair when he got there. I turned, leaning against the desk. He allowed his gaze to travel from my face to the plunging neckline and down to my stomach. His eyes started to roam upward again but stopped when they arrived at my breasts. Unsurprisingly. My nipples were practically begging for attention.

Putting my hands on the desk, I eased myself into a sitting position on top of it. I set my feet on the top of his thighs, careful to make sure he wouldn't get flashed by that skimpy g-string. His eyes grew wide, and he put his hands on the top of my feet.

J looked down as if to check to see if anything was visible from his angle but turned his attention to my legs when he realized he'd have to blatantly lean back in the chair to find what he was looking for.

He ran his hands up my calves, his long fingers wrapping behind my knees and then traveling to the back of my thighs. He squeezed me and smiled.

"What?" I asked, feigning a slight pout and defensive tone.

J looked momentarily amused with my little game. "You're in great shape. Are you still dancing?"

"For work? Hell, no. For exercise, yes."

"It serves you well," he replied and then turned his attention back to my body.

His hands continued to move up the back of my legs until they were met with the desk, and the only way to go further would have been to pick me up.

My feet were gently massaging the tops of his thighs. I could feel the toned muscle underneath the jeans. The same jeans I was hoping to see on the floor before too long.

My desire for J had reached a tipping point. Feeling faint, my head was spinning, jumping forward to the moment when I would know all of him.

My feet crept up to the crease between his upper thighs and lower abdomen. His hands were still on me, igniting my skin, and he was still visually caressing the rest of my body. I could see the wheels spinning behind his eyes. It was evident he knew what was coming. What *I* didn't know was how much longer I would have to wait.

With every minute that ticked by, with every touch of his hands, I was relinquishing my control to him. We were reaching his moment to call the shots. My goal had been accomplished by getting us to this point...and the rest was up to him.

His hands moved almost casually up my thighs, sliding across my bare skin in a mirror image of where my feet were placed on him. J's fingers squeezed the flesh of my hips, his thumbs settling into the crease of my legs. Mere inches away. The proximity of his hands to my delicate intersection was causing an undeniable need within me. My body was crying out for him, reaching a crescendo I could not ignore for much longer.

If he would just move, less than an inch, he would be right where I wanted him to be.

Where I so desperately needed him.

"You're trembling," he said, breaking the silence.

"What?"

"You're trembling. Are you okay?" He looked genuinely concerned.

I wasn't okay. Not by a long shot. In the strangest of ways, my head was swimming with the thoughts of a thousand topics while I simultaneously felt devoid of intellectual reason.

"I'm fine, J. Where's your room?" The expression on his face told me he hadn't been fully present, but the question appeared to nudge him back from wherever he had been, so I quickly followed it up with, "You haven't shown me your bedroom yet."

"Oh, right."

With that, he kept his fingers on the top of my legs and pushed himself into a standing position, took a step back, and held out his hand for me to hop off the desk. Taking his hand, I shimmied down, all the while praying my legs wouldn't fail me now. A bigger concern was that what was taking place between my thighs was intensifying to the point of pain. We either needed to get this started soon, or I was going to have to excuse myself to the restroom to clean up.

As soon as I was off the desk, he let go of my hand, but put an arm loosely around my back. This told me his decision had been made and all systems were a go. This also helped to settle my nerves a little, now that I felt certain it was just a matter of time.

As much as I didn't want to, and I wasn't sure where the line would be drawn for my physical patience, I knew I could emotionally wait as long as I needed to in order to give him full control of how this was to play out. He would dictate what he wanted me to do, and I would submit completely to him, leaving no stone unturned, and saying yes to all of his wishes.

I anticipated J's kinks to be relatively tame compared to the limitless possibilities I was aware existed in the vast world of physical desires, but it would go the way he wanted it to, and that was what mattered most.

As I found myself on the cusp of the ultimate intimacy with J, it was not lost on me that all of this could have happened years ago when it would have been okay, and no other strings would have been in the way. But I was a firm believer in things happening the way they should, and apparently this wasn't meant to take place then.

Either that or we totally disregarded fate.

Nat,
Fuck, that was hot!
Okay, mine's attached. A fantasy that was in my head. I'll never do anything with it, though. And don't feel like you have to read it. The writing isn't even that good…it's just something I thought would be fun to do with a woman, but I won't…
J

We walked out of the office and he shut the door behind us. To our right was the last door in the hallway. He kept his arm around me, reached down with the other hand, turned the knob, and casually pushed it open. He leaned against the doorjamb, pulling me a little closer to him, then cocked his left arm around the trim to push up slightly on a dimmer switch. Soft light illuminated the room. I let out a small gasp.

It was a beautiful space.

CHAPTER EIGHT

There was a large window on one wall, which I took to be the front of the house. Two tall, narrow windows flanked the giant bed. I wasn't sure what they overlooked. Based on my bearings in the house, I speculated there was probably a side yard out there under the night sky. There was a large leather sofa under the biggest window with an antique chest in front of it, standing in as a coffee table.

The furniture was bulky, masculine like the dining room, but this was more...forceful. Powerful. The room was big enough to support the furniture, and nothing looked out of its element. The bed was a four-poster, but I had never seen anything like it.

The columns themselves were enormous. Chunky, carved pillars stopping just a couple of feet below the ceiling. It was more dark wood, similar to the dining room table...tasteful, with an elegant combination of past and present. It worked.

Whoever designed this room had made it flow exceedingly well. An interior decorator maybe? Or perhaps he had done it himself. It was possible. What I knew about J ran much deeper than topics such as styles and the ability to decorate a house.

He was resting against the doorway with his arm still encircling my waist, a little tighter now. He leaned into me, gently kissing the top of my head, and inhaling deeply. Keeping his lips against my hair, he whispered, "You smell good."

Instead of saying anything, I ran my hand up his thigh as a sign of 'thank you.'

In that moment, I felt a subtle shift in the atmosphere. The dynamic between us moving, irresistible like the tide. We both sensed the transposition into *his* posture of control. From here on out, he would lead, and I would willingly follow.

His arm pulled me closer, his fingers finding their way under the fabric on the side of my dress. Starting at my hip, he leisurely trailed up until he was at my breast, where he laid his hand, palm against it. I ached for his fingers to wander just a little further.

So close...

My tongue flicked across my lips. I took a deep, unsteady breath while I struggled to control my body. The torrid heat of my intense need was becoming unbearable. My knees threatened to buckle beneath me as I pressed my thighs tightly together.

Less than an inch and the tip of his finger would be exactly where I needed it to be. But J knew this. Instead, he acted to tease me, casually moving his hand under my breast and cupping it from beneath, supporting it and running his thumb sensuously right below the spot that he knew would mentally unhinge me. I had an urge to lean into him, to force my nipple into his hand, but I had promised myself we were going to play by his rules from this point on.

It took all the willpower I could muster to resist the temptation to seize even the tiniest sliver of control back from him.

I put my faith in his ability to be a master of seduction...if he would just let that side of himself surface like I knew he could.

Keep breathing and let him do it his way.

A pang of disappointment ran through me as J slid his hand away from my breast, pressing his palm against my back, gently guiding me into the room. I took a few steps inside and stopped.

He walked around me, moving to a large armoire that, once opened, revealed a television and some other electronic devices I didn't recognize. He had the latest toys and gadgets, and I was far from a tech person.

"Mind if I change the music?" he asked with a glance in my direction.

I couldn't speak. Words wouldn't form. I just looked a little quizzically at him, as the only music I could hear was the distant sound from the living room.

"It's all connected," he explained. "It doesn't have to be – I can play different music in each room if I want to. But I'm just going to override it out there and put on something in here, if you're okay with that."

I nodded absently, my mind still in another place.

We were here, finally. At some point in the not too distant future, my fantasy would be realized. I was finally going to have relief from the relentless throbbing desire. This aching wanton need between my legs would be sated. I would finally have J.

Not the fantasy.

Not the dream.

This was the real deal. To explore and feel and hold and kiss...and fuck.

I heard him clicking things inside the armoire and then the music turned off in the living room. A few seconds later, 3 Doors Down's "The Road I'm On" started playing in the bedroom.

"Is this okay with you?"

"Oh, yeah," I stammered, my throat dry. "I love 3 Doors Down." And I did – it was sexy music as far as I was concerned, and like the furniture, this song worked.

"Well, it's a mix," he said. "But there's probably a bunch of them on it."

I nodded again.

My conversational skills were escaping me at this point, and I hoped he wasn't really expecting me to say anything more. I planned and executed this, and the time had come for the follow through.

I took a step further into the room, but I was staying close to the wall rather than venturing into the middle of the space. J looked over at me, gave me a small smile, and closed the armoire.

With perfect posture, he walked slowly over to a nightstand. I noticed a framed photo there but didn't make an effort to see who was in it. There would be time for looking and asking about that later.

Standing there, he unclasped his watch, sliding it off his wrist and placing it in a small tray that looked to also contain some change and a money clip.

Watching him from behind, I was struck by his physique and the power that emanated from him. He seemed totally level, not phased at all by the inexorable rise in the tension in the room. His time to establish control had arrived – and he was comfortably settling into the role with finesse.

With his back still toward me, J put his hands on his hips, appearing to be lost in thought for a moment. All that could be heard in the room were the low tones of the music, the lyrics floating through the air like a feathery whisper.

Startling me with a quick movement, he reached one hand over his shoulder, pulling his shirt off from behind. My mouth fell open and I was locked in place. Lust was clouding my thoughts, leaving my tongue feeling dry. I swallowed hard, attempting to regain some composure, grateful that he couldn't see how much I appeared like a smitten little girl.

I was a million miles from the seductress to whom he had opened his front door.

He was arranging his shirt right-side out, triceps flexing with each small movement. I fought to maintain focus on what I knew would be our next step, but his back muscles held me mesmerized. The trembling returned, and I was suddenly feeling wholly inadequate.

J tossed the shirt on a chair next to the nightstand and turned to face me. I felt out of place. My arms hanging at my sides, standing there like I was an eighth grader waiting for him to ask me to dance. The fire below my belly was becoming an inferno, growing more unbearably intense with every passing second his hands weren't on me.

He studied me, his expression inscrutable. I was assessing the situation and trying to figure out my next move, but my brain was no longer cooperating. Should I walk seductively to the sofa, or lean sexily against the wall? Something. Anything to get myself out of this self-consciously goofy stance.

While my cognitive abilities tried desperately to catch

up to the events that were now transpiring, J, without any warning and with the swiftness of a panther, was in front of me. He picked me up and pushed me firmly against the wall.

This was it.

My rational mind shut down, and instinct took over as my legs wrapped tightly around his waist, arms reaching over his shoulders as my fingers wove through his hair. I couldn't help but let out a small whimper of need. My ankles locked together behind his back, and with thighs spread wide, I was intensely aware that my yearning entrance was now open to him, pressed against his stomach. Only the sheer fabric of my tiny g-string prevented my clitoris from rubbing directly against his muscular abs. I found myself desperately wishing the useless material wasn't there at all.

I was reacting before I could form coherent thought. J had seized my ability to think straight, and I had gladly surrendered it. My head tilted, forcing my back to arch, and I cried out. There were no words, only a release of pent up desire. Animalistic sounds calling for the relief I so desperately craved.

He held me against the wall, watching, but didn't make a move until I started to grind against him, my body writhing sinuously with a will of its own. He leaned harder against me, forcing my head upright again, subtly restricting my movements. I loved it. We were eye to eye now, and the look I saw in him was raw.

This was the J who had invaded my dreams. Unfettered by his inhibitions. Totally free.

"What do you want?" he asked, his voice husky as his eyes bore into mine.

I was completely and utterly lost in him. Only one word came to mind, and I whispered, "You."

Without a thought given to even trying to control my physical reaction to him, I squirmed in his arms and detected his brief, mischievous smile.

Keeping one hand firmly under my ass, his other moved to the back of my head, taking a handful of my hair as he pulled my mouth toward him. He found no resistance from me, and then his tongue was inside me, swirling, just like the tornado of passion that was spinning around both of us now.

No matter how much my eager arms and legs pulled on him, I couldn't draw him any closer to me. He was too strong, resisting me. The frenzied kissing continued, and I used my thigh muscles to push up on his hips, trying to slide my clitoris along his belly. Searching to find the tiniest bit of friction that could relieve the furnace burning within me.

Suddenly his mouth was off mine, and I heard a growled whisper in my ear, "Ohhh, no you don't."

He swung me into his arms and carried me to the bed. There was a strength to his movements, but also a purpose that made me feel I was being handled gently. My legs remained wrapped around him as he cradled my shoulders while laying me down.

J backed away, removing my legs from his waist while bending my knees to set my feet down on the edge of the bed. I groaned, reluctant to yield freedom from the carnal embrace.

My chest was rising and falling with ragged breathing, aching nipples pressing through the fabric of my dress, begging for attention. I felt like I was under water, the sound of a rushing river running through my ears. Time slowed to a crawl as the universe seemed to focus in on this singular moment.

I was acutely aware of J straddling me, unbuttoning

his jeans and slowly opening the zipper about halfway. His erection was pushing out of the top. Seeking to assure myself that this moment was real, I immediately reacted to an almost overwhelming urge to touch it. Drawn to it like a moth to a flame.

He swatted my hand away with a firm, "No."

What??? What do you mean no?? Please don't do that to me, please don't.

J's authoritative personality came as no surprise, but I was unprepared for being left out. Teased. Controlled to the extent of keeping my hands to myself.

With desperate eyes wide, all I could do was watch as those long, sexy fingers found their way into the front of his jeans and stroked the length of his cock, pinching the tip when he arrived there. A droplet of cum emerged. I wanted to put my mouth on him. I'd never felt so thirsty, hopelessly attempting to hold at bay a fervor that needed quenching. I licked my lips in anticipation as I writhed in lustful agony.

This was a torture of passion, and I twisted in delirious protest, but I was pinned beneath him. My thoughts rallied toward rational for just a second to remind me that this was likely as far as J would go in an attempt to edge me. Even so, I felt torn in two by my conflicting desires. My wanton need was warring against trying to comply with his wishes. My trembling hands balled into fists as I fought my biological impulses. But even as I managed to keep my upper body compliant, my hips betrayed me. Intense arousal taking control below the waist as I couldn't help but involuntarily buck myself against him, like an invisible puppeteer was pulling on my strings, trying to lift my body against my will.

He put a firm hand on my side and pushed himself off me, keeping his palm in place to hold me steady. When I rolled my right hip and tried to fight him, he looked at me strictly and said again, louder this time, "No!"

Even though the urges that drove me were desperate, I stopped fighting him and struggled to keep my movements to a minimum. J was at my side kneeling over me, watching me, his expression unyielding.

His finger skimmed my skin moving upward from my trembling stomach, lingering for a moment in the smooth valley of my chest. I knew where I wanted to feel his touch next, and J seemed to read my mind as his hand slipped under the material of my dress to caress and cup my aching breast. The feel of my nipple pressing into the palm of his hand was the purest form of bliss. I growled through clenched teeth, acutely aware that I was behaving like a caged animal. Our eyes locked, he appeared fascinated with my response, allowing for a moment's distraction before he assertively pushed open both sides of the dress, exposing my hard, yearning nipples to his gaze.

I shuddered, feeling suddenly and intimately revealed.

Like a present being unwrapped, and I was the gift within. His gift. Willingly given.

I was sharply aware that in the immediate future I would lie naked before him.

My stomach was a seething mass of nerves and excitement as his hand circled around my right breast while he observed me for a reaction. My response was instant and reflexive. The soft, lingering touch caused me to arch my back slightly, but it was the hard pinch to my nipple that elicited a gasp. What started out as an aggressive grip grew delicate seconds later when he began gently rolling it between his thumb and forefinger, effectuating my back to fully arched. I urged my breasts against his hands, physically begging him not to stop. Mercifully, I felt an equal touch on my left nipple.

I was panting now, focused on the relief I felt to *finally* know the intimate touch of his gentle hands. I tried to suppress the ardent begging that persisted in my lower body, to push it to the back of my mind, but my clitoris was hot, and wet, and throbbing relentlessly. Had J been in the right position for that particular view, I was sure it would have been distinctly evident.

The very thought of that, his face being inches from my sex, just made the feeling of wanton lust all the worse. I was sure my tiny scrap of underwear must be soaked through by now.

The teasing of my nipples continued unabated, alternating between a featherlight touch and a rougher, firmer pinch. All the while, J was watching me with captivated contemplation, clearly enjoying driving me to the brink.

He leaned over, kissing me. Gently at first, with his tongue playfully against mine, but as the kiss lingered, it intensified.

Unable to fight it any longer, I surrendered to the desire that was radiating out from my essence. I couldn't help it. My subconscious had taken over. I planted my feet firmly on the bed and my hips rose urgently. I was dimly aware that my short skirt had slid up my thighs and my damp g-string was now exposed. Not that I cared at all. In this very moment, I wanted him more than anything else in the universe. To my relief, he didn't move to object to this new pose, so I spread my feet apart in an effort to further open my legs for him, as I slowly ground my hips up and down.

The satisfaction I was seeking couldn't be found in thin air, but the reciprocal motion of it made me feel the tiniest bit...relieved.

He was still watching me closely, his gaze stoking the fires within me. All my addled brain could think about was how much I needed his kiss, his touch, his...

And it was then that I realized I had forgotten about the length that was still teasing me from the top his jeans.

I turned my head, searching for it. Finding what I was looking for, I moved my hand eagerly to touch him, but he grabbed my wrist before I could get close. In surprise, I tried to jerk away, but he held me securely. I gritted my teeth and growled my animalistic need once more. A pleading mixture of lust and frustration.

J tilted his head as he studied me, smiled the smallest wry smile, and removed his hand from my wrist. Such a minute ripple in time. I had begged, and he had granted me his permission. A subtle exercise in control that only acted to stoke the inferno within.

Before he could change his mind, I reached out and swiftly unzipped his jeans the rest of the way. I half closed my eyes, his shaft finally in my hand. I held it for a moment, savoring the feel.

It was hot to the touch, and it throbbed and twitched slightly under my gentle grip. My fingers closed around it more firmly, grasping it. Holding onto it like it was the lifeline for my rampant desire, feeling like if I let go, I might drown. I started to work it against my palm. As I slid down the length of him and slightly underneath, he put his head back, sinking his weight onto his heels.

The firm touch on my nipples ceased momentarily as J lost himself in his own pleasure, enjoying my enthusiastic exploration. He soon resumed, although somewhat absentmindedly. I didn't care. We were both settling into a comfort zone of physical escape.

My fingers made their way from underneath him to stroke back up to the tip of his erection. When I reached the head, I pinched him the way I had watched J do to himself. At this, he grabbed my wrist again, forcing my hand away. I found myself hating the empty feeling, and my fingers flexed as if trying to grasp that glorious shaft once more.

"Enough!" J firmly declared.

The tone of his voice startled me, and between that and the hard grasp he had on me, I opted not to fight him this time. With wide eyes, I watched as he lithely hopped over the foot board, stepping around to the side of it to stand in front of me.

He leaned over, slid his hands under my backside, and pulled off my g-string in one smooth motion. I spread my feet again, revealing my final intimacy for him to view. A nervous pride flushed through me as he sighed, and I heard his jeans drop to the floor. Evidently, he liked what he saw.

In what seemed like one motion, he opened the nightstand drawer and took out a condom that he tossed next to me.

As J knelt on the bed in front of me, I could see his cock in all its glory, now free from the denim. It was so hard, and it throbbed and twitched as I visually mapped every inch of it, to the moist tip resting not far below his navel. I wanted him inside of me. I *wanted* him in my mouth. I wanted so many things right then that I couldn't think straight.

J reached for my wrists, and I cooperated, maneuvering into a sitting position. He lifted my dress over my head. As it easily slipped off and was tossed on the floor, I had the stunned realization that I was now naked in front of him.

Totally naked.

"I want you, Nat. All of you." His voice was hoarse.

I was in a daze as his hand found its way to the back of my head. He pulled me forward and kissed me. Lingering, unhurried, and unfathomably deep. As I groaned, I realized that his throat was echoing the same sound back to me.

After what seemed like an eternity, he released me. I settled back onto the bed. Still kneeling in front of me, he urged my legs farther apart, leaned over, and put his mouth on one nipple, drawing it playfully between his teeth as his fingers pinched the other. My hips rose up again, searching. But he pushed me back down with his chest.

The feeling of his skin against mine was launching me into realms of sensation previously unknown. As J moved across me, I was convinced that my body was capable of setting off fireworks.

Is it possible to spontaneously orgasm? Just from being touched like this?

Sitting back on his heels, he slid both hands down to my inner thighs and used his thumbs to expose what he wanted to see. Slowly parting the folds, taking his time, enjoying this exploration of his new playground.

He ran a finger over my clitoris with a featherlight touch, making me shudder. My back arched again. I put my arms over my head, hands gathering and gripping the comforter desperately. Remaining on his knees, he lifted my hips and rested my backside on his thighs, my legs either side of his torso. He tore the condom wrapper with his teeth and pulled it on with practiced ease.

J took hold of his cock and guided it slowly towards my expectant sex, stroking my clitoris with the tip as he did so. And then I felt him there. Right there. Poised. I knew it was time.

I was so ready.

"Please," I whispered. Begging.

As he pushed into me, I felt every inch with an intensity I had never felt before. Grasping the comforter tighter, I cried out as J threw his head back and groaned.

We stayed like that for a few seconds, thoroughly absorbing the first entry, without any motion from either of us. Just his manhood buried deep within my twitching core. Even with no movement, the experience was incredible, and I could feel an orgasm building at lightning speed. He backed out slowly and I whimpered, moving to reciprocate the action. I was expecting him to push back inside of me, and I readied myself to meet his thrust, but instead, he simply said, "Shhhh," and held my hips down.

I was physically shaking with pent up desire. I needed to come so very badly, but wanted it to be on his terms, so I gritted my teeth while trying to weather the storm raging inside me.

Once I settled and it seemed that I was going to stay where he wanted me, he used his thighs to push my legs wider apart. The teasing presence of the tip of his cock edged just inside me was making the struggle to control myself almost impossible. This was the most unhinged I had ever felt in my life. But it was just the beginning.

He reached down and ran his fingers around the part of his cock that had just been inside of me, gathering a bit of my own juices, before placing his wet thumb squarely on my clitoris. I almost wept in pleasure as he began a slow, circling motion. Then, unexpectedly, his finger joined the thumb and nipped my clitoris in a firm pinch. A sharp shock of pleasure shot up my spine, tearing into my mind and making me see stars. The inevitable orgasm jumped several notches closer to manifesting. I wasn't sure how much longer I could hold it back.

Fuck!

But I wanted him inside me. I wanted him to fuck me into that sweet oblivion.

He leaned over and placed his other hand on the bed next to my side. I saw his strong arm next to me and released the blanket in favor of holding onto him. My hands gripped his bicep as he slid a little deeper into me. His other arm was between us, those fingers still stroking the crux that would be my undoing.

I felt the breaker cresting.

I couldn't tell if it started in my toes or my head, but within seconds I was consumed, and he was thrusting deeply into me. Wave after irresistible wave rolled over me. J now had both of his arms on either side of my shoulders, and I was clinging to him tightly, my ears ringing, our bodies finding each other with every motion.

And then his head was back, and his mouth was open in a semi-silent roar. He was coming. I squeezed myself around him, and he growled, thrusting into me deeper, if that was even possible. We had caused our own personal earthquake, the power of it rocking both of us to the foundation.

There was one final push, and a shudder from J, as my shaking body tried to settle.

We were approaching the other side of the mountain, both of us embracing every aftershock, as we took our time to calm ourselves from our powerful confrontation.

Arms locked and holding himself up, J hung his head down toward me, his eyes engaged with mine, telling me what I already knew, before slowly lowering himself to kiss me. It was a long, passionate kiss, and I read his message loud and clear – this had been on his terms.

He had just made love to me...his way.

CHAPTER NINE

My head was reeling and, if I hadn't already been lying down, I would have certainly collapsed. All tension left me as my body eased and sank into the mattress.

J sensed this and nudged me onto my side as he lay down behind me, spooning style, and whispered in my ear, "Not so fast. I'm not done with you, love."

What? What was he doing? We had all night.

My back was settled in against his chest, resting my head on his arm. And then I felt his free hand tracing up the side of my body, beginning at my thigh. After all that had just happened, I wasn't sure what he was expecting of me.

"J, I don't think I—"

But he cut me off, saying, "Oh, you can. And you will."

I can and I will what? Come again? Oh, I don't think so, sweetheart. Can he *come again?* But I remained silent as his hand explored my body.

He trailed past my elbow, running his fingers through my hair, and then gathered it to drape over his arm.

Leaning away, with his palm flat against my skin, J's hands pressed sensually against my back, his fingers tracing tenderly up and down my spine.

I was feeling sleepy and incredibly relaxed.

Maybe he just wants to have some quiet time, I thought. And I was perfectly happy to stay ensconced in his arms for this.

J's finger followed along my neck, meandering upward where he brushed the hair out of my eyes, running his hands through it again. A light touch around my face, down to my chest, and I thought, *Surely, he won't...*

At a snail's pace, taking all the time in the world, he kept moving until he reached my breasts.

Slow and purposeful, his hand circled them, one by one. My nipples were rigid, and I couldn't wrap my head around the reaction I felt. The spontaneous tightening that indicated my body was coming alive again, readying for him to take what he wanted, had returned.

There was no pinching this time, not yet anyway. Just soft, slow caresses that put all of my senses on edge.

I could feel J pressed against my back and the hardening response that indicated his continued arousal. Leisurely, he ran his fingers around my nipples, first one and then the other, alternating back and forth, over and over. The light-headed feeling began again, like I was floating away from reality, guided by his tender caress. Closing my eyes, I involuntarily pushed my ass against him as I felt my desire uncontrollably mounting.

If he keeps this up, I thought, *he'll be right – I can, and I will.*

When he felt me trying to assert myself against him, he growled quietly in my ear, "Shhh."

Evidently, my impatient personality was flaring up.

Yet, while his manner continued to be firm, his touch was featherlight. His lips brushed my neck. The warm breath I felt with each exhalation sent excited chills up my spine. He softly kissed from my shoulder to my ear and then reversed course. Moving slowly and calculatedly, each kiss was perfectly placed as his hand continued the exploratory mission. Every now and then he left my breasts and, palm flat, traveled down my stomach, over my legs, returning to my nipples at his leisure.

J took his time bringing me to the point of no return, meticulously concentrating on what drew out the precise reactions he was seeking. When he was finally satisfied that I had arrived, he backed away from me and prompted me to roll over to face him. Propped on his elbow, using a hand to cradle the back of my head, the gaze we shared caused a flutter of butterflies in my stomach. His handsome face was a study in intensity, mirroring the force I was feeling deep in my center.

I was lying partially on my side, my upper body in repose as my hips turned slightly toward him. He resumed the torturous scouting of the geography of my body, exploring every curve, every peak and valley. Swirling around the soft swell of my breasts, his hands, occasionally rolling one of my yearning nipples gently between his fingers. My hips were moving ever so slightly, thighs rubbing subtly together as my sensitive core searched for him, seeking what I craved.

I had thought I was done.

J had proved me wrong.

Unable to keep my hands off him, I was caressing his chest, slowly, around and around. The hair there was soft and provided a thin covering to his skin that I couldn't stop touching.

He leaned in to kiss me. A long, tender kiss that stoked my burning desire for him to another level. Hooking one leg over his, I pushed toward him, feeling his cock against me. He pressed me to move back a little but allowed me to keep my leg on his.

The thought of going ninja on him briefly crossed my mind. I envisioned myself attempting to quickly lie him back so I could climb on top of him, but I had a feeling this move would be met with resistance. J was still controlling this.

He retreated from our kiss and went back to hovering above me, propped on his elbow. Lying his hand flat against my chest, in between my breasts, he began inching down my stomach, fingers first. I knew where he was going, and I was ready to beg for it.

Faintly, in the background, I heard Chad Kroger singing "Savin' Me," and I got him – I was falling. And J's fingers were going to be my saving grace.

The downward path along my body continued until he was there. Again, right there.

Alternating between watching me and looking at his destination, he slipped two fingers past my clitoris, one on either side, brushing so very close it made me quiver involuntarily. As his probing fingertips reached my eager entrance, I closed my eyes. I felt him slide them inside of me. My head was pushing his hand into the mattress as I pressed myself forward to meet him. I recognized the internal rush of warmth and moisture as my body welcomed him.

Keeping his fingers inside of me, his thumb located my clitoris and begin to circle. My soft sighs became more urgent when I felt his mouth on my nipple. Taking it between his lips, he sucked softly while his tongue brushed across it.

His free hand curved over my shoulder, caressing my other nipple. Flicking across it, and then gingerly pinching it.

It was all too much. I couldn't hold out any longer. Feeling his rigid erection against me, I reached for him, but he closed the small gap between us, preventing me from finding what I sought.

I wanted him to fuck me again, but I couldn't wait for that. My final undoing was when he leaned down to me, whispering in my ear, “Come for me.”

I did.

I had no choice.

Hard and fast and furious. Crying out with each upsurge that rolled over me.

My hands were flat against his chest. I was pushing against him as I braced myself, but he stayed firmly in place, not allowing me to actually move him away.

As the tremors subsided, and I gradually sank back to earth, he took his hands away, sliding them around my back, holding me close for a sensual kiss.

My arms found their way around his neck, pulling him deeper into the kiss, moving my hips against him, feeling his hard cock as I tried to slide him inside of me.

J leaned back from the embrace and gently removed my leg from being hooked over his, saying, “Shh, shh, shh, love. Not now.”

What??

I looked at him incredulously, imploring him to tell me why.

There was a sad look in his eyes when he responded, asking me, “How long do we have?”

It was then that I realized he wasn't aware of my plan. One night together.

“Tonight,” I whispered.

It suddenly sounded terrible. The itinerary had been so clearly mapped out in my head with never a thought given to altering it, but now I could plainly see that one night together wasn't enough. Why had I thought it would work so easily? It seemed simple just a few hours ago – meet J, confirm the chemistry, give him the opportunity to be himself, get my resolution, and...leave. The weight of my one-word answer – "tonight" – tugged at my heartstrings. This was what they meant about the best laid plans...

J looked at me, absorbing our gift of the moment, then nodded and said, "Okay. Later then, love."

He wrapped his arms around me, and we curled up together, taking a much-needed break from our physical activities.

❧

We lay on J's bed, tangled up together, and he was playing a game with me.

"Favorite color?" he asked.

"Black."

"That's not a color."

"Green."

"Favorite movie?"

"Gone with the Wind."

"Favorite song?"

"Too many to pick one."

"Try."

"No."

At this, he started tickling me, telling me he wasn't going to let up until I named a song. Giggling, I tried to get out of his arms so I could scurry away from him, but I was no match for his strength.

Finally, when I couldn't breathe from the laughter, I choked out, in a squeal, "Simply Red – 'Holding Back the Years'!"

This satisfied him, and he stopped tickling me. After a minute of thought about my song choice, he said, "That one goes waaay back."

I was still trying to catch my breath when I explained. "Yeah. I don't know. I liked it then and I still like it. It's just too hard for me to pick one song, but it's all that came to mind when you were torturing me with your...*brutishness.*"

"What? I'm a brute?" he said with mock anger, holding his hand over me, poised for another round of tickling.

"No!" I screamed and kicked at him. But he didn't tickle me. Instead, he held my legs down to stop the attack while he kissed me.

When we parted, I said, "What about you?"

"What about me?"

"What are your favorite things?"

"You know all about me, Nat."

"No. I don't know all those little things."

His eyes locked on mine. "You know all the important stuff. You know what matters."

I suddenly felt honored to be the one person with whom he could be himself. J didn't have much of a comfort zone, even when he was alone. There was so much that raged inside his mind. I knew this, and I was happy to see him so relaxed and seemingly at peace. For now, anyway.

The wheels in his head were spinning again, and I waited to hear what he was going to come up with next. Then he dropped a bomb on me.

"What's your name?"

Ohhhhhhh, shit.

This was something else for which I was not prepared, and I briefly worried about what more could happen that I hadn't foreseen.

My mouth dropped open as I was rendered speechless.

He didn't move a muscle as he waited for an answer.

"J..." and I couldn't say anything more because I had no good response for him. I was still trying to maintain my anonymity, and I was fine with him knowing me as Natalie. Better than fine with it – that's the way I wanted it.

I spent years being addressed by that name at work, so I was used to it. I also loved that this was something that was now his and his alone. I no longer worked in that world. He was the only one who called me by the name now and, on top of that, he was the only one who had ever called me "Nat." It was a J thing, and I wanted to keep it that way.

Finally, I looked deep into his eyes and said, "Natalie."

He sighed. "You know what I mean. I know you weren't using your real name as a stage name and that's all 'Natalie' is – your stage name. Don't you think at this point, now, you could tell me who you really are?"

"No."

That was the long and short of it. I had nothing else to say because there was nothing that could happen to make me tell him. I trusted J, and I was pretty sure he wasn't going to be revealing our intimacies to anyone, so the mutual acquaintance was an immaterial point. I simply wanted to keep things the way they were and had always been. The alias worked for me. This was part and parcel of the chamber in my heart reserved for only J.

He was trying to read me, searching to find out if it

was worth it to push the issue. Finally, to my immense relief, he kissed me and said, "Okay...Nat."

CHAPTER TEN

I made the first move to get up by rolling onto my side then kissing J.

"I'm really happy I'm here with you," I said. He turned to look at me, gazing, with an expression I couldn't read. There was a long pause before he pulled me close and kissed me again.

I scooted to the edge of the bed and slid off onto the floor. Man, this was a high bed! There were two closed doors in front of me. I walked to them, turned to J, and pointed at one.

He was propped up on his elbow, watching me with what seemed like a look of amusement. I felt the fire begin to stir within me again, almost laughing out loud at the effect he was having on me.

He nodded at the door where my finger was directed. "Yup, that's the bathroom."

I opened the other door because the bathroom wasn't what I was looking for. Sure enough, it was his closet, and I stepped in to find myself in what appeared to be a walk-in the size of a whole separate room. It was massive. Closing the door behind me, I was surrounded by racks of his hanging clothes, shoes, shelves of folded sweaters and jeans, and more shelves stacked with boxes.

There were cubbies and drawers built in between all the racks, but the centerpiece was what really had my attention. It was an enormous island with a splattered granite top. A black iron chandelier hung above it boasting lights all around that mimicked the appearance of lit candles.

I had to pull myself away from staring at it to focus on my intended mission.

Running my hand along his clothes, avoiding the temptation to lean into a rack of shirts to smell them, I finally came to what I was looking for – a section of dress shirts. They hung neatly, looking crisp and pressed. I found a black one – exactly what I wanted – and took the super soft shirt from its hanger.

As I put it on, fastening just a few of the middle buttons and leaving the bottom and top open in a devil-may-care sort of way, I thought about how much I would really love to see him in this shirt. I had every reason to believe he wore it extremely well.

Shaking out my hair a little, I checked myself in the full-length mirror leaning against the wall, then walked back out into the bedroom.

J was wearing boxers now and lying back on a big pile of pillows.

Oh, my goodness, you sexy man.

When he saw me, a smile slowly crept onto his face. I pranced on tip toe to the bed, leaned over to kiss him, and spun away quickly before he could get his hands on me.

"Fuck!" I playfully heard behind me as I left the room with the intention of making use of the bathroom down the hall.

I didn't want to use his en suite – this one would give me more privacy, and I could take my time knowing I wasn't keeping him from something he might need in his own space.

I went to the kitchen first to grab my purse off the counter, then back down the hall to the bathroom he had showed me on the house tour.

Closing and locking the door behind me, I leaned back against it. I suddenly felt like I was going to collapse. My mind was reeling, and I didn't know if I wanted to laugh or cry...or both.

J was everything I had imagined him to be – sexy, soft yet firm in his desires, smart, deeply thoughtful as I could see in his eyes, sexy...did I mention that already? A fleeting thought raced past me that we had the potential to be great together. If only we could explore each other enough to find out. But that wasn't going to happen.

I went to the vanity to get cleaned up. Everything I had in my little purse had been put in there for this night, and anything extra and unneeded – cash, cards, my license, etc. – had been removed.

When it came to the identifying information, J had never struck me as the type to be a snooper, but it would be just like me to spill everything on the floor. My clumsy ways always had a knack of making an appearance when I least needed them to.

I removed my keys, setting them on the counter, to gain access to my toothbrush and found some toothpaste in a drawer of the vanity. While I brushed my teeth, I combed my hair and took out my personal wipes along with a little bottle of body spray. I also took off my bracelet and earrings and dropped them into my purse.

After I was satisfied that I was cleaned up and presentable, I took a little lacy white thong out of my purse then put everything else away. The white lace would contrast nicely with the black shirt.

Even though I was swimming in his shirt, and it hung halfway down my thighs, with most of the buttons unfastened, he'd be treated to glimpses of the thong because I hadn't closed all the buttons.

I rolled up the sleeves, double checked my hair and makeup, tucked my purse into a corner of the vanity, and walked out into the hall. Was he still in his bedroom? I decided to start there. Sure enough, I found him coming out of his bathroom wearing flannel pants. No shirt.

The sight of him stopped me in my tracks. He was stunning, with an expression and stance that exhibited confidence without an ounce of ego.

J stopped as well and slowly looked me up and down. He smiled while walking to the bed where he picked up a t-shirt that he promptly pulled over his head. It was tight enough to see his muscles, but not so tight that it looked uncomfortable.

The heat between my legs was building stronger. I knew I was ready to go, but I was committed to taking our time again. Let the fire rage...we would extinguish it when we were ready.

J,
Same! Your story is...fuck...hot...!!
Now I want to do that...with you...
Nat

He came toward me, put his strong arms around my waist, and pulled me to him, kissing me first on the forehead, then on my hair.

I had my arms wrapped around him, shamelessly running my hands over his tight ass.

I pulled back just enough to look up at him. "So, I guess I was wrong about your office."

He looked down at me, frowning slightly. "What do you mean?"

"Well, now I know that *this* is the room where the magic happens."

He threw his head back and laughed. "You're crazy," he said lightheartedly as he pulled me closer again.

I giggled. "I'm okay with that as long as...you're into my kind of crazy."

"Oh, I think it's safe to say I am *really* digging your kind of crazy." He squeezed me and took my hand. "Come on."

He led me back to the kitchen, where he stopped and put his hands on his hips, looking around.

"What's the matter?" I asked.

"I don't know where we left our glasses. Fuck it."

He opened a cupboard to get out two more – a wine glass for me and a rocks glass for him.

I heard the music drifting down the hall from the bedroom and, as he was pouring fresh drinks, I asked, "Mind if I turn that off and play something?"

Focused on the glasses and bottles, he answered, "Nope...hang on a sec."

J stopped what he was doing and opened another cupboard where there was, surprise surprise, more tech. As he fiddled, I heard the music in the bedroom stop, then there was a faint hum that seemed to come from all around us.

He saw me searching for the source of the hum. "I turned it on for the whole house so it will play everywhere."

"Ahhh, cool," I said, entering the living room and approaching the touchscreen near the stereo. A couple of taps and then Michael Crawford's voice was coming in full surround as he sang "Music of the Night."

J walked in carrying the two glasses. He stopped to look at me.

"*Phantom*? Really?" he teased.

"Yeeesss," I answered, pretending to be hurt. "Do you know the words to this? I think it fits quite well," I said, putting my hands on my hips while taking a playfully defensive stance.

He walked to me, handing me the wine. "It's been a while, but I'll play along."

He leaned over, kissing me sweetly on the cheek before going to sit on the couch.

"Start it over."

I tapped the screen to play the song from the beginning. When I turned back to J, he was sitting in that damn pose again, leaning back with his arm across the top of the couch. Why did I find that so maddeningly fucking hot?

My legs felt shaky for a minute. I had to pause to compose myself before making my way to the chair where I had been sitting earlier in the evening. Bending one knee to tuck it under myself as I sat, that's when J was granted the first glimpse of my white thong.

He stared at my midsection as I moved to sit, and then raised an eyebrow at me but didn't say anything. He was listening to the song. His eyes moved back to my legs for a few seconds before he turned his head to look straight, giving his full attention to "Music of the Night."

I wasn't sure if I should be feeling differently about it, but I absolutely loved that he wasn't afraid to look at what he wanted to see. Stare, even. Having no shame in doing so was yet another super fucking hot quality of his. And that was exactly where I wanted him to be because I was pretty damn certain that he didn't normally openly study anyone like this, take what he wanted, control the type of sex he was going to have.

Michael Crawford was gearing up to the final lyrics. J was still listening, showing no expression.

I sipped my wine, looking around the room. There were framed photos on a table about ten feet away. I made a mental note to look at them. I wanted to ask about the people who were important enough to him to make their way into a picture frame, positioned on display. I longed to know as much as I could about his daily life before this came to an...end.

The song was over, and J looked at me, nodding. "I see it."

I shrugged. "I don't know. It popped into my head, and I love the song. The whole musical actually, and it seemed appropriate. I like situational music."

"Have you seen the musical?" he asked.

"Mhmm. A couple of times." I took a sip of my wine. "The last time was about seven years ago. I had front row, and it was fun because I could see the orchestra pit. And then the chandelier dropped literally right over my head."

"Don't say 'literally.'" J rolled his eyes jokingly. "What the fuck is it with that word these days?"

"Oh, I know. I agree, and I try not to do it, but it's hard when *everyone* around me is using it to death." I paused. "Like, *literally* everyone!"

J laughed, shook his head, and then took a long drink from his glass.

"Lucky glass," I quipped.

When he looked up at me, I ran my tongue around the edge of my glass.

"Could you try to behave for just a *few* minutes?" J asked playfully.

He got up and went to the stereo where he switched the music over to his mixed playlist.

"Why, J, whatever do you mean?" I asked with an exaggerated batting of my eyelashes.

He rolled his eyes. "You're going to drive me crazy. First that dress. And now what's the deal with those..." He flicked his hand in the air at me. "Those...panties?"

With my chin down, I slowly turned my eyes up at him, smiling wickedly. "Wanna see 'em?"

He sighed and threw his hands up in the air. Then, taking a firm stance, he said, "Yes." Before I could figure out what to do – were we heading back to the bedroom? – he continued. "But not yet."

Fair enough, and it was what I wanted to hear. The atmosphere felt more relaxed now, so I hoped to talk to him for a while before we ventured into the next escapade.

Nat,

Hmmm. Maybe. You're the only one I'd consider letting in again to that extent. Hell, I'm surprised you made it this far.

But then we'd have to meet...

J

I got up and walked over to the table with the photos, leaning over just a bit to look at them. Immediately, I spotted one person among those featured who couldn't go unnoticed to me. All I could do was hope my poker face would serve me well.

J came up behind me and put his hand on the small of

my back. Without needing to be prompted, he started telling me about the people at whom I was looking.

"That's my family on vacation. Mom, brother...brother's boyfriend. At the time. Me, of course."

I stared, openly absorbed in seeing them together. The physical resemblance was there, but the night and day personalities remained a fact.

Looking at the family photo turned J thoughtful about his brother for a moment. "Mark lives in the city. I try to see him whenever I go in. Good guy. Way more outgoing than me and likes to know a little too much about what I'm up to, but a good guy."

I wasn't sure what J saw in my expression, but I hoped my poker face was holding its own.

Shifting my stance, I turned to the next picture.

"That's Rebecca." He stopped, looking uncomfortable before continuing. "My girlfriend...and me in the city together."

Even though I had been told that what he had with her wasn't much of a relationship, they'd been together a long time, nevertheless. I did my best to remain expressionless, not wanting to show any emotion that might increase whatever guilt he might have already been feeling. It must have worked...

"This one is an old pool buddy of mine. I still see him once in a while."

Having successfully skirted around Rebecca for the time being, I waited for him to get to the one I was really curious about. It was a picture of J, standing and laughing, with a stunning brunette dressed in a long, slinky strapless black gown. When I first spotted the photograph, I thought for sure she was going to be the girlfriend, but Rebecca didn't hold a candle to this woman.

She was remarkably beautiful, and I didn't even have

to meet her in person to see the confidence flowing out of her. Here she was standing with J, looking carefree and so happy. What was the story with *her*?

He saw me looking. "That's Alesandra – my agent."

His *agent?* That woman should be *starring* in the films he writes, not sitting behind the scenes representing the writer. Even her name was sexy.

"She's beautiful," was all I could muster.

"That she is," he said. "And a real shark in the industry. I'm lucky to have her on my side."

I felt the most ridiculous pang of jealousy.

Don't be silly, I thought. *You have no claim to him...and you never will.* But I felt intimidated knowing he was so close to such an exotic creature.

He worked with beautiful actresses all the time, of course I knew that. But this was different because he was clearly friends with Alesandra. They looked like they had a connection.

As an afterthought, he added, "She's also a total fruit loop. And gayer than gay could be."

"Oh, really?" I said...just to say something while trying to conceal the relief I felt to hear about her preference for women.

"Yup. And British. Absolutely despises men...as far as the idea of being with one goes. She probably gets nauseous just thinking about it. You know how the Brits can get away with saying anything, no matter how crass? They can come out with the craziest shit that an American wouldn't be able to pull off on their best day, and it sounds like a normal comment coming from them."

With that, he launched into an Alesandra impersonation, complete with a perfect English accent: "'You know, darling, I don't know how you walk around with that thing between your legs. It's positively gruesome, don't you know? Such a shame that men evolved with a dick. A good muff is all anyone needs. You should just cut the fucking thing off and put it in a box. I don't know what you'd do with it. Bury it in the backyard, perhaps. But, I'm serious, you really should just get rid of it. You'd be much happier if you did.'"

He stopped and shrugged as if to say, *"That's Alesandra for you."*

As my shock started to fade, I fell into a fit of laughter. It didn't take long before tears were streaming down my face, and I had to hold onto his arm to steady myself until the fit passed. I thought it was hysterical. And his execution was impeccable.

When I managed to compose myself again, he just chuckled. "You'd get along with her very well. You're both crazy." He laughed again. "I can just hear that."

Another Alesandra impersonation: "'She's just darling, sweetheart. Is she straight? Please don't tell me she's straight – I don't think I could bear it. Should I fuck her? That would fix it. One romp with me and she'll be forever changed and enlightened.'"

I laughed again. No offense to beautiful Alesandra, but no woman was going to be able to drag me away from my attraction to the male physique. Especially after tonight.

I leaned into him, putting my arm around him, a gesture of my commitment to the straight life.

J draped his arm over my shoulders, and I felt the pressure of his toned muscles. It was a delicious weight.

Kissing the top of my head again, he asked, "Are you hungry? I could cook something."

"J, I honestly don't think I could get down one bite right now. I'm a little...preoccupied."

He laughed. "Me too. Maybe later. I'd like to cook for

you."

It was something so simple, but to me, it was such a sweet thought. I squeezed him to express my appreciation.

J,
I'm thinking about taking a break from the club. Focus on the business to get it off the ground. Maybe do a little traveling...
Nat

Walking to the windows at the back of the house, I looked out, although darkness was the only sight to observe. "Do you have one of those enormous yards that everyone else around here seems to have?"

J gave a small shrug. "Yeah. I guess."

He paused, thoughtful, before walking over to French doors on the far side of the room and flipping a switch that shed a glowing carpet of light over the immediate backyard of the house.

It wasn't just one big, obnoxious spotlight. Instead, the switch illuminated a series of small lanterns near the ground, spaced out evenly all around a large flagstone patio, continuing on to a walkway that encircled an enormous pool. It was beautiful.

The path was landscaped on one side with various plants and flowers, a thick padding of red mulch matted in between each tuft of color.

In the distance, beyond the pool, I could barely make out what looked to be some large trees scattered throughout the property.

The pool itself was impressive. The lights shone on the water, giving away a Jacuzzi, diving board, and a waterfall that was created to look like a natural stone formation. Water was running down the rocks, landing with a splash into the pool where there was a cove for swimmers to hide under the cascade, offering them a sanctuary of privacy. I couldn't stop my mind from wandering, briefly fantasizing that it would be an excellent place to be naked with J.

To the back left of the pool, I saw the vague shape of a building that I suspected was a pool house. From my viewpoint, it looked big enough to have a changing room and shower, but there also could have been a whole separate living space out there.

Closer to the house, on the patio, there were two seating areas – one with a large table and chairs, and another with what looked like actual sofas and armchairs. The foundations for the furniture appeared to be heavy, outdoor wood, but there were also comfortable cushions and throw pillows. I'd seen appointments arranged like this in catalogs and always wondered what happened when it rained.

"J, this is really amazing," I said.

"Thanks. It's nice to have it for swimming laps."

Swimming laps – he was too much. All of this and he probably never entertained out there. No barbecues with friends on a sunny Saturday afternoon. No pool parties with rambunctious games of water volleyball. Nope. J was swimming laps...all alone.

He had himself convinced that he liked things this way, but I found myself speculating about how much of it was buried pain and silent suffering.

I knew that brilliant minds like J's had a tendency to take things to heart in the extreme. What the rest of the world would process and move beyond was mulled over...and over and over...by people like him. What afflicted him internally was probably a big source of his creativity.

I had always known this about him, but standing there, surrounded by his things, in the place in which he hid from the outside world, I hit a new level of understanding about him. And I wanted to be near him.

I couldn't save him. Not that he necessarily needed saving, but I wanted to be a source of comfort. For tonight, at least.

I felt an ache in my heart, knowing this was going to be the only time we would have together.

CHAPTER ELEVEN

Wanna go for a walk?" J asked. He gave me a once-over, standing in front of him, wearing only his shirt, and then said, "Never mind. It's probably too chilly."

"No, I'll be fine." He looked hesitant, so I nudged him with my hand. "Come on. I'll be okay. I promise."

He unlocked the door, holding it open for me to step out into the cool night air. The stones of the patio felt chilly against my feet and, without thinking, I pranced and said, "Oooo!"

J took hold of my elbow, trying to steer me back inside the door. "Nope. Forget it. I won't have you catching cold out here."

I pulled away from him, shook my head, and took several steps out of his reach. He sighed, recognizing I was going to take a walk with or without him. I turned my back to him, taking in the sight of the backyard as I heard the door softly close behind me.

The waterfall of the pool lent a peaceful serenity to the atmosphere. I thought, if I lived here, it would be a sound I'd never tire of hearing.

J stood next to me, taking my hand in his. His fingers linked with mine, and it felt right and natural to be there with him.

"Do you spend a lot of time out here?" I asked.

"Sometimes. Coffee in the morning, that sort of thing."

And the laps, I thought to myself.

"It's completely secured with a privacy fence," he added.

Of course it was. If there were any chance of someone catching a glimpse into his private world, he wouldn't spend one second out here. The fence afforded him the safety of knowing his yard could be an extension of his house.

Nat,

I'm home tonight if you want to write. I didn't go to pool league. I should have, but I just didn't feel up to it. Don't give me a lecture about getting out there - just wanted to let you know I'm around if you want to chat.

J

Still holding his hand, I walked toward the water. We were taking a stroll together...and I liked it.

It was after Labor Day, and I wondered when he closed the pool for the season. As if reading my mind, he said, "I keep it open until it becomes too cold to swim during the day."

I nodded as we walked, smiling to myself while I reflected on J's refusal to adhere to the typical northeast pool closing practice. Let everyone else shut it down at

Labor Day – he'd swim as long as he damn well pleased, weather permitting.

Coming around the far side, I could look out on the rest of the yard and had a better idea of the amount of shade trees that could be seen in the distance. There were several from my vantage point, all very big. Old trees left to stand as this affluent neighborhood built itself around them.

As for the privacy fence, I couldn't see far enough in any direction to make it out.

Once we were upon the pool house, I stopped in front of it.

"I didn't bring the key," he said, understanding that I wanted to see it. "Another time. Or...well..." he fumbled.

I tried to save him as I simply said, "It's okay," and walked a little faster to move away from the structure that had caused a temporary hiccup.

It couldn't be seen from the main house, but on the other side of the pool house was a large outdoor kitchen. In the dark, I could just make out that it was well-stocked with all the necessary equipment – a large built-in grill, gas burners, plenty of counter space, a small refrigerator, sink, and even an oven. Stone pillars led up toward the sky to secure a roof over the whole set-up. I doubted this area ever saw much use.

Again, demonstrating his view into my mind, he remarked, "This was all here when I moved in," thereby confirming my speculation that it wasn't something he used often, if at all.

I watched steam rising from the water as we got closer to the waterfall. Letting go of J's hand and leaning over a large slab of the rock formation that came up to my waist, I reached under the flowing water, letting it spill over my hand. It was heated. Warm mist landed in the tiniest of droplets on my face, and I giggled as it tickled my skin.

J stood behind me, putting his hands on my hips. When I turned to face him, he was looking down into my eyes. We searched each other for several seconds before he leaned in to kiss me, softly at first. I put my arms around his neck, pulling him closer. Our fervor intensified before he lifted me to sit on the large stone. His hands slid down to part my legs so he could stand between them, pressing against me.

Our lips separated, and I felt J's tongue softly brush my neck. Tilting my head back, I savored every kiss, as I heard him whisper, "Nat..."

His hands found my ass, and he moved me closer to the edge of the rock. Through the flannel, I could feel his arousal, and my thong was instantly dampened with a surge of excitement.

"J...whatever you want," I whispered.

I was pretty sure he already knew that I was going to allow him to make all the decisions, but this confirmed it.

Through the fabric, I felt his rigid shaft pinned between us. A flickering thought gave me a vision of one particular intimacy that I was hoping to initiate. When the time came, I would hand over control of that as well, following any guidance he wanted to provide.

Pulling my thoughts away from my one wish, J said, "Not here. I'm not prepared."

Of course. The condoms were in the bedroom.

I let out a heavy sigh, not meaning to imply frustration with him, and he said, "Sorry."

"Don't be silly."

Putting my hands on either side of his face, I pulled him in for another kiss while doing my best to avoid pressing too firmly against him. We needed to stop getting ourselves worked up out here. I already knew that, when we went back in the house, I was going to begin my efforts to satisfy my one specific craving.

Our lingering kiss came to a slow end when J pulled away to put a little space between us. Positioning his hands back on my waist, he helped me down from my seat.

This would have been an excellent venue for our next experience together, but we both knew that it would not do either one of us any good to let our passion override our common sense. Or, at least, what little common sense we had left between us.

J had my hand again and took a long pause, gazing at me, before we continued our walk around the other side of the pool.

Here, there was a long row of lounge chairs, each with its own cushion. When we reached the seating area, I stopped and asked, "Do you mind if we sit for a minute?"

I wanted to take in some more of the serenity of his yard before we returned inside.

"Sure, love. But are you sure you're not cold?"

"I'm fine, J. I'm an outdoorsy kind of girl, and I like it out here."

I picked the chair nearest us at the end of the row, positioning myself to sit all the way against the back of it. Instead of choosing his own, J sat down at the foot of mine, picked up my feet, and put them in his lap.

He felt the chill of my toes, prompting him to take them between his hands, massaging them. After wearing the stilettos that I was no longer accustomed to, it was a great feeling. I let out a little moan.

We sat quietly while I looked up at the night sky, observing that, even with his close proximity to the city, I could still see some stars. It was a beautiful evening.

As I star-gazed, J was exploring my toes.

"You have sexy feet," he said. I abandoned my surveillance of the sky and looked at him with a smile. He shrugged. "Did you know that?"

Other than a couple of rare customers I had at the club who had a foot fetish, I'd never really given it much thought.

"No, I didn't," I responded. "But thank you. I think."

He laughed. "I'm not normally what you would classify as a 'foot guy,' but your feet are definitely...sexy."

I raised an eyebrow at him, giving him a sly look. "Let me see your feet."

"Oh, no. We're not getting into all that. Take the compliment and move on," he said with a chuckle.

Even though he wanted to close the conversation, he continued to rub from toes to heels. His hands felt amazing. Once in a while, he trailed away, running his palms up my legs, applying just the right amount of therapeutic pressure.

J,

Have I lectured you? I'm so sorry if it came across that way. I just worry about you. And I want you to be happy. You have pool league again on Thursday, right? Maybe you'll feel up to going then.

I'm home, too - pick a topic and let's run with it!

Nat

"Do you have to travel a lot?" I asked, curious about the demands of his career now that he had attained such a unique level.

"Yes. More than I would care to, if I could help it."

Despite his desire to keep to himself, I recalled that J

had an exploratory side. If being on a crowded airplane was what it took for him to visit a new locale, he would do it. His whole family appreciated taking in the sights of the world, and they often did it together, as the photo in his living room indicated.

"I thought you liked to travel," I said.

"I used to. Now there's so much of it for work. And it takes its toll."

I wondered how many people out there thought that he was living the life of Riley when the truth was, he would be perfectly happy to just stay home and write.

"Hey," he said, "want to hear something cool?"

"Absolutely."

"So, there's a possibility...a small possibility...that I might be a producer on the next film."

"Really?? J, that's fantastic!"

From his struggling, up-and-coming years and everything he had told me in our emails, I knew that learning the many different facets of the industry was a direction he hoped to one day take. Back then it was the stuff his daydreams were made of.

"Thank you. Being able to do that would make the traveling worth it."

"I'm sure! When will you find out if it's going to happen?"

"Should be next week."

"Well, I really hope it works out for you," I told him, and I genuinely meant it. I made a mental note to pay attention to his next film and look for his name on the producer credits.

He nodded. "Thank you." He ran his hands up my legs again. "You're cold. Let's go in."

I finally conceded that I was getting chilly, and he held out a hand to help me up. When I stood, instead of continuing to hold my hand, this time he put an arm around me, pulling me close to him. I wound mine around his back. We started walking toward the door, still out for an evening stroll together, just taking our steps a little faster this time. I had to admit I was looking forward to getting back into the warm house. Not as much because of the nighttime chill, but more because I wanted to instigate the urge that struck me during our waterfall embrace.

We made our way across the patio again. When we reached the door, J pushed it open, putting a hand on the small of my back to urge me in first.

I stepped in, J following closely after as he closed the door behind him. I turned to face him, finding him leaning back against it. Seizing my opportunity, I reached over to the wall, turned off the switch that lit up the yard, and prepared to flip a different one for him.

CHAPTER TWELVE

My arms wrapped around J's waist, and I pressed my cheek against his chest as my fingers trailed up and down his back.

We stood there enjoying the moment for several seconds, J's hands caressing my shoulders, before I pulled back and looked up into his eyes. Gently cupping my face, he leaned in to kiss me. It started out slow and soft before gaining momentum, and then it took a turn. We were ravenous again. I wanted to climb up and wrap my legs around him.

The deep, masculine scent of his cologne pushed me over the edge, causing my patience to wear out. Taking him by the hand, I walked him to the big armchair that had been my earlier living room perch.

Putting my hands on his chest, I gently nudged him to sit down. He did as instructed, eyes intently focused on me, wondering what I was going to do.

I stood in front of him, unbuttoned the three buttons

that were fastened on the shirt I was wearing, letting it hang open to reveal only a thin line of skin.

His eyes traveled from my face, down my chest to where my breasts were hidden behind the open shirt, to my stomach, before resting on the skimpy, white lace. He sat forward, reaching for me, but I swatted his hand away. There was a low growl before he leaned back, resting his arms on the side of the chair, clearly complying with my authority for the time being.

I braced my hands on his knees, easing myself down in front of him. He now realized what was coming and briefly closed his eyes in anticipation of the ecstasy that was imminent.

Stretching my arms forward, I pushed my ass back in a semi-cat's pose. Starting at the waist of his lounge pants, my hands slid underneath his shirt, slowly moving up his stomach to his chest, where I spread my fingers and let them run over his nipples. He sucked in a quick breath and shuddered faintly.

A little tug upward on J's shirt gave him the signal to sit up, allowing me to pull it over his head. When it was off, he took it from me and tossed it to the couch.

I was about to prompt him to lean back again when he acted quickly and, pulling open the front of my shirt, revealed my breasts. He leaned down, taking them in his hands, lowering his mouth to first one nipple, and then the other.

My back arched, offering myself to his ongoing ministrations as J continued to lick and suck, each flick of his tongue carrying me farther away from my plan. Caught between my conflicting desire to give or receive, I forced myself to refocus. It took an act of willpower, but I managed to pull away, setting my sight once again on my intended task. After all, this would be the only time tonight when I would be attempting to take an ounce of control.

I gently pulled away and put my hand on his chest to push him back into the chair. He frowned, but obliged, again placing his arms on the sides.

So fucking sexy.

I slid forward again, stretching up to caress his nipples as I lowered my head to pull on the waistband of his pants with my teeth. He moved his arms to reach down, but I firmly held his hands and kissed his stomach. Once I was sure he would comply and stay still, I released my grip on his arms and slid them under his backside, pulling off his pants. J picked himself up just enough from the chair to allow me to slide them down.

Sitting back on my heels to take them all the way off, I absentmindedly threw them in the direction of the couch where his t-shirt had been tossed. Clearly opting to forego boxers when he dressed, he was naked in front of me. Mine for the taking, exactly how I had imagined it.

My shirt had fallen closed, so I opened it slowly as I knelt in front of him, leaning over to allow my breasts to brush gently against his cock. He was every bit as hard as he had been when I first felt him inside me...and I was ready to take all of him into my mouth.

Expecting him to close his eyes, it was a sexy surprise when he continued to watch me. This voyeurism that I had come to know as typical J fashion. Fuck, I *loved* that about him. After getting used to displaying myself naked on stage, exhibitionism played naturally into my wheelhouse. It turned me on, causing my heart to race just a little faster.

With our eyes locked, I extended my tongue toward him, gently licking at the base of his cock before slowly moving up the length of his shaft. He sucked in a sharp breath, so I repeated the motion.

When I reached the tip, I placed a hand firmly around the base of his erection and steadily lowered my mouth onto him. Tucking my other hand underneath his ass, he briefly arched his back and tensed before sinking into the chair again, settling in to enjoy the focus that was all his. This was exactly where I wanted J, and my primary goal was to make this everything he could have imagined. And then some.

I worked slowly, methodically, taking all of him with each downward movement. My breathing remained steady as I felt the head of his manhood sliding into the back of my throat. There would be no tripped gag reflex – I wouldn't allow it. The level of intensity of this act overshadowed all other thoughts and feelings.

I continued gradually, swirling my tongue around him as I went, sucking each time I came to the tip.

Glancing up, I saw J watching me, so I took my mouth off of him and ran my tongue up the length of him again, feeling every vein as I licked. He kept his eyes on me, naturally. I resumed sliding all of him into the back of my throat, keeping him at a comfortable angle so he could see everything I was doing.

My pace remained slow and steady until I sensed him tensing again. I felt him further grow and harden in my mouth. Moving a little faster, I knew he was getting close when his hands wrapped around the back of my head.

He ran his fingers under my hair, folding them behind me, pushing me down to take him even deeper. I did, and I could feel him throbbing in my mouth.

His hips raised up to meet me, and I tucked both of my hands under his backside as he fucked my mouth. Ravenously, I took every inch of him.

My own lust made my heart race as I felt the pulsing

and sticky dampness between my thighs. I thought about reaching one hand down to search for some relief, but decided instead to remain completely focused on J.

His hands grasped my head more firmly as he pushed harder, moving faster and deeper with every jolt of pleasure that overtook him. He growled my name. I moaned against him.

I took all of him, each time, until the one last thrust, when he groaned loudly. A second later, I tasted his sweet, salty cum flooding down my throat while I hungrily swallowed as he shuddered against me.

J yelled, "Fuck!"...and I didn't stop. My tongue circled the head of him as I sucked the last drop. He flinched in response.

While trying to relax, he put his hands on my shoulders, giving a gentle push to let me know he wanted me to stop. Sitting up, I licked my lips.

He was out of breath, staring at me, and I suddenly wasn't sure what I should do next. I rested my hands on his knees, staying in position, leaning back on my heels.

After a long minute of examining me, he shot forward, took my face in his hands, and kissed me. A firm, deep kiss. When he was done, he took my hands and pulled me to standing with him. And he hugged me.

"Nat, that was...incredible. I mean...I don't know what else to say. Fucking incredible."

I giggled, stepping back from him as I licked my lips again, but I suddenly felt shy and wasn't sure what to say, so I said the only thing that came to mind.

"Yes, well, there certainly is a lot to be said for the oral aspect, isn't there?"

"Definitely. *A lot* to be said."

J was looking into my eyes. I could still glimpse a remnant of the passion that had been there when he came only moments ago. I was feeling happy that he had gone along with my plan. I felt that it had been a success. More than a success, if his eyes were truly windows into his thoughts.

He sighed and put his hands on his hips. As stunning as he was and as much as I didn't want him to cover up, he was glaringly naked, so I went to the couch, picked up his shirt and pants, and handed them to him.

"Thanks," he said while stepping into the soft flannel bottoms. He looked at the t-shirt for a second then tossed it back on the couch.

Okay, I will definitely take him shirtless.

I looked around for my wine glass, found it, and took a long sip, then declared, "As you have probably gathered, I think you should tell Alesandra that under no circumstances are you going to bury your dick in the backyard."

He laughed loudly. "Well, thank you. Yes, I'll definitely let her know it's your preference that I keep it."

"Oh, it's more than a preference...it's a demand," I said, smiling coyly.

He looked thoughtful for a minute, almost distant. "So, does that mean you're going to want to do this again?"

What? Oh, man, I don't want to talk about this right now.

"J...let's not...not now. Not yet," I said, imploring him to put those details on the back burner.

"So, just tonight, right?" he continued, disregarding my begging eyes.

I nodded. I had made that promise to myself for not only family, but my own sanity as well. I just wasn't cut out for an ongoing affair. I didn't think J was either. This was the only way...for both of us.

He absorbed this information, and I was sure he knew taking this any further wasn't possible for me. Or for him. Finally, without saying anything, he sat back down in the armchair and patted his legs. Picking up his message, I set my glass on the coffee table and curled up in his lap.

His arms enveloped me while I snuggled against his chest. In that moment, the entire world could have stopped outside his front door, and I wouldn't have cared. I listened to his heartbeat, timing my breathing with his.

"Tell me what you're working on," I said when I was satisfied we were completely in tune with each other.

He took a deep breath, throwing my synchronization efforts off course. "Oh, it's this story about a couple."

"Really?" I asked, knowing romance wasn't normally his thing.

"Yeah. They're kind of crazy."

Okay, well, that made a little more sense. It would have a quirky and twisted plot, I was sure.

J continued. "Well, actually she's the crazy one. He's perfectly normal, but she causes all sorts of trouble that he gets caught up in."

I sat listening, feeling happy that he was comfortable telling me about his new creation, wondering if anyone else had heard about this yet.

"So, he's just this average Joe, you know? Nothing special, nothing out of the ordinary. And then he meets this woman online."

Wait – what? Now I was *really* listening.

"And, you know, they drifted apart, and he tried to get on with his life. And then one day, out of the blue, she's on his doorstep, totally batshit crazy and rocking his world."

"Jack *Perry*!" I screeched as I swatted him on the arm.

He laughed as he gathered my hands in his and kissed them. "Using my full name now, are you? I must be in trouble!" he laughed again.

"Yes! You're a bad boy," I chastised, but turned my face toward his looking for a kiss.

He leaned into my lips then put his forehead against mine. "Thanks. I try."

I swatted him again before settling back into his arms.

I began to wonder if this would be something he would write about. Surely, not. Romance just wasn't his genre.

His telepathy was working overtime again when he said, "I would never put this on paper. No one needs to know."

And I knew J wasn't just talking about us – he was also talking about himself. After I left, he would go right back to his usual ways, and nobody else would ever know the sensual side of him. I was sure of it. This could have given me a little ego boost, if I had let it, but I was thinking more about him and how sad it was that he would never have a woman in his life with whom he could physically explore and share moments like this.

I had known going into this that, in all likelihood, I wasn't going to teach him anything about sharing himself with someone again. Old dogs, new tricks, and all that. Without a deep communicative and intimate connection to another person, he had the ultimate self-defense mechanism.

If I was being perfectly honest with myself, now that I had experienced the physical side of J, I wasn't sure how I felt about him taking what was ours and attempting it with someone else anyway. This was wrong; my selfish thought process. I would be going back to my own life soon enough. I just couldn't help wishing he would tuck this night away and revisit it from time to time, without trying to reenact it with Rebecca, or anyone else for that matter.

The rational part of my brain told me it would never happen. My emotional side was being greedy and jealous.

I thought about the irony of it all. When I first set out to contact J all those years ago, I didn't know that what he had going on was a deep-seated wrestling match with his desires. And there I was, selling fantasies for a living. Who better to open up to than an anonymous stranger who was also a professional in the dark world of sex? Which led me to become the only one who knew. I was still the only one, right?

That made me wonder if J ever hired someone. He had the money to call up the best escort agency in the city and have a beautiful woman delivered to him with the strictest of confidentiality.

No, I quickly decided. That definitely was not his style.

We had a connection that encompassed all of this, but also so much more. We could talk about anything. Above all else, it was a friendship first.

We sat in a comfortable silence, J playing with my hair and me tracing my fingers over his chest and arms.

The music was still playing, and his tastes were all over the board. So far tonight, I had heard 80s, 90s, there was an electronica song, harder sounds, a couple of disco tracks, and even a classical arrangement. I liked it. And I liked knowing him in this way and on this level.

I was settling into him, starting to feel sleepy again, when he broke the silence. “Nat?”

"Mhmm."

"I have to tell you something. And I'm not sure you're going to want to hear it."

I froze. Now I was wide awake. What the hell was he going to tell me that I wouldn't want to hear? Did he want me to leave? Something worse?

I picked my head up off his chest, pushing back on him a little so I could look into his eyes as I braced myself for the news that was coming.

CHAPTER THIRTEEN

Jsat looking into my eyes, seemingly preparing me for the worst, before he finally said, "I am *definitely* hungry now."

Oh, my God!!

"Jack Perry!" I screeched at him again.

Now I was mad, and I was going to playfully smack the shit out of him! But before I could make a move, he stood up, cradling me in his arms, lifting me off the ground. My legs started kicking, and then he was kissing me. Though I was shrieking behind the kiss, my impish resistance was melting fast. Finally, I surrendered myself to him wholly, his lips and tongue carrying me away on a little wave of passion.

He carefully let my legs drop down as he continued to hold me off the ground around my waist. Our lips stayed locked together while he skillfully maneuvered his way into the kitchen before setting my feet on the floor.

Though his kiss had soothed me somewhat, I was still

lightheartedly annoyed with his little tease, so when he pulled back from me, I swatted him. This resulted in a quick peck on the forehead before he turned to survey the kitchen, giving some thought to what he wanted to eat.

"So, are you hungry yet?" he asked.

"No, thanks. I think I'm still preoccupied," I replied with a hint of sarcasm, but my irritation had completely waned in the warmth of his arms and lips.

Coming up from behind, I put my arms around him. "Hey, on second thought, do you have any fruit?"

"Fruit? Like, apples?"

"Apples, oranges, berries. Whatever."

He took my hands from around his waist and kissed both of them.

"I'll look," he said, going to the refrigerator.

Observing him execute this most basic task reminded me of the passion I felt simmering below the surface.

"I'll be damned," he remarked as he was digging through the refrigerator. "I have blackberries. I didn't think I'd have any, but I do."

"Sold," I said.

He took out a colander, placed it in the sink, and emptied the container of berries into it. Turning on the faucet, cold water washed over them until he interrupted the flow to fill an empty glass. Leaning against the sink, J drank it all and then held it out as if to ask me if I wanted some. I nodded, so he filled it again and handed it to me.

As I sipped from it, he looked alarmed for a second. "I'm sorry – I should have given you another glass."

"Why?" I asked as I lifted it to my lips to take another drink.

"Most people don't like that...sharing glasses."

I giggled. "J, I just sucked your dick and gladly swallowed your cum. I think we can share a glass."

J laughed hard and shook his head. "I guess when you put it that way..."

He turned off the water and tapped the colander against the side of the sink. Covering a plate with a paper towel to absorb the drops of water on the blackberries, he poured them out onto the plate, set it on the counter near me, then popped one in his mouth.

I took a berry, savoring the bittersweet flavor for a moment before swallowing it.

Putting my palms on the counter, I lifted myself to sit. It was then I realized my shirt had been hanging open all along, so I re-did the same three buttons I had originally closed.

Nat,

You know the Al Stewart song "Year of the Cat?" Give it another listen.

J

J stood eating berries and watching me, always with the wheels spinning behind those deep, soulful eyes.

We had established something – a comfort zone of sorts – and the timing felt right to dive into a deeper, more personal conversation. There were a couple of elephants in the room that could only be ignored for so long.

"So, what's up with Rebecca?" I asked.

He looked down at the berries. "What do you mean? Nothing is up with her."

"I mean you've been with her for ages, and y'all never got married, right? And she's clearly not living here. I'm just curious how it's going."

"It's going. There isn't much to say."

I wasn't going to let him leave it there, simply because I wanted to know more, so I remained quiet in an effort to prompt him to keep talking. It worked, and J continued.

"She doesn't want to be here, and I don't want her here. It is what it is. We're fine. We get along fine, do things together, she comes over once a week. She's independent and so am I, so it works like this."

"Why wouldn't she want to be here? And why don't you want her here? That sounds kind of harsh."

"I don't mean it like that. She likes her space, and I like mine. I honestly couldn't imagine sharing the house with someone else. I keep odd hours, need to be able to do what I want to do, when I want to do it. Anything else is a disruption of my process."

"Your creative process," I said.

"Yeah. I don't know. Like I said, it is what it is. I had that bad marriage – I think I told you about it way back when – and I'm not a fan of the institution because of that. So, Rebecca does her thing and I do mine and we get together once a week. Make dinner, watch a movie, fall asleep. Once in a while we go out and do something. Status quo."

Fair enough. I was satisfied with his answer, although it left me with some residual questions about why J perpetuated such a seemingly benign relationship. He had given me what I was looking for, though, so I didn't press the topic.

He looked up at me, then quickly down at the berries again. With his focus fixed on what was in his hand, J asked, "What about you?"

"What about me?"

"You're married. And here you are. What's your story?"

I sighed, knowing full well I couldn't quiz J and then skirt around my own situation. Quid pro quo. But I didn't know where to begin.

He gave me a thoughtful glance, and ate a couple of berries before saying, "So, is this a boredom thing? An 11-year itch, so to speak?"

"Oh, my God, no, J. This is the fulfillment of something I've been thinking about for over a decade. One thing has nothing to do with another. You and I should have...done something...about this a long time ago."

He nodded slowly. "You're compartmentalizing. Putting him and me into separate boxes."

"Okay, I guess. Isn't that the way these things go? I don't know – I've never done this before."

"So, why are you doing it now?"

"I'm not bored. That's not it. Things just got...complicated." I stopped there, weighing the details, trying to determine how much information was warranted. I put another berry in my mouth, sucking on it to buy myself a few more seconds before I resumed.

"Rob..." I started.

"Rob," J repeated, as if absorbing the name of the man who was unsuspectingly on the hurtful end of our time together.

"He made some decisions without me. Kind of big choices that affect our family." My last word hung heavy in the air as it grabbed J's attention.

"Family. As in...kids?"

"One, yes," I answered truthfully.

There was a slight cringe to J's expression as he nodded slowly, processing the realization that his situation and mine were two very different scenarios. Unlike Rebecca, my husband couldn't be glossed over like he was simply a habitual figure in my life. Nor could my son, for that matter.

Feeling that I hadn't yet hit the mark of too much information, I continued. "There's a family business, on Rob's side, and when his dad retired last year, Rob's time invested in running it changed. It didn't have to, but he opted to take a role that required near constant travel. Without talking to me."

"So, he's never around," J surmised.

"Right, but that's not it. He made the decision and put all the company wheels in motion to take on that position before he even said the first word about it to me. And then just came home and announced it like I hadn't been there all along."

"That must have been a hell of a fight."

"There was no fight, J. We don't do that. For whatever reason, even though we've always ruled on these types of things together, he made the call without me. He chose to go on the road and spend most of his time removed from our family without my input. His decision – no fight necessary."

"But you talked..." J trailed off.

I knew what he was saying. He wanted to know if I was the type of person to outwardly accept it without expressing myself while inwardly stewing. Doing so would mean Rob was in the dark about how I really felt. It also meant I had essentially run away from home that weekend to live out this fantasy, never having given Rob the chance to set things right. That wasn't my style.

"Yes, we talked. A lot. Rather, I talked about how I felt...and he talked about the company."

I left it there while J appeared to think. "That must put a lot on you."

I gave him a raised eyebrow in reply.

"A lot of responsibility, I mean. It leaves you to do

everything by yourself. Right?"

Although I hadn't given it much thought, J was correct. The side of myself that was determined to always make sure everything was just right, with or without help, had apparently mechanically kicked in when Rob made his independent career choice. The past year *had* been very demanding for me.

"I suppose so, J. But things need to get done. Life is handling responsibilities, so I just do it."

The look on his face told me he had more on his mind. While I accepted this conversation as inevitable, I didn't want him focusing on my life too much. I also didn't need J to hang out his marriage counseling shingle. We had one night to enjoy each other and let the story play out. Dwelling on the serious shit would put a damper on that.

I moved forward with the intention of bringing the focus back to us. "Anyway, that's when the dreams started."

"The dreams?"

"About you, us, what if-ing myself to death."

This was the first J was hearing about how he invaded my mind. Silently, I prayed that he wouldn't ask for specific details about the subconscious thoughts that drove me wild, ultimately bringing me to his door.

Thankfully, he let it go, presumably able to deduce for himself what kind of fantasies I was having to be propelled to this extent. He slid the plate closer to me. "Here." Then, abruptly, he asked, "Are you curious why I gave in to this?"

I looked at him and wanted to say no because this felt like a continuation of the conversation I was hoping to end, but before I could answer, he went on. "I'd be lying if I told you I haven't thought about you over the years.

My initial knee-jerk reaction to you being here needed to be put in a box of its own so I could do the same thing you're doing...finish the story."

I nodded. I got it. And I was happy to feel the shift of attention away from my circumstances.

"Actually, I'm more curious to know why you let me walk in here, unannounced, no introduction."

He smiled, gave a short chuckle, and came over to stand in front of me.

"Well, to begin with, you're hot as fuck," he said as he moved in to part my legs, leaning against me, placing his hands, palms flat, at my sides. I didn't say anything, and J continued. "You also don't present as a serial killer. Even if you were, I think I could take you."

He flexed a bicep as he said this and then laughed.

I giggled and J cocked his head, looking thoughtful. "And, last but not least, I have enough curiosity in me to kill an entire family of cats."

"No offense to Fred," I said.

"No offense to Fred," he repeated. "It's being a writer, I suppose. I can't let things go, and I just have to *know*. You know? As much as I hide away from the world in here, I don't turn down interesting experiences when they present themselves. Especially if said encounter arrives on my front porch...and then marches into my house."

We both laughed, but he quickly came back to the moment, looking at me quizzically, as if he really wanted to know if all of that made sense. It did, and I told him so. He was pleased with that and kissed me softly.

"I've missed you," I said on an impulse.

He looked around himself, then back at me. "Where did I go?" he laughed.

I shook my head. "No, I've missed *talking* with you. Or

writing to you...whatever. I've missed our 'talks'" – and here I did air quotes – "about everything and nothing."

"Yeah, I really liked that time, too."

```
J,
"Year of the Cat"... Am I the cat?
Nat
```

He grew thoughtful again, a wicked look creeping into his eyes, before he slowly said, "If you're a good girl...maybe...I'll write you a nice email."

```
Nat,
Of course you're the cat.
J
```

"If I'm a good girl? Really? Pffttt," I said mockingly, waving a hand at him.

But he wasn't playing. Something was on his mind, his eyes deep pools of calculation.

I sat there waiting to find out if J was going to tell me what was going on inside that sexy brain of his, when he suddenly scooped me off the counter. I let out a small scream. My arms were still getting settled around his neck to hold on when we were already making our way down the hall, his long legs taking big, purposeful strides.

The door to his office had been pulled closed earlier, but not shut all the way, and he kicked it open. Carrying me inside, I saw the lamp on his desk was still dimly lighting the room.

Without hesitation, he walked over to the enormous chair that was in front of his gaming television. In one swift movement, he gently set me down with his left arm while grabbing a game controller off the seat with the other hand, which he tossed on the floor.

I sank into the chair, thinking how much bigger the thing felt now that I was sitting in it. My feet didn't even touch the floor. I also realized it rocked, and as I settled into a comfortable position, it leaned back slightly.

I sat there with no idea what was going to come next, looking up at him as he towered over me. He was fixated on me. As much as I wanted to know more about the room and what went on there when he was alone, I couldn't pull myself away from him to attempt any observations.

J's intense stare was hypnotic, and I was too entranced to know how much time ticked by before he leaned over, placing both his hands on the arm rests of the pillowy chair, and kissed me.

His lips found my neck, and briefly brushed along my skin before I heard his husky voice in my ear as he whispered, "Now, Natalie, you are going to sit here like a good girl...while I eat your sweet, little pussy."

Every fiber of my body sprang to life. I tensed in anticipation. He slid himself down the front of the recliner, settling onto his knees. I had my arms on the sides of the chair, just like he had when I did this to him in the living room. The only difference was he had been anxious to touch me, and in contrast, I didn't feel like I could move a muscle.

He unbuttoned the three buttons that were keeping my shirt closed and pushed it open, once again revealing my breasts to him. I could feel his bare chest against my legs, and I trembled.

He took my nipples between his fingers, running his thumbs across them. It was a light touch, and my back arched as I felt the clenching of my inner self reacting to him. Caressing across my breasts, moving his hands down to lift my ass, he slid off the lacy thong. As he did this, I had to lean back in the chair, which positioned the most sensitive part of me directly in front of him.

My panties were off and tossed on the floor. His hands rested on the top of my thighs while he sat back on his heels observing the scene. His touch was hot against my skin, prompting a sensual overload as every inch of my body vibrated beneath the surface.

J took my hands in his, guiding them toward my breasts. I knew exactly what he wanted, and I accommodated, running my fingers across my nipples. My entire body tightened at the sensation. I whimpered in need, writhing slightly.

He knelt straight up, swiftly pulling down the waistband of his pants, exposing his perfect erection to me. I moaned, desperately wanting to abandon my breasts in favor of touching him instead.

He stroked.

I frowned.

A high-pitched noise of frustration escaped my lips. He slowly smiled, pulling the waistband of his pants back into place.

"Don't like that, do you?"

I shook my head no as my lower lip formed a small pout.

While I had said there were no restrictions to my night with J, being relegated to the role of observer was not a plan I had anticipated. Hard limit number one...unlocked.

My hands were still on my breasts, but I had stopped with the teasing and touching during J's little game. He reached over, indicating I should continue before he sat back on his heels again, focusing his concentration on the sweetness that was about to become the focus for both of us.

He slowly spread my legs to the sides of the chair while also scooting my backside closer to the edge, and when he leaned into the front of the chair, it reclined so that I was in the perfect position for this.

Glancing up at me to be sure I was still doing as I was told, he turned his attention back to my parted thighs. He was in the motion of leaning forward when he paused and whispered, "You will watch me."

What??? My head jerked up to look at him.

"You will *watch* me as I pleasure you. Do not put your head back. Do not close your eyes. Just. Watch."

I'd never thought about that before, but the very idea of it made me feel like I was going to come unhinged on so many levels. Wanting to comply, I pushed my ass down just a little, and with the angle of the chair, I had a clear view across my stomach.

He moved down, looking into my eyes the whole time. When he was almost there, I saw his tongue reach out, licking leisurely across my clitoris.

A sharp spike of ecstasy forcefully rippled outward from where his mouth performed the euphoric task. My belly tightened. My hands tingled. My breath caught while I simultaneously moaned and panted. On impulse, I dug my head back into the chair, closing my eyes.

J stopped, sitting on his heels again. "Ah-ah-ah," he crooned in his deep, sexy bedroom voice.

I looked forward, wondering how I was going to get through this the way he wanted me to.

He leaned down and licked. Somehow, I managed to keep my eyes on what he was doing, as he kept his eyes on mine.

Slowly licking, and then his whole mouth was on me and he was gently sucking. I was making short, faint sounds, my head reeling. Every inch of my body was on fire. I couldn't focus on my breasts anymore, and whether he liked it or not, I put my hands on the armrests of the chair, bracing myself. He didn't stop to reprimand me but continued on with the soft lapping pattern. Up and down, honing in on every nerve ending that held the key. Alternating between licking and softly sucking. All the while, I watched his every move.

The build formed in my hips mere moments before my thighs began to tremble. I was going to come hard, and it was going to happen soon, but I was doing my best to hold it off for just another minute.

And then I felt him slip a finger inside of me. I tightened around him. He pressed up against the front of me as he swirled his tongue around my clitoris. And with that, he pushed me off the cliff.

I threw my head back – his rules be damned – as my hips drove upward, pushing myself against his mouth, and I exploded...hard. Two of his fingers pinched my clitoris as his tongue found its way inside of me, circling and absorbing every bit of my climax. My whole body was vibrating, each cell burning and fixated on what had just taken place.

He slowed to a stop, sat back on his heels again, and placed the palm of his hand firmly against my trembling center, a steady pressure, as if attempting to help me descend from the peak of the volcano. Inch by inch, I began to relax, sinking into the chair.

I hadn't thought it possible, but I was spent. I needed a break.

J read my mind and stood, leaning to kiss me on the forehead before walking to the couch where he grabbed the plaid throw blanket. He stood over me, snapped it open, and let if fall on me.

After arranging it to ensure my feet were covered, he kissed me on the forehead again.

I wanted to respond. I wanted to kiss him on the lips. I wanted to reach up and pull him onto me so I could feel him inside of me again. I wanted to speak and tell him that he single-handedly had the ability to make the planets align. But I didn't have one ounce of energy to do any of those things.

I think I may have managed a small smile before my eyes closed. I felt myself drifting, as if on a raft in the middle of the ocean, alone and sleepy, with only the sound of the water gently lapping against my rickety vessel.

CHAPTER FOURTEEN

I don't know how long I slept. Coming out of the fog, I heard the sound of clicking on a keyboard and faint, distant music. Stretching a bit and feeling a little too warm, I pushed the blanket off of me.

J,
I registered for a benefit 5K in Tallahassee that will take place in a few months. Are you thinking of going to Florida any time soon?
Nat

Turning, I saw J sitting at his desk, typing furiously. The indistinct tunes were coming from headphones he was wearing.

I stayed as still as I could, watching him until he stopped to run his hands through his hair. Mid-stretch, I reached my arms over my head, causing him to turn sharply to see what had caught his peripheral vision.

When he saw that I was awake, he smiled warmly, took off the headphones, and came to my side, brushing the hair out of my eyes.

"Hey, beautiful," he whispered. "How are you doing?"

"Mmmm, a little hazy, but good." I motioned to the desk and said, "You didn't want to rest?"

He looked over to where he had been. "Oh, no, I'm good. I had some stuff I needed to get down right away."

"More scenes with the batshit crazy lady?" I asked.

"Exactly. She's taken a turn for the worse and things are about to get *really* out of hand."

I winked at him and stuck out my tongue. J wrapped a large lock of my hair around his hand, gently pulling my head back to kiss me.

I felt warm and happy, stretching again before retracting into a fetal position, tucking my feet under me.

"What do you do when the brilliance hits and you're not able to get to a computer?"

He laughed. "Well, that's one of the reasons I don't leave the house." After making a silly face, he followed up with, "No, I just do what I have to. Make a note on anything. Cocktail napkins work great."

I smiled as I thought of him being struck with a great scene or bit of dialogue. The world he was in fascinated me, and I really was so happy that it had all worked out this way for him.

Now that J wasn't wearing the headphones, I could clearly hear the song that was playing through them. Pushing myself up from the chair, I asked, "Hey, can you put that on the speakers?"

"What? Oh, the music? Sure."

He went to the desk, flipped a switch on the headphones, and the music came pouring out of speakers embedded into the ceiling of the office. The song was finishing as this happened, and I frowned.

"Oh, you want *that* song," he said with a wry smile, stepping back to the desk where he clicked something on the computer, starting over Lifehouse's "First Time."

Finding the three buttons again to close my shirt, I walked over to where my panties had landed on the floor. After sliding them on, I turned to give J a mischievous grin.

It only took a second for the lightbulb to flicker. "Oh. No, Nat, I..." But his words trailed off as I began to move my hips in rhythm with the song.

J stood still, watching me. Taking his hands in mine, I continued to sway while stepping side to side. He was shaking his head no while I was nodding my head yes, causing both of us to laugh.

Holding onto him, I kept dancing, becoming more animated, until he finally relented and joined in with an exaggerated sigh.

We were moving against each other and then he was twirling me. I tried to spin him, but he was too tall, and we ended up in a tangled mess, giggling like school kids. Silly fun with J felt like the most natural thing in the world.

By the time the chorus started for the last time, we were hopping around, dancing and laughing...and nothing else mattered.

When the song ended, I playfully fell into his arms. He wrapped them around me as we slowed to a sway. With my head against his chest, I listened to his heartbeat while his fingers slipped under my hair to caress the back of my neck.

Reaching up to take his face in my hands, I pulled him toward me for a kiss. What started out soft and simple quickly turned into something long and deep. He picked me up so I could wrap my legs around his waist. I felt his erection pushing against me, which only served to once again ignite the fiery sparks within me. It was a biological reaction that I couldn't have prevented even if I had wanted to.

He held me for a minute while kissing me, but he didn't let it escalate further, and then my feet were on the floor again.

I was a little surprised, but I could tell he wasn't being distant, so I chalked it up to J having other plans and went along with it.

In just a few short hours, I had learned that, in the middle of the night in J's house, anything and everything was fair game.

Stepping away from him, I picked up the blanket from the chair and began to fold it. I felt it snatched from my hands and turned to see J holding it out of reach, staring at me.

"What are you... Nat, what are you doing?"

"Give me that," I said, leaning for the blanket. "I'm going to fold it."

"Holy shit. No. You're not."

One swift flick of J's arm and it landed on the couch in a pile. I wasn't used to this...but I didn't have time to give it much thought.

He put his hand behind me, pulling me in for a quick kiss before taking my hand to lead me out of the office and back to the kitchen.

Casually approaching the plate of blackberries, he scooped up a handful then leaned against the counter. J stood there, putting them to his mouth one at a time, chewing slowly and thoughtfully, before he took another from his hand.

I suddenly felt awkward and didn't know what to do

with myself. The possibility of overstaying my welcome made me feel self-conscious. It occurred to me that I should tell him what my own time schedule was for the next morning. But in that moment, I wanted him to speak first, to tell me what was going on inside his head.

Nat,
I'm actually due to make a trip down there. Do you happen to know how far your 5K will be from Jacksonville?
J

He was watching me, as usual, and after a minute, held out his hand with the berries. I took one and put it in my mouth, sucking on it instead of chewing right away.

"What do you do?" he asked.

I looked up, a little surprised at the question and then smiled slightly, happy for these conversational junctures.

"I run a small advertising agency out of a home office," I said.

"Really." It wasn't a question.

"Yeah, no big deal. It brings in some money and makes me feel productive. That's all I really want these days."

"I want to ask how you went from planning to run the most elite escort agency in Louisiana to that," he said, "but something tells me you don't want to get into it."

"Well, like I said, I probably would have gotten into trouble with that escort thing, so everything worked out as it should, I think. I couldn't be where I am today on a personal level if I had started that business. And I'm happy."

"Really." Again, not a question.

"Yes, really," I said. "Look, J, I need for you to know

something. I'm going to say it, and I don't want to get into any great detail or anything, but I *am* happy. Showing up here and...doing all of this" – I waved my hand between us – "probably makes you think otherwise, but I really like my life. I love my family. Robert is a good man."

He absorbed that for a minute, while munching on berries, and finally said, "A man who left you and your child all alone. How much weight are you pulling without help, Nat?"

This again.

I knew where J was coming from. There was nothing accusatory in his tone, so I took it for what it was – the words of a concerned friend. Additionally, he was right. A lot had been heaped onto my plate as a result of Rob's decision, forcing me to become even more independent.

"I've always taken care of myself."

"I don't doubt that," J replied, still looking skeptical about my home life.

My chest tightened, and I felt a catch in my throat. I was heading down a path I didn't want to go. Not in this place. Not with J.

I was more than aware that Rob's determination with the family business meant he hadn't considered the impact it would have on me. That stung in ways I didn't care to admit...to anyone, least of all J.

The vow to myself years prior was solid – I would take care of myself regardless of the choices other people made. What I never expected when I took that vow was to have someone like Rob in my life. What further took me off guard was for him, after all these years, to branch off, leaving me feeling hurt and vulnerable for the first time since we met.

Take charge and carry the weight...that's what I do, I

thought, although I wasn't about to verbalize it.

I had a suspicion that J was aware that what I was saying didn't scratch the surface, so I searched for the words to steer the discussion back to where it had originated.

"Anyway, the advertising plays on my former career in marketing," I said, clearing my throat. "You did some marketing for your mom, right?"

J gave me a small smirk, knowing exactly what I was doing. "I did, yes."

"I guess you don't have time for that anymore with everything else you have going on."

"Yeah, no more of that for me, but I try to help her with advice whenever I can. Mostly internet issues and social media."

The mention of 'social media' made me giggle. What had we called Myspace in those days? I couldn't remember if the term was around back then.

"What?" J asked, hearing my small laugh.

"Social media..."

He smiled. "Myspace."

I nodded.

"I hate the social networks these days," he said. "It's so much work to keep up with them, but it's a necessary evil."

"Agreed. I did enjoy the Myspace days, though." I flickered my eyebrows at him.

"Well, yes. Simpler times, I suppose. Although I never expected it to bring us...here." His words lingered, and he squinted a bit, waiting.

My court, meet ball.

"I just...needed to know, J." There it was. I couldn't think of anything else to say.

I loved my husband despite the decisions he made, but I needed to know what would happen if I spent just a little time with this man who made me burn deep down inside when I thought about him. And, although I wasn't going to vocalize it, I was still confident that I would be able to walk away from J without looking back or pining over him or whatever it was people did when these things happened. When they found themselves quickly embroiled in a love triangle. I had every intention of going back to my life, while J had Rebecca over for dinner and a movie. And that would be that.

"Closure," J said.

"Exactly."

"The final chapter."

"Okay, if you want to use your...professional lingo," I said with a smile. But J wasn't smiling.

"What if I didn't need...or want closure?"

I didn't like the way he said this. It made me feel selfish for executing this plan without consulting him and taking his needs into consideration. But that wasn't J's fault. It was my own.

I spent a few seconds wrestling with the idea that I had been thoughtless in this quest before I finally said, "We would have had a glass of wine, talked a bit, caught up, you know...and I would have left."

"Just like that."

"Yes, just like that. I never would have pushed myself on you."

"But seducing is okay."

When I looked into J's eyes, I could see something playful dancing behind them.

"Seduction and pushing are two very different things," I said.

His eyes were searching mine again, and I was waiting to find out if my last statement was enough or if he needed more.

"Seduction by the woman who has a hang-up of her own," he remarked, confirming that his idiosyncrasy was still in place while leaving me puzzled regarding whatever quirk of mine he thought he had discovered.

"I have a sex hang-up? That's news to me," I said, trying to exude confidence as I mentally ran through a fast forward play-by-play to try to find what I had done to cause this belief.

"Mhmm. Someone gets *very* fussy when she isn't hands-on."

Ohhhh. That.

I blushed a little but decided to take a flirtatious tone while I fought fire with fire. "Don't you *want* me to be hands-on?"

"Oh, of course. Your hands have been a wonderful experience so far. I'm simply intrigued by the frustration it causes you. It's a turn on, actually."

That made sense. While J wasn't into anything hardcore – not that I knew about, anyway – he did have that controlling streak, and I had enough experience with the more intricate kinks to know that dominant personalities liked to see their partners squirm.

"I'll try to respect your vexing shenanigans, but I clearly prefer to be an active participant," I teased.

With the smallest of wry smiles, he nodded and turned his attention to the blackberries again.

Grabbing the last several from the plate, he tipped a few into my hand as he nudged me to turn around, walking in front of him down the hall, back into the office.

On the way there, I veered off into the bathroom in the hallway. Before I could walk through the door, he tugged at the back of my shirt, pulling me in for a kiss. His tongue danced with mine as his palm pressed firmly against my back. When he released me, I felt giddy, but I managed to smile at him and say, "Be right back."

"Hurry."

I needed just a few minutes to compose myself, both physically and mentally.

Taking a tissue from a box on the vanity, I set down the blackberries while I went to work on getting myself cleaned up. With the help of the personal wipes and a washcloth, I took another birdbath. A double-check of my makeup told me all I needed was a little powder, which I applied and then put back in my purse. A quick dab of perfume rendered me ready and presentable again.

But my head was whirling with a fast-paced buzz of activity. I gripped the counter to steady myself, dropping my head to stretch my neck.

My expectations for this night had been exceeded. I couldn't have asked for more from J. He was open and sharing. He was comfortable, not just with himself, but with me, too.

I thought about the conversation we just had – closure. It wouldn't be long before the depth of the night would be replaced with the rising sun, and it would be shortly after that when I would have to make my exit. Did I feel like I had achieved my goal?

While everything that happened thus far had been more than I had hoped for, now there were feelings prodding me from within. Feelings that far surpassed those of the friendship J and I had developed in the past. Feelings that concerned me. Feelings for which I had not prepared myself.

If I was compartmentalizing, I would have to find a chamber inside of myself for these emotions. But I couldn't take the time now to identify the right location for them.

Trying not to think about the morning, I gave myself a pep talk to live in the moment.

Taking the berries from the tissue, I headed back through the long bathroom and out to the hall where I made my way into the office.

J,

Tallahassee to Jacksonville? Not far... two or three hours. What are you thinking?

Nat

I hadn't realized it until I stepped back into the room, but he must have shut off the music throughout the house while I was sleeping because it was only playing in there now. I recognized Oingo Boingo's "When the Lights Go Out," and made a face before I could stop myself.

"Right. You don't like Oingo Boingo," he said, reaching toward the computer mouse to skip the song.

"I'm sorry. I don't know what it is," I said. And then, as a consolation, followed it up with, "But I love Danny Elfman as a composer."

He gave me a funny look. "For someone who doesn't like them, you know enough about them. What do you like that Danny Elfman has done?"

A test? I'll play.

Without missing a beat, I said, "Well, this is probably going to sound really cliché, but Beetlejuice is my favorite."

He raised his eyebrows. I did know what I was talking about.

"I can always recognize him within a few notes when I'm watching a movie, and I like everything he does. It all has a similar sound, but I like it. At the end of the day, though, Beetlejuice was just perfect, in my opinion.

Everything he wrote for it fit in every scene, giving it a creepy yet fun sound."

J stood staring at me. Not watching or thoughtfully looking – staring. I put the last blackberry in my mouth and smiled at him. One long stride and he was in front of me, kissing me, taking the blackberry from my mouth into his, where he sucked on it for a second with his lips still on mine, then swallowed it.

As he had earlier, he picked me up so I could wrap my legs around his waist. I felt him against me again, hard and ready.

Still locked in our kiss, he carried me to the couch where he sat down, my legs still around him, and laid back. It was just like my vision from earlier in the evening, and I tensed with the excitement of living out the fantasy.

I was straddling him, sitting up straight, letting my fingers trail from his chest down to the top of his pants. I could feel all of him through the soft fabric, and I was about to slide a finger in to find the tip of what I wanted when he took my hands and said, "Not yet, love."

The look on my face changed from impending ecstasy to hurt surprise, and he followed with, "Soon."

That was not what I wanted to hear, but I had to accept it. His way...his terms. For the time being, I was going to have to try to ignore how badly I wanted him...again.

He pulled me to lie down next to him, and I slipped between J and the back of the couch, on my side, one of my legs hooked over his. My free hand immediately found his chest hair and ran slow circles through it.

"What did I make you miss out on tonight?" I asked.

"Hmmm?" J responded as he settled in to relax.

"That phone call. I'm sorry if it was something

important."

"Oh, no, it wasn't. I was supposed to get together with someone for some pre-production discussion, but it's not a big deal." He was quiet for a minute, but his train of thought had been shifted to shop talk. "It's actually not even pre-production. More like speculation at this stage. But Jerry tends to get ahead of himself with these things."

I was so proud of J for being such an icon in this industry that was a mystery to me. He had come so far and learned so much.

"I don't know how *any* of this works," I said.

J let out a heavy sigh. "Lots of politics, love."

I couldn't imagine J playing that game very well. Not that he *couldn't* do it, but I knew it was the sort of thing he hated, and I was pretty sure it frustrated the shit out of him. It was a hell of a world to be in for such an introverted man.

"Are you happy, J?"

He tilted his head toward me to kiss my hair. "What? Right now? Fuck, yeah."

"No. I mean, are you happy? With everything?"

"Oh. Sure. What's not to be happy about?"

That was a loaded question. If I answered it, we would be dredging up the past, delving into the deep stirrings within that haunted him, so I simply said, "I just want to know that you're...happy."

J was silent for several minutes, and I thought he had put that talk to rest, but then he said, "I know what you mean. And I appreciate it. I'm as happy as I'm going to be. And that's good enough for me. As long as I can keep writing, everything will be fine. I don't know what I'd do without my writing, though, I can tell you that."

His comment scared me. It made me worry that the

day would come when he wouldn't be one of the most sought-after screenwriters in the industry. Then what?

"But, J, you know this can't last...forever," I said with more than a hint of concern in my voice.

"Oh, I know that, love. The next flavor of the month will come along eventually. But I don't care about any of that anymore. I don't need the money, and I'm getting tired of the games that are played in the business. I just have to write. You know? As long as I can write and be proud of it, even if no one sees it, I'll be happy. Without that...well...there's nothing here for me."

In that case, there wasn't anything to worry about, right? He was a writer, and if he didn't hinge his success on making a movie or being published, he would always be able to write. That was a choice he could control. Or so I thought.

"I try not to let it worry me too much, though," J followed up.

I was confused. "Let what worry you?"

"The writing. Not having it. Losing it."

"I don't understand. You said you'd keep writing even if it wasn't as a career anymore."

"That doesn't mean it'll always come to me, love. Sometimes the words just don't work."

Now I thought I understood. "Writer's block."

"Well, yeah, that's a thing, but it's temporary. I'm talking about a more permanent problem."

J saw the concern on my face. I couldn't hide it, and I didn't know what to do with what he was telling me. If something happened to his ability to write...what would that mean?

"J..."

"Nothing to fret about, love. Like I said, I don't give it much thought. Just keep doing my thing and love that

I'm able to send these quirky little stories out into the world. I still find it hard to believe that people want to know about the madcap mishaps that run through my head, but I'll enjoy it while they do."

I relaxed a little and moved my worry to the back of my mind. It certainly didn't seem like J was ever going to have an issue, especially since he loved it so much.

"You could always take a dive into the world of erotica. I think you would be *quite* good at it," I teased.

He laughed. "After tonight, I think I have enough material for a whole series."

I put my arm around him and pulled him closer.

"Honestly, Nat. I would never do that. I want you to understand I wouldn't do that to you. Or us."

"J, please. I know, and I trust you. I wouldn't be here if I didn't."

At this, he reached his hand down to pull my chin to his face, gazing at me intently before bringing me into a deep kiss. Beneath my leg, I could feel him stirring. And I was pretty sure he'd had enough down time...and that 'soon' had arrived.

CHAPTER FIFTEEN

I didn't let the kiss linger for very long before I swung my leg over and straddled him again. He folded me into his arms, pulling me close to continue our kiss.

My hands were braced on the arm of the couch over his head. He was holding me tight, my breasts pressed against him. I felt my inner core tightening, causing me to physically respond by grinding against him.

J obviously had a little voyeur in him, so I wanted to sit up straight to offer a play-by-play view of what I was about to do. Pushing against his hands, he released me, allowing me to move upright.

Just when I thought I couldn't possibly be more excited to fuck him there, on his couch, in this position, I felt my eagerness mounting even more. The dampness between my thighs intensified

He had his hands on my hips, spurring my mind to run ahead of me. Carnal daydreams of him guiding my movements. Up and down, however fast or slow he wanted me to go.

I caught myself grinding again.

We were looking into each other's eyes, and I began to unbutton the shirt when he grabbed my wrists, sat up, and said, "Oh, hell no."

At this, he scooped me up into his arms, rendering me helpless and succumbing to his strength and will.

J held me tilted toward him as he carried me into the bedroom. I could feel his chest against the bare skin that was exposed above and below the three buttons. The intimacy of it made me tremble.

He set me down on the bed but held me behind my back to keep me in a sitting position while he swept pillows out from behind me and onto the floor. Leaving one soft, fluffy pillow in place, he laid me back on it. J didn't make a move. Instead, he looked down at me, lying in wait for him and whatever his next wish of the night might be.

In my self-conscious position, I tried very hard to conceal the disappointment that I wasn't going to get my way – to be on top of him on that couch.

My position dismay didn't last long, though, because I knew whatever J had in store for us would be every bit as good, if not better, than my idea. So, pushing the couch fantasy aside, I readied myself for what would be coming next. The anticipation alone was enough to send small bursts of pleasure throughout my body, making me wriggle on the bed.

He dropped one hand down to my face and traced along my cheek up to my bangs, where he brushed the hair out of my eyes. Then he followed down the center of my nose until he reached my lips, his finger lingering there. Instinctively, I swirled my tongue around it. J closed his eyes and let the feeling sink in before continuing down across the length of my neck.

When his hand arrived at my chest, he shifted his eyes from my face to the buttons on the shirt. Sliding one hand underneath the fabric, he cupped my breast and pinched my nipple. I jerked in response, my back arching, but as quickly as his hand had been there, it was gone again.

Gliding out from beneath the shirt, he skillfully undid the three buttons in quick succession.

Glancing first back to my eyes, he returned his attention to the shirt and opened it. I had lost all ability to stay still. Squirming, I was moving my hips to find him, but gained no response to that.

J stared, bold as brass, at my breasts before running a hand carelessly over them then turning to walk away. I reached for him but was successful in only grazing his skin as he moved out of arm's length.

Taking his time, he went to a dresser where he opened a drawer and removed something that I couldn't see. I heard a small clinking sound as he closed the dresser. Then he walked painfully slowly and in no hurry at all to the closet.

Once he stepped through the door, I could no longer see him, but I heard a swift swishing sound. My mind and heart were racing. I had no idea what to expect, but I stayed still, waiting to find out.

When J came back into view, the items he had gathered were in his hands, held slightly behind his back as he had his hands placed on his hips.

I had complete free will and could have jumped up and run to him. Or even run away, for that matter. But I was locked in place, waiting for his desire to be revealed to me.

He watched me with curiosity for a few seconds

before returning to the bed. One of the items was placed on the nightstand, but he was blocking my view. I would have to wait a bit longer to see what it was. The object he was still holding now dangled in front of me. The clinking sound I heard was a belt buckle.

I instantly had visions of spanking running through my head, but before I knew what was happening, he was pulling my hands over my head, using the soft leather of the belt to secure me to the bed poster nearest me. J made short work of it and was done almost as soon as he started.

I hadn't expected this. Did J's kinks veer off toward dominant more than I knew? Nothing about him scared me, but I was on alert, physically and mentally. My body was begging for more; my mind was swarming with questions.

While I knew quite a bit about the world of bondage just from having a broad variety of conversations with Dominant customers, my personal experience with it was limited. Some short-lived scarf play in my late teens and early 20s after a popular movie had made us all curious was the extent of it.

I pulled on the trappings very slightly. I didn't want him to see that I was checking it, but I was curious to know how stuck I really was. Pretty stuck.

My back arched, presenting hardened nipples in his direction, while I parted my legs just enough to feel cool air against me.

Turning to take the next item off the nightstand, I saw he was picking up a necktie. I was just starting to process the thought of being blindfolded when...he put it into my mouth, lifted my head, and tied it behind me.

Wait...what???

It wasn't tight enough to hurt, but when I tried to say

something, I learned that anything I managed to get out was going to be a jumbled mess, and he wouldn't be able to understand me. Where was he going with this? Wasn't I supposed to be allowed a safe word or something like that?

He leaned over me, kissing up my belly to my breasts. My eyes closed when I felt the soft sucking of a nipple. I squirmed, moaning loudly behind the makeshift gag. I ached to touch him, but there was no such luck in my present position. And I sure as hell couldn't verbally protest.

J stood up, stepped back, and assessed his work. My nipple, still wet from his mouth and exposed to the air, felt painfully abandoned. He turned as if he was going to walk away again, immediately sparking thoughts of being kept there, in that position...for God knows how long.

After just a few steps, he faced me again and, running his fingers under the waistline of his pants, dropped them to the floor, revealing his rigid length. I involuntarily kicked my legs, desperately wanting him closer to me, longing to touch him.

He smirked at me. And I wanted to smack him. Didn't he realize what this was doing to me? Didn't he know that I *needed* to be able to feel him? My hands, my mouth, were crying out for him

Slowly, as if without a care in the world, J climbed on the bed, kneeling in front of me. I thought maybe he was just going to fuck me, using the belt and tie to cause heightened excitement. It would be *very* frustrating to have him inside me if I couldn't touch him, but I could already sense that hindering my movement was ramping up my senses.

Interesting.

Observing him before me, I felt a clench, followed by

a dewy trickle. I was just happy believing he had the intention of doing something about this right away.

Instead, what happened next was so far beyond frustrating that I found myself screeching through the tie and pulling against the belt. I even tried to kick at him to make him stop, but he pushed my legs together, sitting on them to hold me down.

Once I was secured in place, he went back to doing what he had started to do to cause the disruption – he was touching himself. Long, slow strokes up and down his cock. And it was different than before. He was being more thorough, less teasing, giving me every indication that he intended to finish what he started. All while tormenting me.

I should be doing that! I wanted to scream at him. *We just talked about this! Are you fucking kidding me??* But I was stuck beyond stuck. Just the way he wanted it.

I wanted him to take the control that fueled his fire. I wanted to be the one to give him that freedom. Of course I did. But being removed from the equation hadn't been part of my plan, and this time it appeared that my entanglement was going to be the catalyst to his climax. I was going to have to sit, watching him pleasure himself, without being able to do a fucking thing about it.

I knew I wouldn't be able to stand this...*anything* but this. He could tie me up and keep me here, fuck me day and night, and I would obey his every command. But there was no way I could get through watching him bring himself to orgasm while I was restrained, unable to touch him, unable to even beg him to stop. I *needed* to be the one doing this.

I didn't even care about my own deep desires at this point – I just had to have a physical role in it where J and his pleasure were concerned.

He kept his eyes locked on mine as he skillfully continued to stroke. His other hand reached out to pinch one of my nipples, and I bucked as much as I could move with his weight holding me down.

Stroke, stroke, stoke – up and down...it went on and on. This was my ultimate torture.

As he straddled me, pushing down on my legs, I could feel him brushing against me. But my position prevented me from finding the friction I needed to reach any level of satisfaction. Every muscle in my body was tense to the breaking point, and I kept up the screeching through the motherfucking tie, even though it did no good.

I'm going to bite this fucking tie in half, I thought. *And then I'm going to spit on him. How dare he do this to me? He knows I'm not here to be a spectator!*

The muscles in his arms flexed as he stroked, and I was going to come mentally undone. Unhinged. He was going to get a fucking earful when this was over!

And yet, even though what started as frustration had turned to fury, I could feel my body's continued response. I desperately wanted him. If I could spread my legs just a little bit, I could push up, rubbing my clitoris against him. But that wasn't going to happen. I was pinned.

Now, not only was I mad at J for making me watch as I remained trapped, but I was also angry with my own body for reacting to him regardless of the exasperation. It was a testament to how badly I craved him.

He took his hand away from my breast, continuing to stroke with one hand while he ran the thumb of his other hand over the tip of his cock. Pushing up to the tip, I could see a small drop of semen glistening at the edge, then trickling over.

I wished the daggers that were shooting out of my eyes could strike holes in him.

I wanted him so badly that I actually felt a tear fall down my cheek. The last thing I wanted to do was cry in front of him, especially in this scenario, giving him the satisfaction of knowing that this was indeed my greatest weakness where he was concerned. But I felt a sob beginning to form in my chest. I knew if he kept this up much longer, forcing me to watch, I wouldn't be able to control the flood that would follow.

My one, lone tear didn't go unnoticed to him, and he wiped it away.

Suddenly, he let out a long, low groan, and I thought, *This is it. This fucking bastard is going to come right in front of me.*

I prepared myself for the reaction that I wouldn't be able to hide from him, but instead, in one quick move, he pushed his hand behind my head, unfastening the tie.

As soon as I felt it loosen, I was ready to hit him with both barrels, but he was off my legs and pushing his cock into my mouth before I had the chance. And I took it. Hungrily. Ravenously. I took it like a starving, wild animal. All that was missing now was that I couldn't touch him, but I wasn't even thinking about that because at least I had a piece of him. The piece that I wanted in this moment.

As he knelt in front of me, I opened my legs now that they were freed. While I couldn't find any real satisfaction in that, I was able to thrust my hips in unison with the myriad of passionate jolts I was feeling.

J pushed himself into my mouth, over and over, holding onto the headboard, groaning, almost growling, while he did so. Then, swiftly and without warning, his mouth was on mine and his firm body was sliding down me. As I was sucking on his tongue to replace what I had just lost, I heard the tearing of the condom wrapper and felt his hand between us as he put it on. A mere second later, he slid insistently inside of me.

At this, he threw his head back and yelled out, but he wasn't coming yet. He moved from side to side a little, and then in and out.

My feet were planted on the bed. I raised my hips as high as I could to make him go as deep as possible. And he did. With a slow ferocity, we met over and over again. I couldn't get enough of him. And then...

He was out of me again, and I was about to say, *What the fuck?*...when he flipped me over.

The belt had been fastened in such a way that my wrists moved with it, and I didn't feel any extra tension when I was turned on my stomach.

He reached under me, pulling up on my hips so that my knees went beneath me, and my ass was in the air. My hands searched for the top of the headboard. He leaned over my back and helped me up so I could find it. I settled on my knees. When he was satisfied that I was where I wanted to be, he simultaneously entered me and reached his hand between my legs. I cried out from the shockwave brought on by the butterfly stroke of his fingers.

His other hand was holding me firmly on the side of my hip, pulling me to him with each thrust. I fired back against him, urging him as deep as possible.

Having my hands locked in place made all of it even more tantalizing. I was unable to touch him, but being at the mercy of J's desires heightened my senses in a way I had never felt before. And I liked it.

His fingers swirled around my clitoris in a flurry of sensation. I couldn't even tell how many fingers he was using, but the fuel had been ignited. I dropped my head, allowing the gradual build to overtake me. Losing myself in the delicious tension as I tightened around him.

We met again and again, savoring the seconds leading into it. Then came the full force of it as our orgasms began the unmistakable steady climb.

I lingered at the top, allowing the wave to shudderingly consume me from head to toe. In what seemed like the murky distance, I heard the low growl that turned into a roar as J did the same.

It was tumultuous, both of us simultaneously giving in to the sensations that rocked us from the center outward.

J kept moving in and out of me, more slowly now, until our orgasms subsided and all that was left were post-ecstasy tremors.

We were both shaking and panting. He dropped his head to rest on my back. We were sweaty, and I don't know how long we stayed like that before I felt his hand blindly reach up to undo the belt.

Those deft fingers immediately found the right spot. In one movement, it was loose, and I was free. He pulled on the straps that had been created by wrapping it around my wrists, and I dropped my hands to the bed, collapsing when my shaky arms weren't able to hold me up.

We fell together before he rolled off to the side, putting his arms around me. I turned to face him, burying myself in his chest. Our breathing was slowing to a normal speed. Our hearts beat in time with each other.

He backed away enough to put a hand on my face, brushing back my damp hair.

I couldn't manage to get my head focused on any one thing, so I opted to replay what had just happened. The culmination of his teasing had been an epic conclusion of which I couldn't possibly complain. It had been worth every second.

He buried his face in my neck and murmured, "I love your scent."

I could smell his cologne, an earthy fragrance that was probably shampoo, and his natural musk. Taking in the three distinct scents, I closed my eyes and breathed deeply.

I wanted to say something to J. I wanted to tell him, *I love you.* Because, in that moment, I did. But such a proclamation would be pointless, so I remained quiet.

We stayed on the bed together, getting lost in each other, without a concept of time. Our hands explored, caressing, both of us too spent to turn it into anything sexual. It was sweet, caring, gentle. My fingers played with his chest hair while his fingers ran up and down my back.

It was the way couples behaved when they were at the beginning of something big. But this was the beginning and end all at the same time. We weren't going to address that for a few more hours, though. At least if I could help it.

CHAPTER SIXTEEN

J shifted onto his back and gathered me into his arms. I gladly moved into a restful position in the crook of his shoulder, my hands still traversing every part of him that I could reach. I wanted to absorb as much of him as I could.

He ran his hand gently up and down my back, occasionally sifting through my hair.

All of this, us in that moment, was the axis of the planet. I hoped the other Earth-dwellers, if there were any of them left outside those walls, appreciated that we were single-handedly causing the rotation of their planet. Nothing could break this spell...until J said...

"Nat?"

"Mhmmm," was all I could muster.

"I'm going to cook something, and I'd like for you to come into the kitchen with me. Are you hungry yet?"

Again with the food thing. I assessed what I was feeling on a basic need level. I definitely needed more of *him*, but to answer his question, the best he was going to get from me was that I'd pick at something.

"I'd love to help you cook. And I could eat a few bites, but nothing big, okay?"

He thought for a second. "How about eggs and toast? And bacon?"

"I could eat a little of that."

I was one of those women who couldn't eat when there was something this monumental going on. He was probably one of those guys who ate no matter what.

Nat,

Same - I'm sorry you had to cancel your plans for the 5K. And same - I'd really like to make this happen at some point.

J

He got up from the bed, disrupting our peaceful contemplation of each other, and asked, "You want to shower?" When I didn't answer right away, he said, "You're welcome to whichever bathroom you like. Towels are in the linen closets, and I'm pretty sure they all have shampoo, soap, and whatever else. If you need something you don't see, just ask...I'm sure I've got it somewhere."

I was listening to him talk about something as practical as stocking bathrooms, and it made me giggle.

J shrugged. "The housekeeper takes care of that stuff, but she's usually good about having it covered."

I should have expected he would have a housekeeper, but it was also surprising with the reclusive lifestyle he led. Without thinking, I blurted out, "You have a housekeeper?"

I couldn't be sure, but I think he may have blushed a little. He busied himself with putting his flannel pants back on.

"Yeah. Just a few days a week. She does the shopping and cleaning. Laundry. Whatever. It's not a big deal."

It occurred to me that J might be feeling a little too aware of his celebrity status with this conversation, and I fumbled into, "Oh, of course. No, that's great. I was just wondering how it works out with your creative process and all that. Doesn't she get in your way when you're trying to write?"

He shook his head. "When she shows up, I go out walking. We have these cool trails around here, and I walk the river for miles. She always works on the bedroom first. If I get back and she's still here, I shut the door and go to bed while she finishes up."

"You just go to bed in the middle of the day while your housekeeper is working in your house?"

This seemed so incredibly odd to me. I mean, hey, it was his house and who was paying who here? So, he could do what he wanted, but I couldn't wrap my head around it.

He shrugged. "It kind of comes with the territory, Nat. I told you – I keep odd hours. Hell, sometimes when she shows up, I've been up all night and I'm already in bed for the day. Fuck the walk, you know? So, I lock the door, and she knows to stay out of the bedroom and not make too much noise. She works for an agency that sends sane people like her out to crazy people like me...so she's used to the madness. Thank God."

He had his pants back on, and his arms were crossed across his chest.

"Well, cool," I said. "Send her to my house when you're done with her."

He gave me a stiff smile and turned to walk into the closet. Where had his t-shirt wound up anyway? So much had happened since he took it off that I forgot which room it had landed in.

J emerged, pulling another shirt over his head. This one was a tight tank top. I didn't know what was worse – his bare chest or this. He was stunning naked, but he wore his clothes so well that it was hard to say which look I preferred.

No matter – anything he did was going to drive me wild, and I already felt the stirrings of my body coming back to life for another round. Would he be up for more? He hadn't slept yet, came three times already, and now he was about to eat. Isn't that how this worked for guys? Have a lot of sex, stay up too late, eat, and then pass out?

"So, anyway, if you want to take a shower, help yourself to whatever you need." J finished the original conversation while at the same time putting an end to the housekeeper discussion.

"I'll take you up on that," I said. "But I need to get my bag out of the car first."

"I'll get it. Where are your keys?"

I had to think about that for a second, then remembered. "In the hall bathroom."

I started making my way for the door to retrieve the keys when J stepped in front of me. He leaned down to give me a quick kiss on the lips. "I'll take care of it, love."

I thanked him, but I wanted to say a lot more than that. I wanted to tell him I thought he was amazing, and not just in the bedroom. That he was so much more of a man, a gentleman, than I had expected. I should have known J would be like this. He had always come across as the type of guy who would be courteous, doting even. It just wasn't something I was accustomed to, especially over the past year.

"That's the bathroom," he pointed to the door next to

the closet. Glancing over his shoulder on the way out, he added, "*If* you want to use that one," before walking away to get my things.

```
  J,
  Do you realize we say 'same' a lot? It's
like we're one person. :)
  Nat
```

I stepped into his private bathroom and let out a little gasp when I saw the size of it. It was a beautiful room. A sanctuary.

There was light grey paint on the walls, lots of dark cabinets that were similar to the kitchen, and an enormous claw-foot tub. Next to that was a shelf with all manner of bottles. I wondered if he ever took the time to soak in the tub, imagining him stretched out, relaxing and contemplating his next written move.

Across from the tub was a wall with an opening, and I guessed that was the shower. Beyond the entrance, I could see smooth stonework on the floor with distressed tiles of deep greens, blues, and purples on the walls.

In one corner of the room, there was a large built-in that had stacks upon stacks of big fluffy towels lining the shelves. Next to that were two doors. A quick peek revealed a linen closet, housing more towels and necessities, and a water closet. Beside that, tucked into another corner, was a chair.

J walked in with my overnight bag, placing it on the counter.

"I thought you might need this too," he said setting down my purse next to it. "Your keys were on the vanity in the other bathroom. I didn't go into your purse."

I looked up at him. "Really, I wasn't worried about that."

"Well, my mother taught me to never go in a woman's purse." He smiled.

I'd like to meet that woman, I thought. *She did a damn good job.*

We were locked in a gaze when it suddenly dawned on me that he might want to take a shower, too.

"Do you want to join me?" I asked. "Or I could use another bathroom. Whatever works for you."

"Yeaaaah," he said, dragging out the word like he was thinking.

Yeah, what? I should use another bathroom? Or he was going to hesitantly join me?

I could feel babbling coming on, and I already knew from experience that I couldn't stop it. "I mean, I'll use the hall bathroom. It's not a big deal. The shower in there looked great. Here, you take this one, and I'll just move my stuff back over there to give you some privacy."

I shifted to pick up my bag and purse, but his hand shot out, grabbing my wrist.

"Nat, stop. I was just thinking that I wanted to get in the kitchen because I'm starving but showering with you is too tempting to pass up."

I looked up at him sheepishly. After everything we'd done, how was it that my nerves were still at a breaking point?

The lights in the room were bright, so he used the dimmer switch to turn them down. I loved that he could soften the glow to suit the mood in every room.

We stood, looking at each other, for what was probably only a few seconds, but felt like a lifetime.

There was intimacy...and then there was *intimacy.* What we had experienced thus far was closeness in the form of sex. The shower situation would up the ante to another level. This was going to be the ultimate form of exploration.

J grabbed a towel from the big stack on the shelves and rolled it over the wall rack beside the shower, next to another towel that was already there. Turning to face me with intensity in his eyes, I felt like I was going to melt.

I was still wearing the shirt with the three pesky buttons open. J slipped his hands inside and under the shoulders of it, pushing it back slowly, relishing the unveiling of what was now becoming a familiar canvas for him to paint his desires. It dropped to the floor, leaving me standing nude before him. My body on display for his lustful scrutiny. My nipples hardened, the skin around them crinkling with nervous anticipation of what was to come.

Sliding my hands under his tank top, I started to pull up, but being too tall for me to lift it over his head, he had to finish the job.

My fingers found their way under the waistband of his pants and, with just a little push, they fell to the floor.

He took my hand, leading me to the shower entrance. Stepping inside first, he turned on the faucet. The water roared to life. While he was fussing with the temperature, I stared in awe at the size of the enclosure we were in. There was enough room for three or four people in there at least. With tables and chairs. And a dance floor.

He could have a party in here, I thought. If I didn't know him better, I would have questioned what might have taken place there with anyone else.

“Test this,” he said stepping aside from the stream of water.

I put my hand under it and told him it was good.

“All right...ready?” he asked.

I gave him a confused look, and he turned a dial.

Suddenly, there was water everywhere. It continued to spray from the wall in front of us but was also flowing from the walls all around. I felt like we were caught in a rain shower.

Laughing, I put my hands out to feel it as my hair fell into my face.

"Pretty cool, huh?" J said while also laughing.

"*Very* cool," I responded.

He was looking at me intently. When he finally broke the gaze, he brushed the hair out of my face, kissed me, and said, "I want to wash your hair. Is that okay?"

Nobody had ever wanted to do that before. I had to think about it for a second. It was such a sweet gesture, leaving me feeling speechless, so I just nodded.

He moved the shower dial again. The water on the right side turned off, giving us a place to stand where we weren't getting rained on from every direction.

J put his hands on my shoulders, moving me so the warm water from the other side was still cascading over the front of my body. Stepping around to stand behind me, he gathered my hair in one hand, chose a bottle from the long built-in shelf, and poured shampoo into the other. While he lathered my hair, I recognized the same earthy scent I had become familiar with over the events of the evening.

He twirled my long locks up to the top of my head, and his fingers grazed the back of my neck, causing me to shudder.

"Are you cold?" J quickly asked.

"No, I'm good. Your fingers should be a registered weapon."

"Oh. Did I hurt you?"

"No, J. They just do things to me that should be illegal."

At this, he laughed and stopped what he was doing to run his fingers teasingly up and down my back, from the nape of my sensitive neck to the curve of my buttocks.

I gave an exaggerated shudder. "I'm going to get out if you can't stay focused on your job."

"It's my job to wash your hair, is it?" he asked playfully.

"Yes, sir. You started this, and now I'm standing here with a head full of shampoo, so get cracking on it, mister."

I reached behind me and slapped him on the ass. J let out a frisky yelp before pushing himself against my back. It was then that I realized his cock wasn't fully ready for me again...but it wasn't at rest either.

I smiled, warmed by our playfulness while feeling euphoric about my clear effect on him.

He went back to work on my hair. I closed my eyes, feeling my body relax as he massaged my scalp. He worked slowly and meticulously...and I would have been perfectly happy to spend the rest of my life, standing in J's shower, letting him do this.

CHAPTER SEVENTEEN

After J was done washing my hair and it had been rinsed, he handed me a bottle of conditioner. "This is all you, love. I don't know how this one works."

I took the bottle, put some conditioner in my hand, and worked it through my hair. My mind wandered to thinking about why he had conditioner in his shower if he didn't use it, but then I remembered – *Oh, right. The girlfriend.*

Several hours ago, I couldn't have cared less about her, but now she was nagging at me. Jealousy was creeping around me, needling at me. It made no sense because I was getting exactly what I wanted – one night with J. She had him all the time and didn't take full advantage of what was right in front her. Did they even have sex when she came over for her weekly visit? He had said it was dinner, movie, sleep. If there was sex, it was boring. She didn't *know* him.

Did he even open up to her about his work, how he felt about ideas, or any of the thoughts he had during his self-imposed solitary confinement?

Nat,
We do say 'same' a lot, yes. But we're not the same person. You don't like Oingo Boingo and I honestly don't know how I can still speak to you after such a confession. Because of my deep admiration for you in all other aspects, I'll continue to try to work through it.
J

I needed to get my mind off that topic, so when I was done running the conditioner through my hair, and while I waited for it to be ready to rinse, I said to J, "Your turn."

I picked up the shampoo bottle, and he turned so I could work on the back of his head. Tilting himself back to make it easier for me to reach, I slowly but firmly worked the shampoo through his hair, kneading his scalp as I went.

Even with his short hairstyle, there was still enough of it for me to play with. And I did. I weaved my fingers through methodically, absorbing every bit of this very personal moment.

I was enjoying taking care of J in this manner. This was a very different form of intimacy. It felt private. A shared time for us to focus on our basic human necessities together. It was simple. And loving.

And then I heard the snoring sound, coming to me loudly over the raining water.

What the...?

"J...?"

"Shhh. I'm in a trance."

"Oh, for goodness sake!" I said, giving him a little shove.

He turned to me with a chuckle for a showery kiss.

When I was done and told him to rinse, he hung his head under the water for several seconds, rubbed his hair vigorously, then raised up and shook himself. I fell into a slight daze as I watched this sexy move until the mist sprayed all over me, snapping me out of it.

I giggled as I wiped it out of my eyes. He stuck his head under the water again and did another doggie shake, so I screeched and swatted at him.

He laughed while grabbing me around my waist to pull me close. With the water raining on us from two directions, we fell into a deep, slow kiss. I wondered if he was going to make love to me in the shower... but we faded out of our embrace.

J said, "Alrighty, next," before leaning over to grab a washcloth from the shelf. He applied a little body wash, a splash of water, and then massaged the soft fibers to get a froth of bubbles going.

Holding it out toward me, he asked, "You or me?"

Does he mean the washer or the washee?

Before I could clarify, and while I was hesitating, he stopped waiting for an answer.

"Me," he said with a quick nod.

He stepped toward me and began running it over my shoulders from the front. The cloth was extremely soft, and I closed my eyes while giving in to the cottony caresses.

J moved at a crawl over my shoulders and neck, then down my arms. Lifting my left arm first, he worked the underside before doing the same thing with other. When he was halfway done with my right side, I realized I was making him hold up my arm with no help from me. I had turned to putty in his hands.

Momentarily drifting off into a daydream, I fantasized about what might be coming. But as the washcloth began to cross over my breasts, J spoke...

"How are you feeling?"

Because of where my train of thought had been, I gave a little snort. "That's a loaded question."

He smiled. "Insatiable."

As the washcloth continued on its inexorable journey, my stomach came next before he squatted down in front of me to wash my legs. At my ankles, he lifted each leg, running the cloth along the bottom of my feet.

Despite the warmth of the water, my body shivered. I looked down at him, crouching before me. My fingers swirled through his hair.

"Hey, now. You're going to hypnotize me with that."

"Hey, now. You've been doing that to me all night," I teased.

J's eyes were locked on mine as he stood to full height. "Have I now?" he asked, putting his hand on my arm to turn me around.

Sweeping my hair over my shoulder to the front, he moved along my neck and downward. When he reached the small of my back, I felt his foot between my feet, prompting me to stand with my legs farther apart. Shifting into the position for which he was looking, his knees were against the back of my legs as he squatted again.

Going straight back to my ankles, he started to work his way up this time. At the back of my thighs, I felt the cloth gliding in between my legs. I knew where he would be arriving soon. Tensing with the expectation of it, he inched along until I felt his fingers through the fabric...on the spot that made my legs feel weak.

His touch was maddeningly gentle. Slippery, soapy

fingers lightly circling around me.

"You're a wicked man, Jack Perry."

"Me? Who plotted this whole situation?"

"I have no idea what you're talking about. This was all a spur of the moment decision to simply stop by and say hi."

"My ass," he laughed.

J mercifully backed his hand out from between my legs, gently returning to my shoulders. I placed my feet closer together and turned to see him running the wash-cloth under the water.

He handed it to me. Of course I wanted to return the favor for him. The thought of exploring every inch of him made me tingle in all the right places.

I held it out to him as he poured more body wash onto its soft surface, repeating his process of running it under the water and then lathering it.

In an effort to do something different from the map J followed over my body, I started out by turning him around, with his back facing me. Beginning with his feet, I followed an upward course, working gently and slowly.

A question had been playing in my mind, and curiosity finally got the best of me. "Do you wish I hadn't come?"

I patiently waited for an answer as I caressed upward over his whole back, moving in small circles and from side to side, occasionally applying light pressure to his muscles, where I could feel he was harboring some tension.

J groaned. Planting his feet on the floor, he dropped his head and placed his hands on the shower wall in front of him, bracing himself in a slightly leaning position. This was his sexiest pose yet. It wasn't until I felt the warm water splashing on my tongue that I realized I had let my mouth fall open as I brazenly stared at him.

I tried to stay focused on washing him while massaging his unyielding muscles at the same time. I felt the smallest trickle on my inner thigh that I knew had nothing to do with the water.

"Not for a second, Nat. I went into this blind, obviously. Not knowing what to expect. But I wouldn't change a thing. No regrets."

I stepped in closer to him, at his side, as I slid up his stomach to his chest. J maintained his stance, but turned his head toward me, kissing me deeply.

I wanted to duck under his arm and position myself right in front of him for the taking, up against the shower wall. But I also wanted to continue my mission to care for him, so I sighed as I briefly leaned into him before breaking away from his kiss.

"How about you?"

I finished with J's back as I thought about how to answer him. There was still an undercurrent of guilt running through me, but in the moment, as we were, sharing this time together...no regrets.

I worked on his arms from behind, going over the top first, then nudging him to lift them as I worked the underside. He was too tall for me to hold his arms up for him as he had done for me.

As I finished with that, I came around to stand in front of him. His eyes were boring into me. He put a finger under my chin to lift my face, softly bringing his lips to mine.

We slowly moved apart, and I went back to my project of focusing on his body. His irresistible, sexy body.

"I'm the mastermind of this operation, remember?" I finally answered him, giggling. "And I am very pleased with the execution of the mission."

"A special forces quest – Operation Stalker!" J laughed.

"I am *not* a stalker!"

"Oh, you may not have stalked, per se, but you're definitely stalkery," J said, followed by more laughter.

I stuck my tongue out at him. He responded by holding me against the wall and tickling me.

Grasping on to his shoulders, I lightly nipped at him with my teeth.

"Ohhh! And a vampire, to boot!" he joked. "Watch yourself, Nat...you know what they say about writers."

"No, J. Enlighten me," I said while kissing the spot where I had bitten him.

"Don't piss us off, or you could find yourself meeting a fateful demise in the next story."

"Well, if I see your next movie only to discover a character who resembles me has been killed off, my fictious self will definitely be coming back to stalk you."

"I sense a series coming on..." J said, looking thoughtful.

I winked at him. "Glad I could be an inspiration."

Turning my attention back to his body, I used the washcloth to soap downward to his chest. His head tilted back, and over the sound of the water, I heard him making low, deep noises.

Continuing south to his stomach, I felt his firm muscles. I loved that he had what I considered to be perfectly muscular abs – strong, with only the hint of a washboard.

Finishing there, I squatted in front of him, starting back at his ankles, working my way up with the intention of saving the best for last.

It had not gone unnoticed to me that he was growing hard throughout this whole activity, but I was trying not to think about it. Now, in my present position, it was right in front of me. I wanted to drop the washcloth to the floor and take him into my mouth for the third time tonight. Resisting the urge, I stayed focused instead on the task at hand.

Sliding slowly up his legs, I advanced in an orderly fashion; up to one knee, then to the other, before proceeding higher. When I arrived at the destination I had been anticipating, he moved his feet apart without needing to be nudged.

Coasting up his right leg to the top of his thigh, I put my hand underneath him, cradling him with the soapy cloth. His hands moved to the top of my head, where he stroked my hair, keeping it out of my face. I looked up at him and should not have been surprised to see him staring down at me. I held his gaze for a few seconds before turning my attention back to gently washing the firm focal point.

I absolutely expected J to take my head in his hands, assuming control of the moment, forcing my eager mouth onto his swollen manhood. However, if he was tempted, he managed to fight the urge. He seemed to be enjoying our relaxation time as much as I was. Which I found arousing in and of itself.

Knowing that we had not just bedroom chemistry, but also a compatibility bond was comforting to me. We were more than just sex, and it eased my conscience a bit to know I hadn't made this decision for something cheap.

Finishing up with my current exercise, I stood and handed the washcloth back to J. He draped it on a shelf before turning back to lift me off the floor. With legs hanging down and water streaming all around us, I folded my arms around his neck as we fell into a long, passionate kiss.

When it was time to release me, he put me down asking, "Ready to rinse?"

I reached up to touch my hair, realizing I had forgotten all about the conditioner. "Yup."

J stepped aside, allowing me full access to the showerhead nearest me, and watched with fascination as I washed away the solution.

"Not too familiar with lady hair care practices, are you?" I asked with a grin.

"Nope. Definitely not my forte."

"I'll have to get you a subscription to Glamour."

"I'd appreciate that," he said, tossing his head back while using a hand to flip his imaginary locks. "Finally...someone who gets me."

I laughed. "On second thought, I think I prefer you just the way you are."

I was done rinsing, so I stepped up to him, tickling my fingers across his abs while standing on tiptoe for a quick kiss.

J moved under the streaming water, washing away any residual body wash. He was looking thoughtful.

"So...really?"

"Really what?" I asked, confused.

"Just the way I am. Even with all of that?" He waved his hand in the direction of the bedroom.

It was time to get out, so J turned around once more under the water, and then leaned over to shut off our rain shower jets.

He went past me, kissing me on the forehead as he did, and reached out of the shower entrance to grab a towel off the rack.

Half turning, he handed it to me, and I absentmindedly wrapped it around myself. He reached back, taking another one for himself and wrapping it around his waist.

The sight of him standing there, dripping wet, wearing nothing but a towel, flipped a switch within me.

He was right. Insatiable.

He stepped out, wiping his feet on the rug in front of the shower entrance. As he moved toward the vanity, I followed and did the same. He took his place in front of what must have been his favored sink. Opening a drawer, J pulled out a comb and ran it through his hair.

I needed to take care of some basic tasks as well, but first I wanted to give my full attention to his question.

"Yes, J...really. None of this came as a surprise to me, you know. And however kinky you think you are – to the point of worrying about it – trust me that there are far darker realms out there."

"Oh, I know that. To both your points." He paused a moment, seemingly gauging his next words. "I'm pretty close to a guy who delves into what I consider a world of fetishes and eccentricities. I'm not sure I'd ever go that far, though." He chuckled and then said, almost to himself, "Never thought I'd even go *this* far again."

Giving J a moment to see if he wanted to continue, I opened my bag, taking out a hairbrush and a hairdryer. I hadn't packed much for this one night, but I definitely made sure to cover all the necessities just in case.

Sure enough...

"As to your other point, it was pretty evident when you got here that you remembered everything. I guess I was just wondering how you feel. You know...now. Not that I want a full-scale evaluation or anything. But considering *your* little...quirk. Which you never told me about, by the way."

With his last statement, J assumed an exaggerated

stance with his hands on his hips followed by a quick wink in my direction. He was done with his post-shower tasks, so he turned, leaning against the counter.

"My quirk?" I knew what he was talking about, but I didn't quite know how to explain it. So, I stalled.

I took off the towel, running it over my hair, trying to remove all excess water. When I was done with that, I wrapped it around myself again and fastened it just above my breasts. I sneaked a quick peek at J to find that he was watching me closely, appearing momentarily distracted.

He cleared his throat. "We don't have to talk about it, Nat."

"I'm fine. I just thought it was self-explanatory. It's been a long time to wait to...watch."

J tilted his head from side to side, stretching his neck.

Plugging in the dryer, I set it on the counter while I got to work brushing out my hair.

"I'm not a control freak, if that's what you're thinking."

J gave me a small eyeroll with a big smile.

"I'm not! I just...I don't know, J. Like I said, I've waited a long time for this." So much for epic musings.

If I was honest with myself, J was probably right and there was likely a lot more to my quirk, as he called it, than I was willing to address in that moment. Mainly because it was also probable that it had something to do with my home life. However, elaborating on why I felt so strongly compelled to be an active participant where J was concerned would set us on a course for one of those intense conversations I had been trying to avoid.

We were quite the pair. A psychologist would have a field day with us.

"I'm just happy you felt...comfortable with me," I said,

fully aware that I was spinning the topic back to him.

"Ditto – it's been a long time coming for me, too."

I was done brushing my hair, so I turned to face him. "Vanilla?"

He gave a small snort. "Vanilla...yeah. Damn near driven snow is more like it."

We gazed at each other for a moment before J pushed himself off the counter. Scooping up the clothes we had been wearing off the floor, he walked behind me, trailing his fingers along my back as he left the bathroom.

J,

Sorry I didn't get back to you yesterday. Something came up and I was out late. I'm here today, though.

Nat

Time to blow dry. It was a process because of the length, but I wanted to get it back to the straight style I had it in when I arrived, as opposed to my naturally wavy look.

Just as I was finishing up with some smoothing serum, J returned wearing jeans and a sweatshirt. It made me wonder if he was thinking our night had come to a close.

I didn't know what time it was, but it had to be the wee hours of the morning and maybe he had something to do that day. Maybe he wanted to write. Maybe he was just ready to be alone again.

I was thinking about the clothes I had brought to wear in the morning when he took my hand, leading me out of the bathroom to the closet.

"Whatever looks comfortable to you, go for it. I'll be in the kitchen."

He lifted my chin, kissing me deeply before turning to

leave the room.

Okay, so, we clearly weren't done yet if he was offering me his clothes. I sighed as the damnable carnal aching made its presence known.

Pushing what I was feeling physically to the back of my mind, I set about trying to find another one of his shirts to wear. Even with a mounting need forming within me, I was relaxed knowing we had more time together. And, I had to admit, I was looking forward to finding out what was going to happen next, here in J's house, which had transformed overnight into my own personal pleasure dome.

CHAPTER EIGHTEEN

After a quick application of some light makeup and a once-over with lotion, I decided to put my hair up in a loose, messy style with wispy strands framing my face. The music got louder throughout the house, and I smiled as I thought of J in the kitchen, getting into his cooking mojo. The Goo Goo Dolls were singing "Iris." I shook my head at the irony of it.

Walking out of the bathroom, I noticed that he had taken time to put the pillows back on the bed. My red dress was draped over the chair next to his nightstand with my white thong folded neatly on top of it.

I took in what I was seeing and thought, *It felt like months ago when I had been wearing that dress.*

How could *so* much have taken place in such a short period of time?

The room looked different to me now. I hadn't just been there...*we* had been there...together. The rest of my life seemed thousands of miles away. Another lifetime, even.

These walls now held my deepest secrets. J's walls. Our secrets.

Nat,

I have something to tell you - I met someone. It's not really a big deal. We've just been going for coffee and to the movies a time or two. I'm not sure I even feel anything significant about it, but I wanted to be up front with you.

J

The smell of cooking drifted into the room and snapped me back to reality. The reality that would remain blissful for only a little while longer.

I wandered down the hall, finding J in the kitchen. The music was turned up a little more out there, and I could smell bacon frying. He had his back to me when I walked in, so I leaned against the refrigerator taking in the scene.

His jeans were hugging his ass just right, and I noticed a kitchen towel draped down from one of the pockets. The sleeves of the dark grey sweatshirt were pushed up to right below his elbows, keeping the cuffs away from his food prep activities. J was relaxed, obviously working a system he knew well. The sight caused a flood of the stirring feelings I had been having in the bathroom to return. He was in a zone here in the kitchen. I didn't want to ever stop watching him.

J was headed in a more Epicurean direction than I expected. A loaf of Italian bread sat untouched on a cutting board with a small baking sheet of scattered grape tomatoes resting next to it. From where I stood, what I had thought was bacon frying appeared to be perfectly cubed pancetta.

He popped a tomato in his mouth while turning to get a spatula from a ceramic container on the counter. And he saw me.

I stayed where I was, smiling at him. He stopped short, taking in the sight of me wearing one of his t-shirts...but this wasn't just any t-shirt. This one had been totally bastardized for, no doubt, the purpose of working out. The sleeves were cut off and a v-neck had been cut into the chest of it. It hung on me loosely and casually. His eyes moved over me, then to my hair.

When he resumed cooking again, he seemed distracted as he said, "Hey, love. Hungry? You *have* to be hungry by now."

"I'll eat a little," I replied. "It smells good. And you look like you know your way around a kitchen."

J leaned toward me, giving me a peck on the cheek. "I do like to cook," he said, grabbing the spatula he was after before turning back to the stove.

I stood enjoying the display for a little longer, before snapping myself out of it and asking if I could help.

"How about making a couple screwdrivers?" he replied, nodding his head toward the counter where the wine and bourbon bottles had been sitting earlier.

I saw they had been replaced with vodka and orange juice bottles. "Sure."

Having already seen him fetch glasses earlier, I opened the cupboard where they were and took down two tall ones. I filled them with ice from the icemaker on the freezer door then got busy mixing the vodka and juice. When I was done, I set one down for J near the stove.

"Thanks, love," he said, turning away from his cooking for a moment to kiss me on the lips.

"What do you have going on here?" I asked. It looked like he was going to an awful lot of trouble, and I was going to feel bad when all I would do was pick.

"I'm thinking eggs over toasted Italian bread with wilted spinach, roasted tomatoes, and a drizzle of pesto." He paused to look at me. "Yes?"

It sounded delicious, gourmet even, and my stomach reacted before I could give him an answer. I giggled.

He smiled and said, "Yes," with a nod and went back to work.

"Okay, but only one egg for me. And one piece of toast."

"I get it. You don't eat." Standing at his side, I thought I detected a small eye roll.

"No, that's not it. I just can't eat much when I'm hyper-focused on something."

"Really." Not a question, but there was one coming. "And what is it you're hyper-focused on?"

"Stop it," I simply said as I walked over to the sink where I saw he had fresh spinach sitting out.

The colander was still there from the blackberries, so in an effort to help, I set about washing the spinach in it.

He glanced over at me before turning his attention back to the frying pan, and then took a long, deep drink from the screwdriver.

I didn't know how he was doing it, but the pancetta looked like it was cooking perfectly without a single grease splatter anywhere. Whenever I cooked anything like that in a frying pan, my whole kitchen turned into a fresh hell mess.

I was still letting the water run over the spinach, so I picked up my glass and took a sip. There was something about the orange juice that gave me a relaxed feeling at this time of night...or morning. And the vodka washed into me, providing a warm steadiness that I needed.

I turned off the faucet, shaking the colander to help dry the spinach.

“Where are the towels?” I asked J.

He nodded toward a drawer to the left of the sink. Taking one out, I laid it on the counter before dropping the spinach onto it and patting the leaves dry.

“Thanks,” he said.

Unfamiliar with feeling so useless in the kitchen, I looked around to see what else I could do. He already had a plate set out with a paper towel for the pancetta.

The grape tomatoes were already prepped on the baking sheet, and I could hear the oven humming. Pointing at them, I asked, “Do you want these in the oven?”

“Sure. Thanks.” And then to follow up, “Five minutes should do it.”

I saw they had already been seasoned with oil, no doubt olive, and what looked to be simple salt and pepper. Putting the tray in the oven, I set the timer for five minutes.

At a loss again for what I could do to help, I walked over to J, standing close enough to be near him without invading his space. Leaning against the counter, I asked, “Where did you learn to cook?”

“My mom. She's a great cook,” he answered. “I don't do a lot of it these days because it's just too damn easy to order something, but I always make sure Lydia gets *some* groceries every week.”

Lydia must be the housekeeper, I thought. And I couldn't help but wonder how she managed to function when she was in his house. When she was dusting furniture while he was tucked into his bedroom sanctuary, sleeping the day away, did she fantasize about going in there and climbing onto that tall bed with him?

I was convinced that every woman who came into contact with J was longing for him in the same way I was. Except Alesandra. She didn't know what she was missing, but I also had a feeling that Alesandra was the female version of J in the bedroom. Or, at least, who J was when he was being himself. I imagined she was a total barracuda and decided she probably left a trail of broken female hearts all over the world. No wonder they got along so well – birds of a feather.

The pancetta was done, and he was transferring it to the paper towel-covered plate at the same time the oven timer went off. I had seen an oven mitt in the drawer with the towels, so I grabbed it to remove the baking sheet. Setting it on a trivet that was already on the counter, I noticed J had drained most of the drippings from the pan and was quickly wilting the spinach in what little had been left behind.

He used salt and pepper grinders to season it, then pushed that to an unlit back burner. Turning his attention to a clean pan, he placed it over the flame, sprinkling it with a touch of what I could see now was definitely olive oil, and cracked three eggs. More salt and pepper before he turned to a loaf of Italian bread. Three swift slices with a serrated knife then it was on its way into the toaster oven.

While J waited on the bread, he turned to me, taking me into his arms, giving me a long, gentle kiss. I was getting fired up, not that I had ever really cooled down in the first place. If I was in control, I would have let the food be damned. My passionate thoughts put me back in his arms, where I could once again wrap my legs around him. When the timer on the toaster oven went off, reality reminded me that what he really wanted to do was eat, so I released him with the hope of more to come later.

He turned off the heat on the stove, took two dishes out of a nearby cupboard, and started plating our food with expert skill.

First, the lightly toasted bread with a drizzle of olive oil. He put the spinach on the bread and the egg on the spinach then crumbled pancetta over all of it. The tomatoes were scattered around the plate. He then opened a small container of pesto and used a spoon to trickle it back and forth across the plate.

Turning to me, he asked, "Want to go into the dining room?"

"Sure," I said. "Do you want me to get utensils or napkins or anything?"

"It's all in there," he answered. And then added with a wink, "We'll use the fancy stuff for this. Come on."

J took both plates. I picked up our glasses, following him into the dining room. Once there, he used his elbow to slide the dimmer switch up, flooding the room with light.

There were no place settings on the table, and I felt frustrated with what seemed to me like a lack of help on my part. "J, let me do something. Please. Where's the silverware?"

"Top drawer," he answered, nodding toward the china cabinet.

I set the drinks carefully on the table, opened the drawer, and took out two forks and knives. Next to the silverware tray was a stack of woven placemats, so I removed two of those as well. Linen napkins were neatly folded alongside the placemats, but I thought it would be silly to use linen for this, so I told him I would go back to the kitchen for paper napkins.

"Nat, seriously, just use those," J said, nodding again in the direction of the drawer. "I never do anything with this stuff. Let's cut loose and go crazy."

He gave a little eye roll. I laughed and busied myself with setting the table while he waited patiently, still holding the plates.

Once everything was ready, he set down the food and went to a dry bar in the corner of the room. When he turned around, he was holding two candle sticks and a lighter. He set them on the table, lit the candles, and then turned the dimmer switch down most of the way.

J pulled out the first chair to the left of the head of the table for me. I settled in, delighted with the illumination coming from the candles and the soft glow of the chandelier.

He went right to work cutting into his food while I took a long sip of my drink. The orange juice was watered down now from the melting ice, but I still got a powerful taste of the vodka. That was what I had been looking for.

Glancing toward the window, I noticed Fred was still exactly where we had left him hours earlier.

J saw where I was focused. "I told you – he'll stay here all night. Lazy bastard."

The last statement was said lovingly. I had no doubt Fred and J were as thick as thieves.

"When does he spend time with you?" I asked.

"If I were writing right now, he'd be on my desk swishing his tail all over my keyboard. That's where we do our male bonding."

I felt another pang of jealousy, wishing I could be the one to sit on J's desk when he was working in the early hours of the morning.

Now I'm jealous of the cat. Holy shit.

J wasn't kidding when he had told me he was starving. I looked over to see he was almost a third of the way done with his meal. Mine hadn't been touched yet, so I finally picked up my knife and fork to cut into it.

"I hope you're okay with sunny side up. I'm sorry – I should have asked."

"It looks wonderful, J," I said. "Normally I'm an over-easy kind of gal, but tonight I'll try anything. I think I'd even swallow the worm."

"I do have tequila in the house," he quipped with a spark in his eyes.

My response was a brief smirk because, as adventurous as I felt, I had no intention of eating a worm, or even drinking tequila for that matter.

Taking my first bite of J's creation, I closed my eyes as I tasted all the flavors. It was cooked perfectly, and it tasted delicious, making me realize how hungry I actually was.

I surprised myself when I thought, *I just might finish this.*

While I ate, I looked at the dry bar where J had found the candles. There I noticed another framed photo. This one was of a man, and it looked quite dated. Taken back in the seventies maybe. Pointing my fork at it, I asked J who it was.

He gave it a glance before quickly returning his attention back to his plate. After a minute, in a distant voice, he said, "That's my dad."

And then I remembered. He had written to me about losing his dad at a young age, around the time he was in college.

"I'm sorry, J."

"You have nothing to be sorry for." I thought that was going to be the end of the subject, and I didn't want to push him to talk about it, but then he continued. "I keep that picture in here because this is where I come to talk to him. All the other rooms have distractions. You know?

Television, stereo, computer...just crap that gets in the way. So, once in a while, I pour myself a stiff bourbon and come in here to hang out with Fred and Dad."

J put his fork down and sat back in his chair. I was holding my breath as the air in the room hung heavy. It felt like there was more to be said. After a quiet minute, J continued about his dad, and I sat perfectly still, knowing this was something he didn't talk about to everyone, if anyone at all.

"It's just fucked up, you know? Losing someone like that? There's this expectation that we'll grieve, go into mourning, whatever...and then we're supposed to snap out of it. I mean, some people just don't...'get over it,'" he did air quotes here and paused. "And then you go to talk about it and everyone's like, 'Oh, I'm so sorry. When did it happen?' And here I am like, 'Over 20 years ago.' And then they don't care. No one wants to hear about something that happened so long ago. And they've all got it figured out...that I should be past it, living in the present, all that."

He stopped there, continuing to stare at his plate, then glanced over in the direction of the dry bar and the photo of his father. "I *am* living in the present. I'm all about being here for today. But some things just hurt for...forever. So, I keep my mouth shut and don't get into it." Making an effort to lighten it up a bit, he concluded with, "Fred knows. So, I do what I have to do most of the time, and then wander in here now and then to toast Dad with Fred."

He looked up at me and smiled. I didn't know what to say.

Finally, honesty seemed like the best policy. "Thank you for sharing that with me. It means a lot."

I was pretty sure there weren't many people in his life

who had ever seen this side of J, and I would take it with me and keep it close to my heart when I thought about him. I wanted to hug him, but I stayed seated, not knowing if an affectionate gesture was what he needed.

"I'm sorry. I didn't mean to go sideways with these depressing thoughts," he said.

"No, you didn't. I get it."

He raised his eyebrows in curiosity.

"My grandfather passed when I was thirteen, and I'm still...processing it."

J propped his elbows on the table, leaning over to listen to me.

"I was this super bratty kid. Like, think Veruca Salt bratty. But I really loved my grandfather. He was this incredibly patient, loving guy. For years after he was gone, my grandmother always said he never loved anyone as much as he loved me. And I was a brat. They put him in a nursing home about a year or so before he died, and they wouldn't let me go to see him. I fought with my parents about it, but no one understood that I *had* to see him. I had to let him know that I was sorry I had been a little bitch. That I loved him and appreciated him."

I stopped there, looking down at the table. From the corner of my eye, I could see J was still focused on me, making no move to put an end to the conversation. I felt like I was throwing my own sad curveball into the mood, so I wrapped it up.

"And then he was gone. Thirty years later and it still haunts me that I was never able to apologize to him. And that he never had the opportunity to know the person I've become." I looked up at J and shrugged.

"And no one wants to hear about it because it was a lifetime ago," he said quietly.

I nodded.

We sat without speaking for a couple of minutes, before turning our attention back to the food. J was almost done. I had eaten about half of mine, which was more than I expected to accomplish.

I couldn't resist sneaking glances at him. His presence was so...powerful. Relaxed, with a confidence that didn't need to be forward, combined with physical characteristics that drew me to him like a magnet. Being within J's private territory routinely made my heart skip beats.

I was trying to focus on this time with him, to sit and talk and just be, but that physical rousing, the need, was still there no matter how far back in my mind I pushed it. I felt like a horny schoolgirl. And all of it had just been heightened by sharing these deeper memories.

J,

I understand. I'm a little jealous because I can't remember the last time I felt this close to someone, but...what are we doing? I don't know.

Nat

J was the first to break the silence. "Tell me about your company."

"There isn't much to tell," I said with a small shrug. "It's just me. And a girl who works for me remotely. She's really cool, and we get along great." Then I added, "Probably because we don't see each other every day."

J was finished eating now while I continued to pick, taking little bites here and there. He leaned back in the big chair, arms resting on the sides. I ignored a vision of the table being surrounded by women who longed to be with him, knowing full well it had never happened and likely never would.

"Do you have a lot of clients?" he asked, prompting

me to tell him more.

"Enough," I answered. "Nothing big. Small accounts, but they're spread out around the country, so I do have to travel a bit. That's how I ended up here."

"You have a client in New York City?"

I laughed. "No. I don't think anyone in Manhattan needs my mom-and-pop services. I have a client in Burlington, Vermont."

He tipped his head to the side. I could tell he was absorbing what I had just said. It meant that I had driven all the way from Burlington to New York to see him. And sure enough...

"Nat, you said you were in the area. Burlington is hardly being in the area."

"Well, it's a hell of a lot closer than Louisiana."

"What else are you doing while you're in New York?"

"Nothing. I have to leave later on today."

At this, I dropped my eyes back to my plate and pushed some food around with my fork. J kept his elbows on the armrests of the chair as he put his hands together, making a tepee with his fingers. I could see him out of the corner of my eye. It was another maddeningly sexy pose.

I thought about how I'd have to go back to my hotel in just a few more hours to try to compose myself before it would be time to catch my flight.

"I'll drive you to the airport," J said, ever the mind reader.

I shook my head. "Thanks, but I have to check out of my hotel and return the car and all that."

I was still staring at my plate, and I felt the sting that was the beginning of tears. I steeled myself to hold them back because this was definitely not where I wanted to go right now.

J had his chin resting on his tepee hands, and he finally asked, "Where are you staying?"

"It's not far, J."

"How much longer do you have?"

"Just a few hours."

He let out a deep breath. "Well, then I think we'd better make the most of it."

He stood and pulled my chair out for me, quickly taking me into his arms as I was moving to stand.

He was holding me tight when his lips found mine. There was an urgency to this kiss; a bigger force to it than there had been before. I settled into him as my body came to life with all the wants and desires and needs that only J could awaken within me to a fervor of that degree.

Even with that delicious physical anticipation, the sting I'd felt in my eyes was still there. I was grateful J was focused on kissing me when I felt one tear escape and fall down my cheek.

CHAPTER NINETEEN

My passion for J was irrepressible and flaring again. It enabled me to put aside the heartache of knowing our time together would soon come to an end.

Still kissing me, J walked backward toward the entrance of the dining room. I stayed glued to him, feeling more than ever like I had to have him, had to be one with him.

J made it out of the room without bumping into anything, but when my shoulder grazed the wall at the entrance, he stopped kissing me to ask me if I was okay. I was fine, of course, but he wasn't taking any more chances of having me navigate the hazards, he said, of his house with my eyes closed. Apparently mapping this unfamiliar location while concentrating on J's lips was a dangerous game for me. In his mind, anyway.

I rolled my eyes at him but let him take my hand to walk me toward the bedroom. He held on tightly, as if together, we were about to jump off Oahu's aptly named Leap of Faith cliff.

Nat,
Same. It feels weird to be out with someone else. I feel closer to you than anyone, even though we've never met. I guess we just keep doing what we're doing with the honesty thing.
Thinking of you a lot...
J

We wandered through the house at a normal pace – not hurrying, but not being as leisurely as our pool stroll, either. I think we both felt a sense of weight surrounding what was about to happen, as this would likely be our last chance to be together. In a matter of hours, everything would turn back into the proverbial pumpkin...the enchantment broken.

I glanced around as we moved, trying to take in anything I had missed. His personal possessions, photos, the fragrance of his home. All night, I had noticed a faint masculine scent throughout the house, as if he had a diffuser placed somewhere with a woodsy aroma dispersing into the air. It reminded me of his shampoo, and I liked it. In it, I found a sense of comfort.

There was artwork lining the walls of the hallway that I hadn't even stopped to look at yet. All of the pieces appeared to be earthy and deep, like J.

As he led me through the house, I was unable to take time to drink in each painting, and I regretted not paying attention to them sooner. If he chose these to hang on his walls, they were a part of him, speaking to what captured his attention. I wanted to know as much as I possibly could about that side of him. The time for having in-depth art discussions had come and gone, though. Now was for us. And only us.

When we arrived at the doorway to his bedroom, J walked in first and spun around to face me, pulling me back into his arms. We were going to take our time but standing there was not where I desired to be with him, so I nudged him toward the bed. I wanted to lie down with him, roll around with him, get lost in him. One more time.

Taking my hint, J led me in the direction of the big bed, keeping his arms around me and his lips on mine.

When we arrived, still kissing me, he reached a hand toward my head, looking for the clip that was holding up all of my hair. Thinking that this might be outside of his wheelhouse, I was about to grasp it and do it myself, but I felt my hair cascade down my shoulders and back. Then, without missing a beat, I heard the clip land with a 'clink' on the nightstand.

J turned his focus to the hem of my shirt, his fingers venturing beneath it. As he brushed my skin, it raised goosebumps, sending shivers reverberating up my spine. All of me was now fully alert. Alive to sensation.

Unhurriedly, as if helping me with a slow strip, he teased the shirt up and over my head. When my body came into view, J paused as he took in what I was wearing underneath. He drank in every inch of me. Fully immersed in his visual inspection. No shame.

Instead of exposed breasts, this time I had on a black lace bra. My skimpy thong had been replaced with matching lace low-rider boy shorts, which clung snugly to my hips.

My body shook as he put his hands on the sides of my waist, running his fingers toward my belly, skirting the edge of the new panties. When his hands were on my stomach, they started to glide up to my breasts and, once there, he trailed his fingers over the lace, without rhyme or reason, sometimes passing over my nipples, sometimes simply caressing my breasts over, under, and around them.

This gradual escalation of arousal was making me giddy. I held onto his biceps with a firm grip to ensure I would be able to continue to stand for this exploration as long as he wanted to keep doing it.

The fire down below was an inferno now, and I urgently wanted him to do *something* about it. Conversely, however, I also didn't want to rush anything.

I let go of his arms, slipping my hands under his sweatshirt, where I put them flat against his stomach, spreading my fingers wide. I was trying to take in as much of him as possible.

He was looking down at me, alternating his gaze from my eyes to my breasts. I moved my touch upward, slowly, stroking his chest and then tickling across his nipples before gliding under his arms to his back. Caressing behind him, I then followed the same map across his body, starting at his stomach again.

After I made a second pass over his chest and back, he took his hands off me, reaching one arm behind his head to pull off his shirt. My eyes ran over his upper body. I was awestruck, once again, that I was here with this magnificent man.

Putting his hands on either side of my face, J pulled me in for a deep kiss. My hands went to the button on his jeans and I slipped it open but didn't touch the zipper just yet. I needed to enforce some self-control. There was something in the air that said this time was going to be different.

I could feel him stirring behind the fabric of his jeans. Dropping a finger near the opened button, I gently caressed the tip.

We were still locked in a slow-burning kiss when J's hands skimmed up my back, where he unhooked my bra with practiced ease. His hands lingered there. There was no hint of haste in his movements. It seemed like forever before he eased his fingers under the straps, gradually edging it off my shoulders.

We stopped kissing for a moment. He took a small step back to watch as I put my arms down, letting my bra glide off them, dropping quietly to the floor. I flicked it aside with my foot and reached for him again.

He pulled me in for another long, slow kiss. I wrapped my arms around him, feeling my breasts pressed against him, desperately wanting him.

His hands were running through my hair. I was doing my best to take in every inch of his back. As our time ran shorter, I was determined to commit every tiny piece of him to my memory.

We slowly backed away from each other at the same time – our thoughts, wants, and needs being totally in step for this dance. I took this opportunity to return my attention to the zipper on his jeans as I steadily eased it down. No boxers again.

Irresistibly hot.

I pushed down on the jeans, and they dropped to the floor. As he stepped out of them, I visually took in all of J in his raw, naked form.

The sight unleashed the damp surge between my thighs while my back arched, urging my breasts toward him. He responded with a gentle roll of my nipples between his thumb and forefinger, charging my body with jolts of electricity.

Pressing himself against me, I felt his cock, hard and pushing on my stomach.

Putting one knee on the bed, he lifted himself onto it, taking me with him. We shifted to the center of the oversized comforter, facing each other on our knees. His arms wound around me, pulling me toward him. Leaving my lips, he moved his mouth down to my neck where he showered me with the soft fluttering of his tongue.

Heat coursed through my body while I battled a contradictory chill.

I reciprocated the action, burying myself in his neck, my hands wrapped around the back of his head as my fingers sifted through his hair. His fragrance would stay with me forever, this I knew.

I felt his palms flatten against my back, and when he gently pushed against me, I knew J wanted to ease me down onto the pillows. As I willingly leaned back, he stretched out with me, settling himself between my legs. The hard shaft I felt resting against the soft lace of my panties was unmistakable, provoking my senses.

My hips naturally rose toward him, feeling the tantalizing pressure where I instinctively wanted it. Grinding, further opening myself to him, longing for his naked skin against mine. Seeking raw relief.

We lay there searching each other, kissing and touching and bringing ourselves to a point of arousal that didn't seem possible after all that had taken place.

I was on fire, tingling not just in all the right places, but everywhere. I could feel how absolutely ready for him my body had become. Now, it was just a matter of waiting for his cue.

As badly as I craved physical relief, I didn't want to break this wonderful soft, sensual moment we were sharing. The memory we were making was more important to me than the impending sexual fulfilment, even though my lust wouldn't let me forget my need.

My hands meandered over every part of J that I could reach. His erection was pinned between us, and he was moving ever so slightly against me, between our soft sighs and heavy breathing.

I had my legs loosely wrapped around his back. J had his arms underneath mine with his hands cradling my shoulders. His lips were all over me, gliding from my mouth to my neck to my chest, and even trailing down my arms.

Despite my determination to forge memories, my desire for him was reaching a tipping point. But just when I thought I wasn't going to be able to hold back much longer, J put his lips to my ear, whispering in his rough bedroom voice, "Make love to me."

I tensed as his words alone almost sent me over the edge.

His weight lifted off me as he pushed himself up on his arms and rolled to my side, reaching over to the nightstand for a condom. He dropped it near the tray that was holding his watch. leaving the drawer open then quickly turning his attention back to me. We fell into a side embrace, me on my left side and J on his right, arms wrapped around each other and legs entwined.

His hands crept down to my backside where he started to slip off my panties. I lifted up on my elbow to make it easier. When they were below my knees, I used my feet to kick them the rest of the way off, not caring where they went.

We stayed tangled up in each other, absorbing every second, until he rolled onto his back, pulling me with him.

I straddled him, sitting right below his erection, giving him space to put on the condom. Even watching him do something as mechanical as that was incredibly sexy.

I almost couldn't bear it. And now, I was finally going to get my chance to be on top of him. I quivered, thinking of J watching my every move.

Moving up, I put my hands on the headboard just above him. He was leaning back on a pile of pillows, which positioned my breasts right in front of him, ripe for the taking. And he did. I felt his fingers softly caressing one hard nipple as he took the other in his mouth, gently circling his tongue around and around. It felt extraordinary, like I had never before experienced such a thing.

As slowly as I possibly could, I slid down on him as his cock slipped inside me. My body was screaming to move faster, the caged animal was thrashing against the bars, but I wouldn't let it happen. We weren't fucking this time, and it was going to take a while before the savage beast had its peace.

When I felt like I was capable of staying steady enough, I let go of the headboard, sitting up straight on him, placing my hands on his stomach for balance. Doing this removed my nipple from his mouth, so he now had both hands on my breasts, slowly moving around them, running his fingers across them.

I settled further down, pushing him as deep into me as I could, as slowly as I could. When I had all of him inside me, I stopped and stayed there for several seconds, squeezing myself around him. J briefly closed his eyes. When they opened again, he was fixated on my face. All I could see in the expressive hazel sea was a deep passion.

When I felt it was time to move up his cock, I pressed my hands gently against his stomach, rising as slowly as I had going down.

J shifted his hands to my hips, taking hold of me,

participating in guiding my motion when he was ready for it. His gaze was locked with mine, watching me the whole time.

I was lost in him, taking all of him with every downward movement. There was no thrusting, no feverish scramble to the peak. This was steady passion, every minute fanning the flames ever higher.

J's hands tightened on my skin. He closed his eyes as he held me down, stopping me from sliding on him for a few seconds.

I knew there was nothing wrong. He was simply trying to prolong our lovemaking, so I waited until his hands signaled me to continue.

As we started again, his hands slid up to my waist, and he pulled me toward him. I leaned into him, placing my palms on either side of his head. My nipples grazed his chest, shooting a tingling sensation throughout my body. I kissed him, long and slow and deep, while I maintained the steady, metronomic movement on his shaft.

When I pulled back, I parted from him just enough to take my lips from his but stayed close enough that our tongues continued to explore each other.

J's hands indicated it was time for me to sit up again and, when I did, I felt myself starting to tighten around him. I knew I couldn't put off the inevitable much longer. He knew, too.

Placing one hand on my ass, he nudged me slightly forward. My clitoris brushed the soft hair of his groin. I heard myself call his name in a rising crescendo.

"J..."

"Nat...fuck..."

His free hand slid down my stomach until I felt his thumb caressing between my legs. The rest of his long fingers wrapped across the top of my thigh, gripping tightly. He knew this was going to be my undoing.

When it happened, there was no controlling anything. I slid down him, hard, slamming him into me as the waves crested, one after another. My eyes were screwed tightly shut as I planted my hands on his stomach, bending my head forward. Sweat-soaked hair fell across my face. I cried out in the throes of my passion. Somewhere in the distance, through the ringing in my ears, I heard J groan.

He took my hands, raising them so we were palm-to-palm. I was leaning into him as my orgasm continued to overtake me. Bracing myself on his hands, I moved faster, grinding my hips with abandon, continuing to come in pulsing bursts all around him. Then, when I was halfway down on him, he pushed into me, unleashing himself with a roar. With this, he let go of my hands, sat up, and wrapped his arms around my back, holding me tight.

We rocked together, continuing to feel the ripples as they flowed over us and through us. I was shaking and clinging to him, perhaps a little too tightly. But I couldn't let go. I was afraid my trembling would become uncontrollable if I did.

As the afterglow set in for both of us and we floated gently back to reality, I shifted to get off my knees so I could wrap my legs around his back. Resting my head on his shoulder, I fell into his arms, where we stayed, breathing heavily, until he rolled us onto our sides again.

We were face to face, tangled together again, hands slowly moving over each other. I couldn't imagine what was left to explore, but I did know both of us were going to stay right where we were for as long as we could.

Every now and then he took his hands off my skin, drifting them through my hair. We kissed. Not the deep passionate kisses that started this, but slow, gentle, thoughtful kisses. I couldn't have asked for more in this moment.

And I truly and sincerely hoped that J felt the same.

CHAPTER TWENTY

We settled into a comfortable snuggle, J on his back with my head on his chest. I had my leg bent, knee pulled up to rest on his thigh, toes running up and down his calf.

"Are you cold? Do you want to get under the covers?" he asked.

I would have loved nothing more than to climb beneath the cozy comforter with him, to stay wrapped in his arms as we both drifted off to sleep. But I couldn't risk dozing off at that point. I knew I needed to get up and get dressed soon.

How am I going to say goodbye to him???

All of my previous thoughts of leaving J with ease were shot to hell.

"I'm good," I said. "Are you comfortable?"

"Mhmm," he murmured as he moved his hands over my hair.

His other arm slipped behind his head. I propped

myself on my elbow so I could kiss him, but what I really wanted was to see him in this pose. I had fantasized about it in his office the night before, and now that I was seeing him like this, it was every bit as sexy as I had imagined. More so.

I put my head back down on his chest, my fingers trailing through the hair they found there.

Behind the blinds in his room, I could see the stirring of dawn outside, but I pushed it away. It wasn't time to deal with that just yet.

Then it occurred to me that he might fall asleep, and not wanting to wake him, I would have to leave without saying goodbye. I couldn't imagine bringing all of this to such a quietly abrupt close.

"J, are you going to fall asleep on me?"

He turned his face to kiss me on the forehead. "Trust me, love...I'm wide awake."

I would have given anything to know what was going through his head, but I didn't want to ask.

My mind was back to that hateful twelve-lane highway, and I was having trouble staying focused on any one thing for more than a few seconds.

The eerie tones of the beginning of Breaking Benjamin's "Diary of Jane" were coming through the speakers. I stayed centered on the anger and pain Ben Burnley put into his voice.

Somewhere along the way, J had turned the music down from the heightened level at which it had been playing when he was cooking. Now, even hard songs like this floated in the background without overpowering the room.

Ben Burnley roared his exasperation with Jane and their complicated relationship, and I thought about how much I would have loved to be able to scream right then.

My whole being was rocked. I wanted to, just for a minute, transplant myself into the middle of an isolated forest where I could yell at the top of my lungs until my throat hurt.

I wasn't angry or frustrated. I was just...different. Changed. And there was a whole swirl of turmoil going on within me for which I needed an outlet.

When Ben wrapped up "Jane," Howard Jones took over singing "Like to Get to Know You Well."

I giggled causing J to tilt his head toward me. "Share."

"You sure do have an eclectic taste in music."

He thought about it for a minute. "Oh. Yeah. I guess so."

Thinking he might be taking my remark the wrong way, I quickly followed with, "I like it. It covers just about any mood or thought."

He nodded but didn't say anything more about it.

"I saw Howard Jones when I was in high school," I continued.

"Really?"

"Yeah. He was crazy good. I remember being mesmerized, seeing him surrounded by all those keyboards. I have no idea how he kept track of all of it."

J didn't say anything at first, and I thought he was ready to move on from the music topic, when he remarked, "He's a really cool guy."

"You met him?" I asked, in too much of a star-struck tone for my liking.

"In London. At a movie premier," was J's simple response.

That should not have surprised me, but I still hadn't given much thought to this world in which J now lived. To me, he wasn't that person – he was just...J.

I reflected back to what he said about having trouble

determining who wanted to be near him for him, and who wanted something. It made me angry to think there were people out there who didn't stop to appreciate J for who he was. I tried to chalk it up to their loss, but that didn't work because it hurt him...and I also found that to be very upsetting.

J was still on the subject of Howard Jones. "There's a lot of talent there. I could never create something like that."

At this, I pulled away from the arm he had around me, sat up, and looked at him with my mouth hanging open.

"What?" he asked, looking truly perplexed.

"Are you *serious*?"

"Yeah. What?"

This silly man didn't even realize how talented he was. How could his success escape him like that?

"J, you goofball, you have movie studios fighting over your work. Do you have any idea how brilliant you are?"

He was lying there, staring at me as if we had had a miscommunication.

Finally, he said, "Well, yeah. That's different, though. I mean I couldn't write music. I feel like that's a whole different type of talent. Taking these instruments, learning them, conjuring up these sounds that no one has ever created before. Bands that jam together and they're all on the same page. It's just...different."

He raised a hand in the air as if to make his point then let it fall on his leg. I settled back into the crook of his arm, resting my head on his chest once again.

"It's all the same, if you ask me," I said.

"How is it all the same, Nat?" he asked, with a touch of frustration in his voice.

"Because *you* are still *creating* something...something no one else has ever written."

"I'm putting words on paper. Piecing together a story that crept into my head. Anyone can do that with enough imagination."

I sighed. Silly, silly man. Reaching up, I ran my fingers across his cheek then down to his goatee, lingering to tickle the slightly rough hair I found there.

"I see you're still not giving yourself enough credit," I finally said.

J didn't persist with the subject, and neither did I. I knew from our year of writing that this was something with which he had struggled in the past, but I was surprised to hear that it was still an issue.

All of those movies, and a book, and he still couldn't see that he had a gift. What came out of his head was desired by millions of people, whether they watched it or read it. The general public looked forward to finding out what his next plot would be. For God's sake, he had *fans*.

We lay there for a while without talking. I was still running my toes up and down his leg. He was still playing with my hair. I could feel that his body was completely relaxed, and I determined that he likely had moved past whatever frustration he felt about our talent conversation. That was an internal J issue. As much as I wanted to, I couldn't help him with it.

J,

Well, on that honesty note, it's my turn to tell you that I met someone. We've only been out a few times. I don't know what to say about it. Feeling kind of confused right now.

Thinking of you, too. Always.

Nat

"Will Lydia be here today?" I asked. "Do you need for me to be out of here at a certain time?"

I knew what time I had to go, but if Lydia was going to show up before then, I should probably know about it, and be prepared for an earlier exit.

"I sent her a text and told her not to come today," he answered.

When did he do that?

I felt like I had disrupted his routine. I told him so and apologized.

"No worries, love," he said. And then added, "It's been a welcome disruption."

His hand was trailing up and down my arm. It all felt so natural, but I couldn't help but wonder if he was going to easily fall back into step with his normal life after I left. I hadn't come here with the intention of causing an upheaval, but would it be a simple thing for J to put all of this behind him?

While I hadn't meant to rock the boat, this had turned into something very much unexpected. Or was it just me?

He reached over to the nightstand and picked up a remote control.

"Shit," he said, pointing the remote at the closed doors of the armoire. He waved the device, attempting to elicit magical results before releasing a small sigh. "I really need to update the house to voice controls so it does this stuff for me. Just want to check the weather," he finished, by way of an explanation.

Gently slipping away from me, softly setting my head down on the pillows, J got up to open the armoire where the television was tucked away.

"The ultimate in lazy," I teasingly remarked.

"Once the yoga's done for the day, you'd better believe it," he laughed.

We were both still naked, and I was reveling in the

sight of him walking through the bedroom, comfortable in his own skin. After he opened the cabinet, he went to the sofa and picked up a throw blanket.

Coming back to the side of the bed, he snapped open the blanket, just as he had in his office when I was dozing after our amazing time in there. Remembering this sent shivers up my spine. My desire for him began buzzing at me again, but I needed to do away with it. The sand was racing through the hourglass.

If I stayed here, my life would eventuate to a perpetual orgasm.

J put the blanket over me, getting into position at my side again, pulling the other half of it over himself. I picked up my head, waiting until he was comfortable, before once again taking my place against his chest.

"Sorry. I had a chill," he told me, as if he owed me an explanation.

"You really need to stop apologizing so much," I said.

"What do you mean?"

"It seems like you've said 'sorry' to me a lot tonight." He thought about that for a minute, so I continued. "I just don't want you to feel like anything you've done has bothered me. Quite the opposite."

I kissed his chest. He returned the kiss on the top of my head. We relaxed in comfortable silence together for several minutes.

"You do it, too, you know," J said.

"I do what?"

"Apologize. For all sorts of things."

"No, I..." I stopped here giving his words some thought.

I could feel J nodding his head as he said, again, in a sing-song voice, "You do it, too."

"Shut up," I jokingly told him and lightly pinched

him.

We lay quietly wrapped in each other, until J finally said, "Same."

"Same what?"

"I don't want you to feel like anything you've done has been a problem for me."

This small reassurance was priceless to me. And I hadn't realized until I heard him say it that I really needed to hear it.

He picked up the remote again, turning on the television and quickly flipping to The Weather Channel. The volume was muted.

"I don't really care about today here – I'm not going anywhere. I just want to see if it's supposed to be warm again this week. And we can check to make sure you're all clear for the flight back."

Unbeknownst to him, J's practical and thoughtful words made me feel emotionally fragile. I no longer lived in a world where someone looked out for me.

A pang of sadness rushed over me as I accepted this temporary gift...and struggled with the permanent loss that was right around the corner.

Nat,
I never know what to do when I'm faced with these crossroads. You know that. And I never want anyone to get hurt. I feel your confusion and raise you some stress.
J

The timing was just right as the forecaster on the screen was going over national weather. I saw that I was going to be flying back to a torrential downpour.

Figures.

J was paying attention. "It looks like you're going back

to some bad weather."

"Mmm, I'm used to it."

"Don't you deal with a lot of flooding down there?" he asked.

Really? Were we going to talk about the weather?

"Yes. It's a pain in the ass," I answered. "But it's home."

My last sentence unsettled me further. Nothing could help me escape the reality of it – I was going home. Soon.

I had been with J for less than twenty-four hours, but in an ironic way, it felt like a decade. It felt like we shared this place, his home. It felt like I belonged. But this wasn't where I belonged, and he didn't want anyone here. Everything was going to be the way it had to be.

"What do you think of the weather up here?" he asked.

"Oh, I love it. I love all four seasons. The humidity down...there...is stifling. It's hard to breathe some days."

"I've been there – have I told you that?"

"You did, yes. Shreveport, right?"

"Yup," he answered simply.

"Well, that's a lot different from where I live. You need to check out south Louisiana. The culture there is unlike anywhere else."

"New Orleans?" he asked.

"Oh, hell no," I said. "New Orleans is fun and all, and there is a ton of history there. But west of there is the Acadiana region of the state, and it's just...a whole different world."

Why had I just said that? What if he took me up on my suggestion and traveled down there? What if we ran into each other?

J wouldn't do that. He wouldn't want to be in that situation any more than I would.

I didn't want to continue with this conversation. And I didn't want to go back to the weather, either. If we had more time, I would have been happy to talk about absolutely nothing with him all day long. But not now.

I felt grateful when Fred wandered in through the door we'd left open, surveying the scene before jumping up on the bed. True to J's word, he had stayed in the dining room all night, and was now emerging with the rising sun.

He sat down next to J, looking at me as if he was trying to figure out why I was still there.

"Hi, Fred," I said, stretching across J to scratch him between the ears.

Fred put his head down, leaning into my hand to let me know this was acceptable to him. J gave him a quick pet down the back before putting his arm behind his head again.

"Does he sleep with you?" I asked. I needed to know the answer to this because it was going to be part of how I would picture him after I left. I knew I would be mentally drawing various scenes of him...often...for many years.

"Sometimes," he answered. "I keep the door closed a lot, but if it's open, he'll come in."

J chuckled and I said, "Share."

"He hides in here when Lydia is doing her thing. I don't know what it is, but, man, he really fucking hates her."

I couldn't imagine Fred hating anyone, so I said, "Did she ever do anything to him?"

"No, no way. She's super cool. And it's actually on her agency profile that she's good with animals." He chuckled again. "I think he just sees her as this monster with the vacuum and mop. I mean, if he's in a room and she has to vacuum, what is she supposed to do? So, she does her thing, and he takes it as a personal threat."

Fred finally decided he was willing to share his best friend with me, and he curled up against the other side of J. This gave me the gloriously sexy vision of J, lying on his bed, one arm behind his head, Fred at his side.

Then I removed Fred from the scenario, and it was just J, his bed, and one of his many poses that drove me wild. In my mind's eye, J was naked, of course. I closed my eyes to better commit this scene to memory. He was hard and idly stroking himself. I couldn't stand the thought of having to sit and watch it without participating, but when I thought about him being all alone, caressing, fantasizing, bringing himself to climax, it shot lightning bolts through my whole body.

Stop...this...now.

Another serene silence took over as J watched for his local forecast, and I daydreamed about something I had just experienced, live and in person.

He broke the reverie, snapping me out of my naughty thoughts. "Do you want to take another shower? You're welcome to it."

I didn't want to verbalize how I was feeling about that, thinking it would sound juvenile if I told him that I never wanted to wash him off of me. I knew I would have to, of course, but I was planning on waiting until it absolutely had to be done.

"Thanks, but I'm good," I said. "Although I definitely wouldn't mind doing that again with you."

He squeezed me, kissing the top of my head, his lips lingering on my hair. Then he put his hand under my chin, turning my face toward his. I felt his tongue sliding into my mouth, and I returned the kiss.

J put both of his arms around me as I rolled over to lie

on top of him. My hands were on either side of his head, and we stayed like that, absorbing this passionate moment. One of the last we would have together.

Our kissing slowed, and I pulled my lips away to give him a quick peck on the tip of his nose. I dropped my head down to rest on his shoulder as his hands smoothed my hair, running down my back, and then he playfully squeezed my ass. I responded with a small squeal, squirming in his arms.

My eyes glanced over at the blinds again. I could see that we were officially in the early stages of sunrise.

The stinging in my eyes returned. I was certain it wouldn't be long before I became unable to hold it back.

Rolling off of J, I once again found my cozy position in his arms. I loved listening to the sound of his heartbeat, his breathing. There were birds chirping in the distance, on the other side of the walls of his home. The walls within which I desperately wanted to stay.

I pictured joggers out on the sidewalk, making time for their morning run before going home to get ready for work. They would pass by his house having no idea what had taken place here last night and this morning. How could everyone out there just go on with life after everything that had happened here? Didn't they know that the planet had shifted?

This was immense. Someone should tell them. They all thought it was just any other Monday, any other normal day. But it wasn't. And it would never be again.

CHAPTER TWENTY-ONE

It was time to get ready. I lay there with J, letting that sink in, but I couldn't take much time with it because of that damnable stinging in my eyes.

I ran my hand across J's stomach and over his chest before I propped myself up to look deep into his eyes. I said nothing.

We gazed at each other for a long time, and then he said, "Oh. Now?"

I nodded. I was afraid if I spoke, the flood would come.

"Okay," he sighed.

He picked up Fred, stood up from the bed, and set Fred back down in a spot where he was out of the way. Unaffected, Fred turned around twice before settling into another comfortable position to continue his nap. I wished I were Fred.

J held out his hand, helping me down from the bed. When my feet hit the floor, I leaned into him, putting my arms around his waist, holding him tight.

I couldn't stay like that for long – I needed privacy...quickly. Sensing this, J scooped up the shirt I had been wearing and eased it over my head, then pulled me back into him for another embrace.

This time, I tucked my arms in, leaning toward him for a few seconds, allowing myself to be completely enveloped in J. But I couldn't stay like that. To have him see a stray tear during tormentingly teasing sex was one thing. This was about to be a lot different, and I wanted to keep it to myself.

Pulling away from J, I walked around him and, without saying a word, entered his bathroom, closing and locking the door behind me. Going straight to the chair next to the linen closet, I crumbled into it. And cried quietly.

I leaned my elbows on my knees, putting my face in my hands. I could feel the tears streaming. There wasn't a damn thing I could do to stop them. So much had happened, and I felt the physical roller coaster I had been on throughout the night shift to a wild ride of emotions.

My heart felt like it had been torn open. There I sat, exposed and bleeding.

I knew I had to snap out of this, but I needed to release at least some of it before I walked out to face J...and say goodbye to him. I couldn't let him see me this way.

J,

Please don't get stressed over this. I never want to be the source of that for you. Things will work out the way they should, I guess. Fate being what it is and all. We both just need to take a deep breath and see what happens.

So, just to let you know, I'm moving, and I might be without internet for a little while. I'll be in touch as soon as

possible.
Nat

I went to the vanity where there was a box of tissues, taking two before going to sit down again.

This was going to be the hardest thing I'd ever had to do. But life needed to go back to the way it was. Contrary to my belief that the world was different, nothing had actually changed for anyone but me...and maybe J. Although I suspected he would be back into the swing of business as usual within a short period of time.

And what about you, Nat? Where will you be?

I would be home, running my little company, taking care of my family, whom I still loved more than anything. I would be happy to be with them, in my comfort zone, laughing and loving and living together. Despite the hiccups my marriage was experiencing, home was where I was needed.

J didn't want something like that anyway. He wanted his peace and quiet...his dinner and a movie night...his bourbon with Fred. I doubted he would ever settle down with someone to truly share his life – he just wasn't wired like that. Maybe at one time, but not anymore.

And even if he did want it, that wouldn't change what was meant to be. I was already living the life I was supposed to have.

Regardless of these truths, my tears continued. I felt so emotionally drained. My thoughts rewound back through the events of our one night together, and I cried harder as I thought about all the things I had discovered about J.

Yet I still felt like I'd barely scratched the surface.

Before coming here, I had already suspected he was a man true to his word. A thoughtful, caring, and considerate man. I knew his demons ran deep, and I contemplated how long it had been for him since he had shown anyone his true self. This made me incredibly sad for him. I wanted to put him in a protective bubble, carrying him with me.

But I *would* be taking him with me. All of him. Everywhere. Not one second of our time together would ever be forgotten.

I sat, still crying, on his bathroom chair. I pictured J in my mind. Not sexy, naked J...just jeans-and-a-t-shirt, gazing-into-my-eyes J...and I knew I had flown too close to the sun. And now I was feeling the blazing burn of it.

I needed to steady myself, accepting what was imminent. Whatever I needed to do to continue with the forward motion of life would come to me. But I couldn't try to work this out here, in his bathroom, with an upcoming flight. And I still needed to say goodbye to him.

Knock it off and get ready for this. Get through it and then deal with the rest of the shit later, I told myself.

I sat up straight, taking several deep breaths. I was strong enough, I knew, to go through the steps of what had to be done. I meditated on that thought for a minute. It helped to calm me, and the more I settled down, the more it helped to make the tears eventually come to an end.

This was a temporary solution at best. A band-aid over an open wound. I could almost guarantee there would be more to flow at a later time, but in that moment, it was time for me to pull myself together, focusing on what I needed to do.

Wiping my eyes and nose with the tissues, I went to the sink to wash my face. The splashing of cold water on my skin woke me up, helping to snap me out of dwelling on the ache that was spreading in my heart.

I leaned over the sink, repeating the motion over and

over, washing away the tears, but it did nothing for the pain and confusion I was feeling. I sincerely hoped none of this hurt J as much as it hurt me.

I stood up, looking at myself in the mirror. My skin was blotchy, and my eyes were red. I didn't think I had ever felt this out of sorts in my life. And that was saying something, considering all the things I had been through up to this point.

After patting myself dry with a hand towel, I opened my bag, taking out the outfit I would be wearing as J and I said our goodbyes. Underneath the clothes was a notebook I always carried with me, and I took that out as well, along with a pen.

I looked around, went over to pick up the chair, and set it in front of the vanity. Sitting down to lean on the counter, I flipped the notebook open to a blank page and started to write.

Dearest J,

You are an amazing man...in every way possible. You deserve everything your success has given you and so much more. I wish you the best that life has to offer. No regrets.

I paused there because I didn't know how to continue. There was so much I wanted to say to him, so much I wanted him to know.

I wanted to tell him that walking away from him was going to be my own personal hell. I wanted to say that I did regret this, on some level, because leaving him was turning out to be so much harder than I thought it would be, and if I had never come, I wouldn't be so sad right now. I wanted him to know that I hoped he wasn't having as hard of a time with this as I was because I never wanted him to hurt like this. Most of all, I wanted to tell him that I loved him.

This wasn't something that had just happened because of our night. I was a grown woman, and I knew the difference between lust and love – this was both.

I think I had fallen in love with the idea of J all those years ago when I was encouraging Mark to speak of him. Then, when I finally developed my own relationship with J through our emails, I fell for real. But the law of the jungle dictates that just because we love someone, doesn't mean we're going to be with them. So, I tucked it away in the place where those things need to go and went on with life. Until this. And now I knew for sure, beyond a shadow of a doubt, that I loved him. And I'd never be able to tell him. It wouldn't do either of us any good.

So, while I wanted to tell J so much more in this letter, I was at a loss for the words. What more could I say that would let him know how important he was to me, without getting too deep? And what if he wasn't feeling any of these things? What if the whole night had been nothing more to him than a fun romp? A way to explore his erotic side without doing it with someone who might judge him?

Here I was feeling this explosion of love for him, struggling with the heartache of never seeing him again, but maybe none of that mattered to him. So many years had passed since our original connection. With all the tenderness and respect he had shown me during the night, I could tell that he valued what we had...but maybe, for him, on an emotional level it didn't amount to anything more than friendship.

Combine that with the girlfriend and his apparent commitment to living alone, and what I saw was myself in love with a man...who was married to his writing. His craft took precedence over everything else. He wasn't going to change that now. Not for Rebecca, or me, or probably anyone else. And I wasn't about to leave my husband, so focusing on what J was possibly feeling was pointless.

I had gotten myself embroiled in this situation, thinking the ending would be a lot easier than this, and now, there I was wrapping myself up into an emotional pretzel. I needed to stop it and just finish the note. I looked over what I had already written.

Is it enough? Should I leave it at that?

No, it was pitiful. I couldn't tell him everything I was thinking and feeling, but I also couldn't leave it with those pathetic few sentences.

I got up from the chair, walking over to the shower, replaying in my mind what had taken place in there earlier.

I heard our banter. I felt his soft caresses.

My thoughts wandered through the course of the evening...

Our walk, hand in hand beneath the night sky.

Silly dancing in his office.

I reflected on the belt wrapped around my wrists, his necktie tightly winding through my mouth. My frustration...

Acts committed in the name of flirtation and seduction. Heartfelt emotions withstanding the test of time.

No regrets.

Nothing he had done tonight...last night...had hurt me in any way. Always a gentleman, J had been warm, thoughtful, and forthcoming. It was for these reasons that I knew I loved him.

The towels were hanging on the rack to dry. I ran my hand over them, feeling the dampness of our rain shower exploration.

I stepped one foot inside the tiled cubicle. Lydia would be there in a day or so to clean it – would she scrub away our time together? I wanted to keep these memories as fresh and vivid as they were, then and there. Brooding over this would not be a healthy way to spend my future, but how could I let go?

In an instant, a thought came to me that frightened me...because I actually considered it.

What if I asked J to keep me here, cloistered away from the world, with him, just the two of us...forever?

I pictured every day and every night being a repeat of this safe haven we had created with each other. J would work and I would...do what? Be his toy? No, he wouldn't treat me like that. But what would I be?

I would be *his.*

I let out a heavy sigh, and now I was the one running my hands through my hair. My exhaustion was starting to hit me. While I felt like I could cry a whole bayou of tears, I didn't have the energy to dedicate to that. It would happen later, on my own time.

Walking back over to the vanity, I stared at the note again. I was sure if the roles were reversed and J was writing something to me, it would be far more profound and eloquent. But I wasn't J, and I didn't have his way with words and, so, I signed off on it...

Love,

Nat

It was time to focus on getting ready. I stared at myself in the mirror for a minute, trying to get my bearings. The face that was looking back at me was a different person. I had something now that I didn't have before – a gift that some people never saw once had been granted to me twice. Genuine love. It was time to go home; back to the place where I had been feeling hurt and passed over, but where the foundation was solid and committed.

I didn't expect anything to change in the near future. So, I would adapt, and put the collective good for my family above all else. And this would forever be my stolen moment.

I stood at the vanity. As I pulled J's workout shirt over my head, my heart skipped a beat knowing his clothes would never again touch my skin. Neatly, I folded it, placing it on the counter next to his sink. I would leave the note on top of it.

Using my personal wipes and some lotion, I cleaned up as much as I could without removing him from my body. I wasn't ready for that yet.

I slipped on clean panties – more boy shorts – and a plain white bra. Pulling on a pair of distressed, hip hugging, boot cut jeans, I then added a loose, peasant-style blouse that turned out to be a lot more low-cut than I remembered.

I thought about tying the strings in the front but preferred to have them loosely dangling. A couple of test movements in front of the mirror told me that it would be safe to leave the ties hanging between my breasts.

I was in the process of sliding a wide leather belt through the loops of my jeans when J's belt antics came flooding back to me again. With a heaviness I hadn't felt in a long time, if ever, I slid back down onto the chair that was still pulled up to the counter.

I stopped to think about if our night together had brought out what *he* wanted. I came here to put a neat bow on our emailing story, but I was also on a mission to help him finally experience what he had desperately wanted back then – to take what he desired when it was being offered to him. I wanted him to feel empowered.

Throughout the course of the night, while I had reminded myself to allow him to plot the scene, it hadn't really been discussed. Now I wanted to know how he truly felt about the lead he had taken during our time together.

I couldn't possibly ask him...could I? No.

I would have to accept all that had transpired as proof that he had shifted during this, done what he had always wanted to do, spoken up, and taken what had been there for the taking.

Maybe his fears and insecurities would continue to keep him from doing something like this again. Maybe his bedroom personality would continue to be held at bay. We had our spell...and I had to go.

I stood up to continue getting ready, finishing with my belt. What I would like to do to *him* with this belt! I pushed that thought out of my mind as soon as it presented itself. The clock had struck, and our time was up.

I wondered where he was in the house, and it dawned on me that this was the longest I had been away from him all night. I didn't like it. It felt unnatural and I needed to be near him again, in the same room, as soon as possible.

Nat,

I know you moved, but it's been a while - everything okay? Send me a smoke signal when you can. I miss you.

J

I took a quick assessment of myself in the mirror and washed my face again. My skin had returned to normal, and my eyes were looking better, less red. Another application of light makeup, then I had to figure out what to do with my hair.

I played around with it down but opted for the messy up-do again. The hoop earrings worked for both dressy and casual, so I put those back on. I left the bracelet in my purse. Still no rings.

I stood there looking at myself in the mirror. Everything was fine. I looked presentable. If this had been a get-ready-and-go situation, I could have walked out right then and there. But it wasn't, and I had to take one final step before leaving this room that had become my temporary sanctuary – I had to set the note in place.

I looked it over again. Still not happy with it, but with no clue what else to say to him that could sum up how I felt, I decided this would have to do. J was the writer – not me. All I could hope for was that he would read between the lines, understanding how deep my river for him ran. His place in my heart was a chamber where I would tuck him away. And no one else would ever invade it.

Would he gather that from my note? Maybe not, but I also wasn't about to write something so revealing to him, either.

I stepped over to the side of the counter where his shirt was now resting, folded. I wanted to take it, tuck it into my bag, and steal away with it. I could see myself occasionally taking it out of a hiding place, reliving all of this love and passion in my mind.

Bad idea.

Frequently worn clothing had a way of absorbing the scent of a person, no matter how many times it was washed. I picked up the shirt, put my face into it, and took a deep breath. He was there...and I wanted to remember this fragrance. If it was up to me, it would be bottled so I could carry it with me always.

I put it back on the counter and picked up the paper with my silly note, wishing I had brought some bright lipstick so I could leave a kiss mark on it.

Stop it – we're not in high school.

I knew that, and I wasn't trying to be even more silly than I already felt, but I wanted him to remember me in every way possible. I wanted him to remember my lips, my hands...my body against his.

Never forget.

As J had said to me the night before, I yelled at myself. *Enough!*

I set the note down on his shirt. I had begun the lengthy process of privately letting go of J...now I just had to go do it in person.

CHAPTER TWENTY-TWO

Carrying my overnight bag and purse to the bedroom, I could see that J had turned off the television and closed the armoire. The pillows were placed back on the bed in a haphazard pattern. The throw blanket had been tossed on the sofa. Lydia would be there this week to fix it. Besides, he had to be tired, and would probably be going straight to sleep as soon as I left.

J,

I'm so sorry it's been so long! Thanks to the move, I haven't had internet until now. How are you? Did you finish the screenplay? I really hope all is going well for you.

So, listen, I don't know how to say this, so I'm just going to say it. It got serious. We're talking about getting married. I know that sounds crazy, and I don't know how to explain it other than to tell you it just happened. I really wasn't expecting it and then...there it was.

Please know that you are on my mind always. If you ever need anything, please don't hesitate to let me know. I don't want to lose our friendship over this – you're far too important to me.

When you get a chance, if you're still speaking to me, please write back.

Love,

Nat

I set my bags down on the bed, took out the sandals I had chosen to wear that day, and dropped them on the floor. They were backless and flat with thin leather straps over the top of my foot. The leather of the shoes matched that of my belt, and I felt that I had been successful in achieving the casual and fun look that I'd been hoping for when I had packed.

Now, the *last* thing I was actually feeling was casual and fun.

I looked over at the nightstand, glimpsing the photo that had briefly grabbed my attention when I was first standing there in J's room. Picking it up, I saw it looked to be dated similarly to the picture of his dad in the dining room.

This one, though, had four people in it – a small peek into J's early life with his family, when his father had still been with them. They all looked happy. And J had been a cute kid. Of course. Likewise with Mark.

I returned the frame to the nightstand with a sigh. I'd wanted to ask him about the picture and the people in it, but the opportunity for that had come and gone. There was no more time for heartfelt conversation or silly banter.

My dress was still draped over the chair. I picked it up, along with my thong, tucking both into my bag. There was a part of me that wanted to leave the panties behind...something for J to remember me by. It was a risky idea, though. Like the thought of asking J to keep me tucked away in his safe haven, this was another foolish proposition. There was no way for me to know if he would be amused by or appreciative of the gesture.

Standing next to the bed, I hesitated, thinking about how there was nothing to commemorate our one night together. There were no pictures, no trinkets, no texts to save. There weren't even emails, since all of that had long ago been deleted. Unable to see the future, we could never have predicted that this would happen. Maybe we should have kept them for posterity.

Then I remembered my note in the bathroom. That would be J's souvenir, if he wanted one. I would simply have my memories.

I scrapped the thong idea. It *was* a bad thought anyway. What if Rebecca stumbled across it? She would be coming over for movie night sometime this week. I doubted she would appreciate it if she were innocently going through his things, looking for something she needed perhaps, and found evidence of another woman.

Now that I thought about it this way, I felt better about what I had written. My note was relatively benign and didn't mention all of the passion we had experienced.

The aroma of coffee was drifting down the hall, and I gave myself one more pep talk to prepare for the inevitable. The feeling of fear was overwhelming me. I was afraid of what I had to do because...I didn't know how to do it. But no matter how much I wracked my brain, I couldn't figure out a way to avoid it.

Taking one last look around the bedroom, I then wandered out into the hall, stopping to stare at the office door. It was slightly ajar. The desk lamp was still glowing.

I should just go in there, curl up on the couch, and never leave, I thought. *No, no, no. I shouldn't, in fact, do that. And J wouldn't want it.*

That thought made me wonder if he was getting anxious for me to leave. He said he wasn't going anywhere today, but he probably wanted to get some sleep.

Acutely aware that my thoughts were taking on the characteristics of a runaway train, I took a deep breath. The persistent speculation that was in my nature was not serving me well here. Placing my thoughts about the office gently at its door, I turned to hurry down the hall.

As I was coming around the corner, a little too fast into the kitchen, I walked right into J.

"Oh, I'm sorry!" I told him.

"Nat! What the fuck? Why are you going Mach ten?"

He put his hands on my shoulders when we collided and stepped back to look at me, giving me the famous J once-over.

"Are you okay?" he asked.

"Yeah, I'm fine. Sorry about that," I said, apologizing again.

"Where's the fire?"

"What? Oh, no fire. I..." I didn't know what to say.

Just let it go, J. Please.

"Are you running late now?"

Oh, for fuck's sake.

"No. I..." I said trailing off again.

All this did was pique his curiosity, and he continued to stand there waiting for an answer. I wasn't about to lie to him, so I told the truth.

"I was thinking I need to go so you can have your house back to yourself, go to sleep, whatever you were planning on doing today."

He took that in and didn't say anything for a minute. He was looking me up and down again, starting at my feet. When he got to my eyes, he frowned.

"You don't need to rush out of here, Nat. Staying up all night is the norm for me, and I'll get some sleep whenever it happens."

I looked down at the floor, feeling silly. What had I thought he was going to do? Swat me on the ass and say, "Thanks for a good time, but now I have to get back to the real world"? That wasn't his style, and I knew it.

Lifting my head to study his eyes, the frown I had seen when he realized why I was hurrying softened. He put his hand on the side of my face, leaning down to kiss me softly.

When he pulled back, we looked at each other, our eyes searching. Whatever else the night had been, it hadn't been awkward. Even my entrance couldn't be described as that. Nerve-wracking, yes; awkward, no. But now we had arrived at the uncomfortable moment.

J broke the silence. "Do you want some coffee?"

He turned to where he had set out a mug for me.

Before he could pour coffee into it, I said, "No. Thank you, though."

"You don't drink coffee?"

We knew so much about each other and yet so little. These finer details were inconsequential compared to what we had done together.

"Not anymore."

I had stopped drinking coffee a few years prior, and I hesitated, thinking maybe I should tell him about that, but then I decided it just didn't matter. I had to go soon...that was all that was significant right now.

J simply nodded, sliding the extra mug next to the coffee pot, out of the way. He leaned back against the counter, folding his arms across his chest.

Good God, please don't stand like that, I thought.

He tilted his head from side to side, stretching his neck. I thought about massaging his back in the shower, wishing I could turn back the clock for just a little longer so I could do it again.

J may have been used to staying up all night, but I wasn't. The fatigue was hitting me. The fatigue, the pain, the desperation to do this the right way. Because even though I didn't know *how* to do it, I knew there was a right way and a wrong way. Exposing myself to J, showing him how much I was struggling with it, would accomplish nothing and serve no purpose.

I was still standing there, holding my bags, when J jumped. "Here, let me take those for you." He was about to set them down on the counter, then thought about it and asked, "Do you want them in the car now?"

I shook my head. *Ohhh, J.*

He set the bag and the purse on the counter, came right back to where I was still standing, and pulled me into his arms. I held onto him tighter than I had all night, my hands running up and down his back, taking it all in again. The muscles that embraced me, every ripple across his shoulders, the fingers that pressed into my skin. His face was buried in my hair.

We stood like that as the minutes ticked by. My heart was racing. When we finally disengaged, J put his hands on either side of my face, drawing me back in for a long, lingering kiss.

Our tongues were tenderly dancing, and I felt the familiar fluttering as my body reacted. I tried to get my mind to explain to my body that it wasn't going to happen again. Not here. Not ever again. But my stupid body wasn't listening.

Our kiss slowed to a stop. I backed away from J, putting my hand on his chest, turning to walk away. I didn't know where I was going, though, so I took a few steps and stopped.

"So...um...do you have everything you need?" he asked behind me.

Turning back to him, our eyes locked before he went back to the coffee pot, leaned against the counter, and ran his hands through his hair.

I wasn't sure what he was asking, so I just said, "Yeah, I'm good." And then added, "I think."

He looked me up and down again. "I like you in jeans. It's a good look."

"Thanks," I said, wiggling my hips back and forth quickly to try to lighten the heavy air that was hanging over the room.

He looked thoughtful for a second. "Well, truth be told, love, I like you in anything. And nothing."

I wanted to be playful and run up to him. Hug him, kiss him, tickle him, even. But I needed to put on my suit of armor to refrain from doing all of that.

I loved that he called me "love." Did he do that with other women?

I gave him a shy smile and said, "Same."

After we gazed at each other for a long moment, he turned his attention to his coffee, took the last sip from his mug, and placed it in the sink.

I walked over to my bag, thinking about taking my phone out and turning it on, but I decided I wasn't ready to deal with that. I would turn it on once I got to the hotel. Maybe catching up on whatever I missed the night before would be a welcome distraction.

J continued to lean against the counter. He folded his arms across his chest, crossing one foot over the over.

Absolutely fucking maddening.

One of us needed to start this, so I finally said, "Okay, well...thank you for...everything." Then I remembered our early morning breakfast. "Oh, I should help you clean up the dining room. I'm so sorry I didn't think of it sooner."

I started to go in that direction, but J took two long strides across the kitchen, grasping my arm to stop me. He was right up against me when I turned.

"Don't take one more step," he said.

"But..."

"No, absolutely not. I will not have you worrying about dishes and shit right now."

Before I could think of a rebuttal, I was in his arms again. He was smoothing my hair down my back and he said, "Nat...I..." before trailing off.

The tears would be coming soon. I needed to go. Just rip the band-aid.

"I know, J," I muttered into his chest. But I didn't. I had no clue what he was going to say or what he didn't know how to say. I could only hope he was happy that we'd had our night together.

I wanted him to be content in life, and I hoped that he felt good knowing he had done this exactly how he wanted to. I knew he hadn't held back, and while we could have done so much more if time was on our side, he handled each of our moments of passion on his terms.

We finally let go of each other. Looking down at the floor, I raised my arms before letting them drop to my legs with a quiet smacking sound.

"Oh, hey," J said, as if he was just remembering

something. He leaned over to pick up a small card off the counter. "I wanted to give this to you. You know, just in case. Like...if you ever...need anything. Anything at all."

He was holding out a business card. When I took it, I saw that it had all of his contact information on it – email, website, social media accounts, and two phone numbers...one printed on the card and one handwritten.

He pointed to the second number, the one in pen. "Use that one – it's my personal phone, and I always answer it because only a few people have that number."

I couldn't think straight. I knew I would never reach out to him, and now I was wondering if he thought I was going to stay in touch.

It didn't matter. Just as I'd left J the note, he, in his own way, had given me a souvenir of our time. Not the card – that was generic. But the beautifully handwritten phone number was a personal touch. Proof that I'd been here. That we had shared something deeply personal.

Even if I never used it, never contacted him ever again, he had chosen to leave the door open to me. There was a lump in my throat as I looked him in the eye.

"J, thanks. I appreciate it. I really do. But..." I couldn't finish. Even in my head, I couldn't find the words to tell him he would never hear from me again. We had arrived at our finish at last. And nothing more would come after this.

"I know, Nat. I just wanted you to have it. Like I said, just in case. I don't want to think of you needing something that I can help with and you can't get in touch with me."

My heart was melting with this gesture. I wanted to tell him so, but the words escaped me, so I simply said, "Well, okay then. Thank you. That's very sweet."

I thought about it for a few seconds before deciding to

do something that had been on my definite no-no list when I first arrived there.

"Do you have paper and a pen?" I asked.

"Sure," he said, opening a drawer that had all sorts of notepads, pens, and pencils. I wondered if he kept items like that scattered about in case an idea came to him. His strategically placed proverbial cocktail napkins.

J handed me a piece of a paper and a pen, and I leaned over the counter writing. When I was done, I handed it to him. "You can always find me at this email."

It was an unidentifiable address associated with my company, but it always came directly to me.

He was looking at it, and I continued. "You know, just in case, for you, too. I mean...this" - waving a hand around - "can't..." I needed to say it, but the pain in my chest was excruciating, and it rendered me speechless.

He was nodding that he understood he wouldn't see me again. And I couldn't imagine what in the world could possibly happen to him that would cause him to need *me,* but giving him a way to find me seemed like the right thing to do.

He was still nodding when he said, "Yeah. Thanks."

We fell into an awkward silence for a few seconds.

"I have to go," I said.

My heart hurt. I moved to pick up my things, and J jumped into action.

"I've got this," he said, taking the bag while I carried my purse.

I didn't want him walking me to my car. I wanted to say goodbye on the front porch, where we first met, and then I would go back out into the world alone. Stepping off the porch with him seemed too...normal. Cue Danny Elfman...the sand worms would get us.

He took my hand, and we walked slowly to the front

door.

"I hope you have a good flight. And that the weather isn't too bad when you get back."

"Thank you. I'm sure it will be fine."

When we were at the door, we both stood staring at it. Outside was reality, and I wanted to stay in here with J and everything this fantasy world we created had to offer.

He put down my bag, and I threw my arms around him.

I love you so very much, I wanted to say. But didn't. The pain in my heart was becoming unbearable. I reminded myself to keep my armor up for just a few more minutes.

He returned my embrace, then put a finger beneath my chin to pull my face to his. One more sweet, long, tender kiss.

We parted, and I quickly reached down for my bag, but he tried to stop me. "No, I—"

I interrupted him. "I can take it from here, J."

He looked deep into my eyes. He knew what I was telling him – stay on the porch. I couldn't drag this out into the driveway.

He opened the door. I paused, looking at the world outside. A Mercedes drove down the street. Everything looked so...ordinary...out there. Another warm fall day that would end with another cool evening. But I wouldn't be here for that.

Staring at the spot where all of this had begun not even twenty-four hours earlier, I felt like an entirely different person from the one I had been when I stood there plotting his first view of my skimpy dress.

I stepped out into the morning sun, and I could hear Marc Scibilia begin in the house – "Rather Be." Once again, the irony absolutely fucking astounded me.

I stopped for a moment, listening to the first verse. Keeping my head down, I focused on the stonework of the front porch, stifling the sob in my chest and feeling my heart break. I *felt* it. Almost heard the cracking sound as I internally shattered.

J came out of the house to stand beside me, and I put my arm around his waist, pulling him close. I turned my face into his shirt, inhaling one more breath of his scent, pulling the fragrance into my memory where it would stay tucked away with everything else we were.

He had his arm over my shoulder. I felt the weight as he kissed me on the top of my head, one last time.

And then...I did it.

I walked away from J.

Heart aching, eyes stinging, believing I knew exactly how our story ends.

Coming soon by NT Anderson...

Acts of Confession

Acknowledgements

My sincerest heartfelt thanks to all who have supported me on this crazy trip that I never thought I'd take. I appreciate beyond words everyone who had a hand, no matter how big or small, in bringing my efforts to fruition.

First and foremost, in addition to their treasured support, I am incredibly grateful that my family hasn't had me committed. Yet.

John Painz, Jon Ford, Hayden Blackwood, David DeWinter, and David Atherton-Cooper have advised and listened to me enough to write a whole separate book.

Danica, Marisa, and Sara are three incredible women who have made the choice to get down in the mud with me every time I've decided to go off-roading. There aren't words to describe how thankful I am for each of you!

My tolerant tech professional and friend, Mark, who goes above and beyond every time, never blinks an eye at my eccentricities, and generally makes good shit happen.

I am deeply appreciative of the wonderful woman and writers who have kept my content creation company afloat while I veered off track. Y'all are truly the most amazing group of talented people I have ever had the pleasure of working with, and I could never thank you enough for all you do.

Many, many thanks to the Twitter #WritingCommunity who has been the most amazing source of love and laughter throughout this process. The support I have found because of this brilliant group is incomparable, and it has meant the world to me.

And last but far from least, to each and every reader who has made it this far, for giving me a chance, I thank you from the bottom of my heart.

About the Author

NT Anderson has lived in multiple countries and states and is currently hunkered down in the Endless Mountain Region of the northeast US. Her chosen professional path was restaurant management and hospitality services until 2009 when she turned her passion for writing into a career as a content creator. In 2019, she took it several steps farther by diving into the world of fiction.

Nikki can usually be found keeping odd hours, spending time with family and friends, talking to the characters in her head by candlelight, and plotting her next adventure. Several furbabies keep her on her toes, including two spoiled dogs, a pudgy cat, and a feisty horse.

She fancies herself to be a pirate, especially on Saturday nights when she breaks out the rum.

Made in the USA
Las Vegas, NV
22 February 2021

18385092R00169